HOLD YOUR FIRE

Hali Mallo

A warning to my father; there is kissing in this book.
Sorry.

x

A thank you to my incredible husband; without your undying love and aggressive support I would have thrown this in the garbage. Love you.

x

TW: Mentions of sexual assault, suicide of a family member, sexual content, and violence

1

My kidnapping was as easy as stealing a puppy from an unguarded backyard. I roll my head back and squint at the fluorescent lights. I could burn this building to the ground and incinerate everyone with a sneeze. It would take nothing but a flex of my hand to save myself and return to my normal life. I don't want to hurt anyone, even if it costs my life.

They tied me to this hard chair at least four hours ago. My restricted shoulders ache like hell. Time is hard to judge in a windowless room. It feels like only moments ago, I was wrapping up my exciting night with Mrs. Evelyn Featherly.

She's a retired teacher who keeps her bespectacled eyes glued to the shopping channel and a big orange cat at her side. She takes decaf spearmint tea with two generous dollops of honey right before bedtime.

When I pulled a lavender-stuffed heating pad out of the microwave, Mrs. Featherly had just finished her cup with a handful of nightly pills. I placed it on her arthritic knees.

"How does that feel?" I asked as loudly as I could without screaming at her. Her hearing aid sat on the table beside her. She looked like an ancient queen reclined in her purple loveseat.

"Very nice," she sighed. Her crepey eyelids sank closed. A shawl she crocheted herself rested on her thin shoulders. The cat lay asleep on her slippered feet. I smiled at the cozy woman, a portrait of peace.

I envy her.

I picked up her empty tea mug and tiptoed out of her gauche living room, careful not to trip over one of her many scattered ceramic angels.

I pumped a blue gob of soap onto a sponge at the kitchen sink and scrubbed away the dark tea and her lipstick stain on the rim. She always wears pink lipstick, even to bed.

The old water heater in the cellar below barely does its job, as the water that flowed over my hands was frigid.

Should I risk it?

I glanced over my shoulder to make sure that Mrs. Featherly was asleep. Her lower jaw sagged deeper with a snore. I typically steer clear of utilizing my power on household objects, but the water chilled my fingers to the bone.

I touched my fingers' pads to the spout's cold metal and focused. My palm glowed with heat. It transferred through the conductive metal, and the warm flowing water washed the rest of the soap suds off the ceramic mug. Goosebumps formed on my arm as I savored the warm water. *Totally worth it.*

A bang on the kitchen window scared me so badly that I nearly dropped the mug.

What was that?

I squinted into the dark yard and flipped on the back porch light. There was nothing out there except overgrown rose bushes and a rusty swing, left to rot decades ago. *Maybe a bird flew into the glass.*

I pulled my jacket on, slipped my feet into clogs, and slid open the back door. The old wood of the deck moaned under my feet as I stepped out into the night. I stood on my tiptoes and leaned over the railing, scanning the grass under the window for a stunned bird.

There was nothing under the window except a neglected flower bed. Then, a branch snapped near the line of trees at the back of the yard. I whipped around.

"Hello?" I called out. Nothing answered me. I shook my head and moved to step back inside when I saw him.

A man in the shadows smiled at me. The porch light cast menacing shapes on his face. My stomach dropped through my ass, and my feet froze.

"Good evening. You'll need to come with us," he said. More figures materialized out of the forest behind him.

I turned to run back inside to protect Mrs. Featherly and call the cops, but a large arm wrapped around my waist and threw me over a hard shoulder. I screamed and screamed, but I knew it was no use. Mrs. Featherly could sleep through a hurricane and that fat cat is good for nothing. I wish she had a guard dog. We were in a tiny neighborless house in the countryside of Maine. There was no hope of rescue.

The rev of a van engine. A hand over my mouth. My teeth sank into warm flesh. Sharp pain in my head. Darkness.

When they grabbed me last night, I hit the top of my head on the side of their van door as they tossed me inside. It wasn't their fault. I thrashed around pretty violently, and I bit through somebody's hand.

Hungry and sore with a busted scalp and throbbing headache, I'm hopelessly taped to a chair in a tiny room like a naughty mobster who disappointed her boss. I wonder if they stole this dirty plastic chair from Mrs. Featherly's patio. Who even are *they*? A criminal organization, no doubt. My kidnapping was fast and well-staffed.

I've passed the time wallowing in existential dread, wiggling, and I even fell asleep for about an hour, proving my sister correct that I can fall asleep anywhere.

My mind has skipped through the stages of grief and landed on the fifth and final stage: acceptance.

I know why I'm here.

I've finally been caught. It was bound to happen.

I knew I wasn't clever enough to hide it forever. They're gonna kill me for sure, and I don't blame them. I've been a danger to myself and others since I was thirteen. Lied hundreds of times to conceal. To my loved ones. To myself.

I'm a loaded gun with no safety.

No matter how careful I am, it could go off.

I have a perpetual prescription for powerful allergy medication to ensure I never sneeze. My hands are always stuffed in my pockets. I rarely drink and have never done drugs for fear of losing control.

I hid fire extinguishers in my car, bathrooms, kitchen, bedrooms, and under the couch. I've taped fire blankets under every drawer in my house and stuffed them in my purse. I own six pairs of oven mitts.

As I test my restraints, duct tape tugs painfully at my arm hairs. I wiggle my hands, grasping at air. Hands that can burn through a million possibilities.

Paper. Wood. Metal. Flesh.

After they kill me, maybe I'll become the local ghost.

I'd like to be a Lady of The Lake in a white dress with long flowing hair. I'll make eighth-graders shit their pants at summer Bible camp.

This is my greatest ambition at the moment since all else seems lost. I'll never become a mom. I'll never see the ocean again.

I'll never see my sister again. And I'll never get the chance to apologize. My eyes start to sting, and I shut them tight to stop the tears before they fall.

But then, footsteps outside the door rip me from my pity party and daydream of future ghosthood.

The metal door screeches open, and a woman enters. I recognize this guard. She gave me crackers yesterday and wiped my blood off my face with a damp cloth when I jolted awake.

My stay has hardly been a four-star experience, but she helped make it survivable.

"Don't speak," the woman says and steps behind me.

My wrists are freed from their restraints. I bring my hands in front of me and rub at the pink marks on my wrists. My shoulders pop, and my back burns from hours of restraint.

"Stand up. Keep your head down and mouth shut."

She moves back in front of me, eyes down, expression nervous. Why is she nervous? It makes *me* nervous.

No time to panic now because Ginger grabs me and roughly guides me out of my prison cell by the elbow. I've been careful not to get caught, but everyone makes mistakes—especially an idiot like me.

The shuffle of my pink work clogs echoes off the cement walls as she guides me down a long hallway. I grimace in embarrassment. I didn't plan on meeting my fate in pink scrubs and matching clogs. We approach a door at the end of the hall too quickly.

It's difficult to draw breath into my frantic lungs, and I lean on her, so I don't slump to the floor in a puddle of sheer terror. She promptly shoves me off.

The fate waiting for me on this door's other side could be gruesome.

Maybe blood will spill from my throat and slip down my chest. Sunlight will shine through bullet holes that tunnel clean paths through my head. A mob boss will exhale white smoke through his teeth and shake his head at my lifeless body.

Ginger shuts the door behind us with a loud bang and a click, locking me in this new, dark prison. Then, white lights illuminate the center of the room with a click.

The edges of the large room are cloaked in thick darkness. I take a few steps forward with skittish caution. A pool of dark water fills the center of the lit space. I step close to the edge and wonder what I'm looking at. I squat down and touch the water with a curious finger. It's so cold it burns my skin. I jerk my hand back and wipe it on my leggings.

"Miss Auclair, pleased to finally meet you."

The voice almost startles me into the water.

"I've known about you for so long. I feel like we're already friends. Do you know what I mean?"

I don't know what he means.

My shaking fingers retreat and curl into my sleeves. A shape emerges from the dark edge of the room and enters the circle of light with me. He's been watching me. He looks fondly at the dark water with a smile. He knows something I don't. At the moment, I don't know anything, and I hate it.

"When I was six, my father held me down at the bottom of this pool until I was on the cusp of drowning. He was a man of harsh methods," he says and shrugs.

I look down at his childhood trauma pool and back up to him.

I have never seen this man in my life. He's tall, blonde, and good-looking for a criminal. Maybe a decade older than myself. He reminds me of someone I've met before.

A sickly sense of deja vu joins the heavy ball of dread in my stomach. The shuffle of papers draws my attention outside our circle of light.

A group of men and women with clipboards and lab coats are watching us at the edge of the room. They feverishly take notes in the dim light. I feel like a lab rat.

"Do you know why you're here?" he asks.

It's the first non-rhetorical question he's asked since I was shoved in here. I clear my dry throat to find my voice.

"No."

"Any guesses?"

My eyes dart to the water, the man, and the lab coats.

He's going to drown me in there. I knew it. I'm going to be the ghost lady of a tiny lake.

He shrugs, pulls his phone out of his pocket, and hands the device to me. A video plays—a video of *me*.

The first clip is shaky. Someone filmed me from my bedroom window. I'm reclined on my bed, a book balanced on my knees, pink socks on my crossed feet. As I read, my pinky finger is lit like a birthday candle, and I make figure eights with it in the air.

It's a bad habit.

The following clip is clearer but black and white. The footage is of a funeral. I swallow hard as I realize it's the funeral of Edward Spears, a client I lost last month. The camera must be a bodycam because it bobs as the spy walks.

They walk past the roses and the cards. Past his open casket. Past the poster board with pictures of travels worldwide with his wife over many decades.

Embracing her in Paris. Kissing her cheek in Rome. Holding hands in Vegas with their heads thrown back in laughter. Eddie was a funny guy. We shared a laugh over my dismal cooking on his last day.

The cameraman walks out of the doors of the funeral home. The camera zooms in on a little blue car in the back of the packed parking lot. A brunette is in the driver's seat. I watch my shoulders shake as tears stream down my face. I remember I had been holding it together well until I saw his new widow touch his casket with a heartbroken wail.

When I'm distraught, my tears can become a problem. Cloud-like puffs of steam float from my eyes. I watch myself punch her dashboard, cursing cancer of all forms and phases. She leans her head against the steering wheel and covers her face with her arms, hiding further evidence of my condition from the camera.

The last clip has the clearest quality. It's the most damning. One of his goons caught a great shot from the window of Mrs. Featherly's kitchen as I warmed her icy tap water last night.

They've been watching me for months.

"That you?" he asks and snatches his phone away as if I've infected it. I raise my eyes to the ceiling, clasp my hands in front of me, and remain silent. He steps back and looks me up and down, shaking his head like a man in disbelief.

The silence is deafening. I feel everyone's eyes on me, adding weight to the enormous lump in my throat, threatening to choke me to death.

The look on their faces is a look I give myself in the mirror too frequently. Freak. Mistake. Monster.

"Mark?" The blond finally turns towards the group. A gangly man steps into the circle of light with us.

"What are her stats?"

"Twenty-four-year-old female, BP is 120/70, pulse was high at 122 beats per minute, her body temperature was also abnormal at 99.7 degrees Fahrenheit," Mark says.

"Blood labs?"

"All normal." This answer is apparently inadequate for the unhinged blond. He looks away from me and glares at poor Mark, who visibly trembles under his direct gaze.

"Do them *again*," he orders through his teeth. He was calm and collected a moment ago, but now he's so pissed his hands are shaking.

"But, sir–"

The blond maintains eye contact with me as he pulls something out of his pocket and flings it at the stuttering man. It slices through his cheek, and a thick teardrop of blood streaks down his terrified face. The small knife clatters against the floor on the other side of the room.

My heartbeat performs a drum solo in my throat as I try to meet the eyes of one of the women off to the side. They keep their heads down and gaze dutifully at their paperwork.

He smiles at me, satisfied with my reaction, then throws his head back and laughs loudly. It's wretched.

It bounces off the walls and into my brain. But nevertheless, it confirms the hypothesis I've been building since he stepped into the light.

He's crazy.

Not just crazy, but, like, *crazy crazy*. Like flay my skin and wear it as a scarf. He'll slowly gouge my eyes and enjoy them with fresh marinara sauce. I've fallen into the lap of a psycho.

Nice going, Ruby.

At least I'll be leaving this world with a good story.

I stopped wanting to die old and gray after a couple years in my profession. I've spent countless times holding dying clients' hands, senile and frail, confined to a bed they hadn't left for years.

"They said you were soft," he says. He smiles at me with unwelcome fondness. My stomach rolls.

"Kazak," a man calls from the group of watchers in the shadows, "get on with it."

Kazak is a good name for a Doberman with a nasty bite. Not a person. I wonder how new parents can look down into their soft bundle of joy and innocence and choose a name like that.

"Cato, don't be shy. Meet my guest," he turns back to me, "this is my younger brother."

Another excellent name for a guard dog. Upon first impression, he sort of looks like one. However, all I can see in the shadows is a good six feet of man. Tall and broad with a piercing stare, he moves slowly from the dark to the light with the caution of a dog approaching a snake.

He fully steps into the light, and I realize...we know each other. We've met before in a bar.

Over a year ago, on my birthday, my tongue was down his throat, and his fingers were tangled in my hair. Lost inhibitions released by a steady flow of alcohol. His eyes slightly when he sees my face, but otherwise, he gives no hint of recognition.

I was never supposed to see him again.

I don't even know his name, but I could never forget his consuming dark eyes, no matter how many vodka cranberries I slurped down. The tall ones always break my heart. I'm a sucker for a kiss on tiptoes.

The real kicker? At the night's end, he rejected me, and I never saw him again.

Until now.

My desperate wish for the floor to open up and swallow me whole transforms into a panicked prayer. This has to be a joke. An elaborate, high-budget, made-for-TV prank.

As he looms over me, it becomes clear that this is no jest.

He's the dark-eyed stranger I let slide into second base. Here. Participating in my kidnapping, interrogation, and expected execution.

I'm going to throw up.

And I'm going to die.

I'm going to throw up and die on the floor in front of these strangers and the hot guy I let fondle my tits on my birthday.

This couldn't get any worse.

Unless the boy who rejected my prom-posal in high school is somewhere in the back, this couldn't get *any* worse.

He doesn't speak, simply looks over my head at his brother. Kazak leans in close, smile gone. His cologne is heavy with the scent of pine. I'm frozen like a baby deer in the headlights of a speeding Ford.

"How did you trick my father into giving you a Dotion?" he asks.

"What? I-I didn't trick anyone!" I stammer, still frozen in place. He grabs me by the face, and I fight back a scream.

"Don't lie to me. How did you trick my father? Did you blackmail him?" he hisses at me through clenched teeth. The heat of his breath burns my eyes.

"N-no, I swear I don't know what you're talking about!" I squeak and back away.

"I think she needs a push, Kazak," a dark-eyed guard at the opposite door cuts in and grabs me roughly by my arm and shoulder.

"This bitch clearly doesn't value her life enough to talk," he painfully squeezes my shoulder harder to hold me in place, "maybe a few pokes with a cattle prod will make her loosen up."

"Shut up, Marcus."

"Bro, what if she sets shit on fire? She's a walking hazard-"

The crackling sound of electricity fills the room. I stare at the lit electric weapon. Kazak pulled it out of nowhere.

"No, wait, sir, I didn't mean any disrespect. Please, I only meant-"

Kazak steps up to us, ignoring him and looking me dead in the eyes again. He turns off the cattle prod but slips it beside my waist, sliding it behind me to reach my guard. He's so close I can smell his pine cologne again.

He flicks the switch on. The lit prod is shoved into the ribs of the guy behind me, who screams right in my ear.

Unfortunately, he's still clamping onto my shoulder with his hand, sharing his electric punishment. The potent shock shoots down my shoulder to my feet. It hurts, but I grind my molars together and stare into the sadist's eyes. He smirks down at me and shuts it off. With a thud, the man collapses behind me. Kazak winks.

The temptation to spit right in his face wars against my common sense. I manage to swallow the urge. I'm not brave enough.

"I didn't ask for this," I say. My hoarse voice does me no favors. His smile falls as if my comment has reminded him of the business at hand.

"I didn't ask my father to create the most powerful Dotion in the world and let it fall into some stupid little girl's mouth. It was supposed to be mine. It *is* mine."

He glares at me like I stole his lunch from the employee refrigerator. He steps closer with his cattle prod still in hand.

"I'll get your power back even if I have to peel it out of your veins," he says.

I look over at my ex-hookup, the younger brother, and beg for help with my eyes. He does nothing.

"Kazak, she could kill us all, right? In an instant. We should give her some space."

One of the few women speaks up in a choleric tone. Long black hair hangs to the edge of her pencil skirt. She taps a pen against her downturned mouth and glares at me.

If looks could kill, I'd be a heap on the floor without a pulse.

But I know why she spoke. I know. She stopped Kazak from shoving the electric rod into my own ribs.

Hushed murmuring and uncomfortable shifting from the members of this snake pit queue me into the fact that they've all been wondering when I will start barbecuing them alive. I find the eyes of Cato again.

They're still cold. For stupid, childish reasons, I thought our history might buy me some sympathy.

The power to raze cities, and you cry steam tears, heat cold water, and do cutesy little tricks with your fingers. Mountains of power, and you don't even have the guts to use it to save yourself. So pathetic. I berate myself.

Kazak nods at the woman who spoke up.

"Sorry. Playtime is over for today," he says. He tucks a piece of my hair behind my shoulder with the tip of the electric weapon.

"Get some rest and have a meal," Kazak encourages me with faux kindness.

"We'll chat soon. Dismissed."

2

I'm roughly led back to my small concrete room. The dark-haired man who was electrocuted with me shoves me in, slams the door, and locks it.

Alone with my thoughts and the folding chair they tied me to last night, I pick it up and fling it at the door with a loud clang. My shaking fingers comb through the roots of my hair. I will die here if I don't calm down and think. I sit on my hands in the middle of the hard floor and squeeze my eyes shut.

In my last year of college, I burned off the tips of my hair after an especially difficult calculus exam. The nervous habit of twisting my dark strands between clammy fingers never crossed my mind as a dangerous habit that could get me caught. I broke that habit by sitting on my hands instead. My fingers prickle with numbness under the weight of my butt.

I picture a dark lake with still waters.

A crane with broad white wings silently glides inches above the surface while tiny silver fish swim below. The water is glassy and dark. Everything is balanced. As above, so below. Calm. Cold. Quiet. Controlled.

A quick knock rattles the door.

An announcement, not permission.

The tall woman from the pool room enters. The one who reminded everyone that I'm dangerous. Her eyes are kind, yet her expression is deadly serious.

"I'm here for a blood sample. Do not resist," the woman says. Her mouth is a tight line as she rubs an alcohol swab in the pit of my elbow. I inhale and open my mouth to speak.

"If you're going to ask me to help you escape, don't even waste your breath," she comments crisply as she gently slips a needle into my arm. Her skill is evident, as I barely feel the poke.

"Am I going to die?" I blurt. I can't help myself.

"Someday."

A ghost of a smile crosses her delicate features. It brings me a strange peace.

"Fair enough," I say.

She takes two vials of my dark blood and shoves them in the pocket of her lab coat. Then, before she exits my room, she turns back and meets my eyes.

"If you take a moment to calm down and think rationally, your problems might melt away."

She slowly grasps the silver door handle and exits the room. Then, with a click of a lock on the other side, she's gone.

Melt away. I tighten my greasy ponytail with dirty fingers and say a quick prayer of thanks for the brilliant woman they sent to take my blood.

I will get my ass out of here, take a hot shower, and hide under my covers for the rest of my life.

My hand grips the metal door handle, and I close my eyes in concentration. Slowly, I allow the warm flow of power to bleed through my fingertips and into the door handle.

I peek open one eye to check my work. The iron handle melts like butter, dripping and smoking on the concrete floor. I gently push the door open. That was way too easy.

The hall is empty, but it won't be for long. I sprint like a crazy woman. I haven't seen a single window, so we could be underground. I keep running through the gray maze of plain concrete walls.

My panic ascends to impossible heights as claustrophobia seeps beneath my skin. Corner after corner after corner. The halls don't end.

I sprint into a random hall, throw myself in an empty room, and slam the door shut. My heart is pounding so loudly in my ears that I'm sure the whole building can hear it.

A minute ticks by. Or maybe a lifetime. I can't tell.

The quiet of this room slowly calms my panicked senses. I release the tight breath I held and flex my tense fingers. Now what?

"You lost?" a low voice questions too close to my head.

I smack my hand over my own mouth to muffle a scream. The room is still empty. Bewildered, I look up at the ceiling and down to the floor, still not seeing a person.

"You're in my office," the voice speaks again. I throw an elbow into the direction of the voice as hard as I can and connect with a solid object. It feels like someone's nose.

"My nose!" an invisible man roars in my face. I scurry back and fall hard against the door. Then he's right there.

The dark-haired man with the name of a guard dog, Cato, holds his nose as thick blood seeps between his long fingers. The same long fingers twisted in my hair and pulled me close a year ago.

He appeared out of thin air. I stare at him with a gaping mouth. Cold eyes hold my gaze.

"You!" I shout and point at his chest like an idiot.

My power came from a cookie I ate on a family trip a decade ago. That summer, my family went camping in our national park. Fishing and hiking filled the long, hot day. My little brother almost hooked me in the eye, and my younger sister put a dead cicada in my hair.

I wish those were the scariest events that happened that day.

Our tired little troop bundled up in blankets and enjoyed s'mores and hot chocolate around the fire that took my dad four bad words and 45 minutes to light.

I should have listened to my mother when she warned me about that second cup of hot chocolate before bed. I was a thirteen-year-old girl with the bladder of a squirrel. When I left the safety of the tent I shared with my sister to find the outhouse, the moon was high, and the deep darkness of the unfamiliar woods made my heart race.

Who puts an outhouse 100 yards from a campsite?

I've always hated the dark. I slept with a nightlight until college. I did my business and pulled my pajama bottoms back on, nearly dropping my Scooby-Doo flashlight in my haste. I must have taken a wrong turn while wiping the sleep out of my eyes on my way back to camp.

Hidden creatures sang a nightly chorus at their highest volume. It was ominous enough to scare any kid, but it was petrifying for a girl with a panic disorder. Their haunting songs sent me spiraling. I walked and yelled and circled and cried for what felt like hours. My mother said I must have been out there at least an hour when my sister woke her and said I hadn't returned. They said the search lasted until dawn when they saw a flare go off and found me huddled until a willow tree.

My father lovingly berated me for getting lost and stroked my hair as I hugged my mother like a much younger child. Nobody questioned who set off the flare. I'm sure if it was brought up today, my mother would wistfully say it must have been a guardian angel. But I knew the truth.

I slumped down in front of that willow tree and hugged my knees. My torrent of tears eventually calmed down to sniffles and shaky breaths. I looked down and noticed a peculiar item in the middle of the woods.

Next to my shoe sat a small, red cookie on a leaf.

Pretty little swirlies detailed the top of the treat and glistened in the moonlight like it had been placed there by faires offering a late-night snack.

It pulled at me. I wasn't even hungry, having eaten three s'mores mere hours before my unplanned excursion. I cupped the intricate dessert in my hand and admired its beauty. Tiny golden details and sparkling leaves shone in the blue summer moonlight.

I don't know what possessed me to eat it. I just popped it in my mouth. What can I say? I'm an emotional eater.

A loud whooshing noise in the droopy willow branches startled me. I screamed and jumped back, throwing my hand in front of my face. A warm rush of power surged through my shoulders, vibrated down my forearms, and exploded out of my hands with a soft whoosh. Two waves of fire consumed the tree.

In the light of the flames, I saw I had attacked an enormous barn owl. It spread its wings wide and flapped frantically, a field mouse squished in its sharp beak.

Little did it know that this night's hunt would be its last. The poor owl was burned alive by my newborn raw power. Its wide eyes looked into my soul and begged for help I couldn't provide.

It thrashed and screeched terribly as it died. The bird eventually fell into a smoldering heap of twitching feathers and spasming flesh at my feet.

A burning inferno reminiscent of a flamethrower had exploded from my child-sized hand. I cried and cried. I choked on hoarse sobs, wracked with remorse for the innocent creature I tortured to death.

As the night sky shifted into gray dawn, I shakily reached my hand up and shot a small flare above the trees. After I was found, we packed up and went home.

I leaned my forehead against the cool glass of a window of our minivan and could still hear the animal's screams in my head. I could traumatically hurt people. Hurt, burn, kill. I wouldn't be able to live with myself if I ever harmed my little brother and sister. I pushed it all down and didn't speak a word of it. Years of nightmares tormented me.

My mind conjured images of the burning owl nightly. Scenes of my family dying in a house fire caused by a slip of my hand danced behind my eyelids every night. They would cry and howl in pain and claw at the windows as I stood outside on the lawn, watching their skin melt from their blackened bones and drip down the glass.

I never played hide and seek again. Or pranked my siblings. I was too afraid of being startled.

As I grew up, the nightmares morphed into images of the government discovering my secret and experimenting on me. They would take me apart and put me back together. Piece by piece, hair by hair.

I would hug my pillow in a desperate fight against sleep before succumbing to another restless night of ash and charred bodies. My weight dropped dramatically, my grades slipped, and my friendly personality diminished to meekness.

Once bright eyes became underlined by constant purple shadows. I hate pictures from those years. I looked like a ghost.

My parents took my phone and books away nightly, convinced they were the culprits of my sleeplessness and behavior changes. They interrogated me repeatedly about if anyone touched me, if I was bullied at school, or if I fought with my friends. I would give them a tight smile, shake my head, and insist I was fine, only tired.

Before the incident, I would hold my sister's hamster, Onion, when she would clean his cage. She was highly covetous of him, so it was a rare treat when she'd allow us a few precious moments of bonding time. I would gently pet his little head, and his warm, shallow breaths would tickle my palm.

Holding a flame in my palm reminds me of Onion. Warm and soft. Weightless and ticklish.

After my incident, I couldn't hold Onion anymore. Intrusive thoughts of turning him into a smoldering piece of burnt meat in front of my little sister made me sick.

The first rule of gun safety is to treat your weapon like it's loaded. I adopted this policy over my own hands. I will point my weapon at the ground and protect everyone around me.

I'll adapt. I'll hide. I'll lie.

At thirteen, I took that solemn oath, staring up at my pink bedroom ceiling as steamy tears rolled down my temple and disappeared into the dark tangles of my hair.

"I think you broke my fucking nose," he says. His red-rimmed eyes burn with hatred as he clutches his face with one hand and leans against the wall with the other. It's balled up into a fist. Tight skin stretched over large knuckles.

"I-I thought you were going to kill me!" I shout in my defense.

"I might!" he growls.

"Let m-me help," I stutter. I don't know why I've offered help besides the fact I have a bleeding heart, and he has a bleeding nose. His expression startles, and his dark eyes narrow. If I wasn't so terrified, I would have laughed.

I'm the least intimidating of the two of us, even with his injury. My hands are trembling. My head is spinning. I'm going to die. He's going to march me to his brother and watch him slice me up.

"Hey," he says sternly, "you need to look at me, please."

I do. A rush of heat unrelated to my power flows to my face.

"You're panicking. I'm not going to hurt you. Can you obey some instructions?" he asks. I nod stupidly.

"Good girl. Open the top drawer of my desk and retrieve gauze and tape, please."

I obey his order with robotic precision, and my breathing slows. Simple, easy instructions. He's not going to hurt me. I'm okay. Everything is okay.

I grasp the opportunity to ground myself and take in my surroundings. As he said before, it's an office with an oversized lounging couch, a generous desk with three monitors, and three bookshelves. Various maps paper the walls. I pull open his drawer and find gauze rolls and tape. I grab them and gesture to the couch.

"Sit."

He obliges but gives me an annoyed glare. *He certainly wasn't this moody when my tongue was in his mouth.*

I can't fight my blush as I kneel in front of him and open a roll of gauze. Prickles run up the back of my neck from our close proximity.

"You have blood in your hair," he says.

I look up, and his eyes are narrowed and focused on the top of my head.

"Oh, um. I hit my head when they grabbed me. It was an accident."

"Idiots," he mutters so low I almost miss the comment. A touch of anger rumbles in his voice. His eyes shift from the top of my head to my face. Why would he care whether or not I was injured?

"You're a strange girl. And stupid. Helping your enemy."

"I know," I agree, shrug, and turn away from him to unroll gauze, unable to look at him and maintain my weak mask of confidence. It's his hard stare that makes my pulse race.

Does he think I could hurt him? I *should* hurt him.

I mean, more than I already have. He's complicit in my kidnapping and weird interrogation. I could have turned him into a pile of ashes when I ran in here if I had panicked and let loose an inferno, but that would have been a shame.

He's pretty. His clean dark hair sweeps to the left and frames deep brown eyes. His jawline is sharp enough to slit my throat. No wonder' drunk Ruby' pounced on him. I move his hand with a gentle touch away from his nose and replace it with a pillow of gauze to soak up the blood. Most of it is leaking from the bridge of his nose. I broke the skin when I nailed him with the point of my elbow, but I don't think I caused any structural damage. I'm so accustomed to caring for the elderly that I expected much more damage.

"It's not broken, but you're probably going to need stitches. Sorry," I say. He doesn't respond. He glares. I awkwardly look away and pretend to be interested in a map on the wall instead. He's so intense.

"What?" he hisses at me. I glance back up at him, wary of his reaction.

"Are you, like, an alien or something?" I ask.

"What?!"

"You heard me." My lips scrunch into an embarrassed scowl.

"I" m no more of an alien than you are, you little brat," he snaps, but I can see a spark of amusement in his face. I raise my chin in defense.

"You can vanish. You were also brooding alone in here before I came in. In the dark."

"I was napping."

"Sure," I say. We sit in loud silence as I open a new gauze roll for him to clean off the nose blood on his hand. He stands and walks over to a wall mirror to examine the damage.

"Get it stitched up, and you'll need to ice it for a few days." I guiltily fiddle with the gauze wrapper and glance up at him.

He stares at me for a moment and aggressively grabs me under my arm. He still has the fresh gauze pressed to his nose with the other hand.

"Hey! Stop!" I gasp and try to yank my arm back, but he tightens his grip on me and shakes his head in warning.

"Shut up."

Cato cracks open his door, and for a second, I worry he will throw me to the wolves. After checking both ways, he pulls me down the hall by my bicep. He opens a new door and pulls me inside.

It's a stinky, empty closet, almost as big as my old cell. The only item of interest is the petite door on the opposite wall. He yanks it open to reveal a garbage chute. My mouth drops open.

"Go on. I never want to see your bratty ass again."

He doesn't have to tell me twice as I jump down the chute. I tumble down the hot tunnel for about five seconds. It smells so bad I could puke, but the elation and hope of freedom keep the bile at bay.

I land in a pile of trash with a crunch and an "oof." A sharp object stabs me in the thigh, but I don't give a damn because I'm free.

I pop my head out of the dumpster and gulp in the crisp fall air. Dying sunlight attacks my corneas. It's the most beautiful thing I've ever seen.

I'm downtown in a dumpster behind an unsuspecting building. I twist and see a familiar flash of blue down the street.

A delirious, happy smile spreads across my face. I shove my hand down my bra and pull out my car key fob and give it a click. My little Honda beeps. They must have stolen it when they stole me. I could cry with relief. Those idiots didn't search my titties when they grabbed me yesterday. I climb out, slip, land hard on the pavement, and immediately throw up.

I don't care that I look like a strung-out coke rat. I wipe my mouth, jump up, and run barefoot down the street. I hop into my precious transport to drive myself home. I smell like the bottom of an old Rubbermaid trash can in a middle school cafeteria, and I couldn't be happier.

3

After a scalding hot shower accompanied by a healthy cry, I collapse into bed and sleep the rest of my Friday night and Saturday morning away with a baseball bat tucked in bed next to me. I checked the door and window locks six times before finally drifting off into a comatose slumber in my warm, safe bed. My sister and I rent this townhouse together, but she's visiting New York City with her girlfriend this weekend.

Around noon, my phone dings with a text. My unofficial boyfriend's name pops up with a request to meet him for lunch at our usual dive. I respond that I'll be there in fifteen minutes.

I glance at myself in our oblong mirror in the foyer before leaving. I don't look like a person that was kidnapped for almost a whole night. Inexplicably, the stress of almost being murdered did wonders for my complexion.

The familiar scent of coffee and fresh garlic bread wraps me in a delicious and welcoming embrace as I step into the cozy diner. My stomach twists as a reminder that I haven't eaten in over twenty-four hours.

Seth is at our usual table and greets me with a quick peck. I return the kiss with a reassuring smile meant to convey, "Yeah, I'm good! I wasn't kidnapped yesterday and spent hours thinking I'd be tortured or drowned. Also, I do not have superpowers I've hidden from everyone I love for almost eleven years. So how's work going?"

An oolong tea, two toasted bagels with cream cheese for me, and a black coffee and cranberry scone for him, please. I dig into my doughy circle as he sips his bitter drink, eyes glued to the TV above my head.

He fidgets with a sugar packet and bounces his knee incessantly under the booth's table. His eyes don't hold my gaze for longer than a moment.

Absently, I realize he hasn't touched me all week except for a peck on the cheek or two. Maybe he's stressed with work or frustrated with his new psychiatrist. He's not my boyfriend yet. We haven't put a label on it.

He manages his family's catering company for a living. Seth and I have known each other since high school and began our relationship this summer.

Seth is lanky and tall with sand-colored hair and a great laugh. I love to make him laugh. There are issues we could work on, but all couples have their problems. I finish my bagel and delicately tap my fingernails on my ceramic mug, trying not to worry too much about his behavior. Maybe I have my anxiety meds in my purse. I could pop a couple to take the edge off this foreboding feeling in my stomach. I roll my shoulders and concede that I'm still shaken up from yesterday's events.

Dotion. I guess that's what my power is called. My curse. That crazy guy, Kazak, wants to take it for himself, even if it kills me. As much as I don't like this, I don't want to die to give it up. I need to lay low for a few days to plan and adapt. I rehearsed my lines of a white lie to perform for Seth on my drive here.

I think a guy has been following me around work and to my assignments. I'm freaked out. I see him everywhere! I swear he took pictures of me leaving work last week, and I don't know what he wants, babe.

Do you think you could stay over and pick me up from work this week? Please?

I can't tell him that I was kidnapped and tied up by an evil group who I think wants to use me for my secret fire powers and that I escaped through their trash, and now I need him to be around for protection. However, I have to come up with an excuse to explain my frequent glances over my shoulder and heightened anxiety. It's a harmless lie. Lying is so easy for me now. Little untruths roll off my tongue like poetry.

With my sister out of town and my parents out of state, he's my only line of defense. There's a lull in the conversation, and our eyes meet. Here goes nothing.

I swallow the worried little lump in the back of my throat with a generous gulp of tea and lick my lips.

"You know, I'm so glad we got to sit down this week and-"

"I think we should stop seeing each other," he interrupts. I snap my mouth closed. His eyes are guilty, and his gaze drops low, staring at my hands wrapped around my mug. Even though my intuition warned me about this, I have to sink my front teeth into my lower lip to keep it from quivering.

"Oh."

That's all I can say right now without bursting into a pathetic mess of steamy tears. Seth gives me an exasperated look as if sitting across from me and dumping my ass is a chore.

"Don't look at me like that. You knew this was temporary," he says and shakes his head as if disappointed that I never caught on to this. His casual cruelty feels like a knife in my ribs.

In fact, I didn't know this was a temporary arrangement. Temporary girlfriend. Temporary bed warmer. Temporary caregiver. Temporary fuck. Is that all I'm good for? My cheeks flush in anger, but I hold back. I release my lip and give him a tight smile.

"Did you meet someone?" I ask. I have to know, even if I end up breaking my heart.

"Uh, yeah. I did. A couple weeks ago."

He rubs the back of his neck awkwardly and looks away. My smile tightens even more with the fresh sting of betrayal.

In the last 48 hours, I've been kidnapped, interrogated, humiliated, escaped death, and now dumped like the trash I landed on last night. It's the cherry on top of the shit storm sundae.

"Okay. Right. I understand. Um, I've got work soon, so I better get going. See you around, Seth. Take care of yourself."

I awkwardly nod and stand to leave. I don't have work until later this evening, but I'd rather be back in that locked room tied to a chair than sit here another second.

I call my best friend, my partner in crime, and my other half as soon as I plop down on my bed.

"What's up, chick?" Her mouth is half-full with food, most likely black licorice twists.

It's her latest pregnancy craving. I sniffle.

"I've been having…" a sob escapes me, "a shit week. Can you come over?"

"Is the sky blue, bitch? Do you need me to bring anything?"

"Pack of Twizzlers and several hugs."

"Be there in fifteen minutes. I'm leaving the office now."

"What about Janet?" I sniffle. Janet is Trish's notoriously strict editor-in-chief at the Harrison Herald, our local newspaper.

"Janet can suck it."

True to her word, as always, in fifteen minutes, Trish Bartlow wraps me in a hug on my front porch. Her hair smells like lavender, clean laundry, and home.

"My poor, little Ruby. Fuck whoever made you feel this way," she mutters at the top of my head.

We go up to my room and make ourselves more comfortable. Trish kicks off her work heels, and I find a fuzzy blanket to wrap around my shoulders like a cloak. I can't tell her about the kidnapping, so I tell her about my short breakup scene at the diner.

"So you got up and left?" She hands me a piece of candy with an impressed smirk. I nod and bite into the treat.

"I love that for you! Ice cold bitch! His jaw was probably on the floor."

"Well, not exactly. That wasn't the point. I...I just had to get out of there," I say.

She nods but gives me a funny look and twists the candy in her hands. I've known her so long that I can tell she's restraining herself from lecturing me about standing up for myself. She changes the subject with swift tact.

"Anyway, did you pick your costume for my mom's Halloween party? I bought the cutest dress that compliments my belly."

Having an obscenely wealthy best friend is a unique experience. The position requires participation in events that I would have never been invited to otherwise. I love to tease her that it's like being besties with a princess. This pisses her off.

Trish feeds my little gecko, Tyrion, another fat mealworm, as I peel open a fancy, albeit slimy, face mask she brought.

"Easy on the treats, momma. He's watching his waistline," I swipe the treat jar out of her generous hands, "and uh, no, sorry, Tee. I was going to work that night. On purpose." I carefully smooth the cold, gooey mask over my face and prepare myself for her imminent backlash.

"What?! Why?"

"The vet said he's a few grams overweight."

She flings a tiny worm at me, and I let out my first laugh in days as the reptile treat almost falls down my bra.

"No, dork. Why aren't you coming?"

"It's not like I have a date. I need the money, and I'd rather wallow in self-pity at home."

"Too bad. You're coming. End of discussion. My mother will assassinate you if you don't make an appearance. You're young and beautiful and hot, and you deserve a break. Also, it's our last dance before the baby comes."

She's been bossy and loving since the moment we met.

She found me on the floor of the seventh-grade girls' locker room, enduring an emotional crisis. She asked me if I was okay and kneeled down next to me. Her eyes were so kind and sincere that I began to cry again. She put her arm around me, and we shared chicken nuggets until the bell rang. Then, she marched me down the hall, arm in mine, assured me I would have a great day, and shoved me into my math class.

The first time I went to her house in middle school was an experience.

Tee led me into their home gym, which was the size of our school's gym. I met her mother, Diana, as she pumped hand-weights to her own award-winning exercise videos. This became a regular occurrence when I visited my best friend's house well into college.

She would always pull me into a sweaty hug, no matter how focused she previously was, and point to a tray of healthy after-school snacks her personal chefs prepared for us. I love her like a second mother, but she's twice as nosy as my own. If I show up without a date to her party, she'll corner me and play matchmaker, a position I don't think she has the hang of based on her last four marriages and two failed engagements.

In between those engagements, Diana adopted a perfect little baby from Korea who grew up to have a heart as big as the sun and a terrible taste in men like her mother.

As Trish babbles about how much she loves my fat gecko, my mind conjures the image of the tall, dark-haired man who called me a brat and helped me escape yesterday. Cato.

He'd be an excellent date for the party. Diana would be ecstatic for me. Too bad he committed a felony against me.

My super pregnant friend lowers herself onto my purple bedspread and lays back with a great sigh. I give her swollen belly a loving pat.

"Is the little peanut giving you a hard time?"

"Peanut? Try cantaloupe. He's been kicking my kidneys around all day," she whines, "and on top of that, Derek isn't answering my text messages. You'd think he'd want to check on the mother of his unborn son," she huffs, her huge belly jolting under my hand. I shake my head and pat the bump.

Despite her perpetual bad decisions and shitty taste in men, I love her like another sister.

"Two more months," I say, an excited flutter warming my chest.

"Two more months," she repeats with a deep sigh. "I always dreamed of a proud, strong husband by my side while I pushed out my first baby. I wanted a little family and not be a fucked up mess like my mom." She bites her lower lip, and I can tell she's fighting back big feelings.

"I'll be right there no matter what."

"I know, you're the best. But, I just..." she trails off and watches Tyrion as he slowly crawls up the side of his glass enclosure.

"Wish things were different." I squeeze her hand with a sad smile.

"Yeah," she squeezes it back, "enough about me, sugar tits. Are you okay? Like, actually okay?"

I swallow a new lump in my throat and nod. I've never wanted to tell anyone more about my curse than Trish. Even my own sister. But I won't.

I've gotten so used to carrying my secret alone. If I told her about it, I wouldn't blame her if she never let me hold the baby. She has enough to stress about.

"My mom hates when you call me that." I wrinkle my nose at her.

"Well, she's not around, so I'll use it as I please, sugar tits."

She grabs the hand on her belly and pulls me down onto my bed, wrapping me up in a tight hug against her side. A few traitorous tears escape, tracing a watery path down my nose.

Thankfully, these ones don't turn to steam. The vice around my heart loosens as a peculiar thought surfaces. When I was tied to that chair for hours, when strangers gawked at me and talked about me like an object in an armory, when I jumped down the trash chute to freedom...Not once did I think of Seth.

"Would ya turn up the thermostat, toots? I'm gonna freeze to death in this damn icebox!"

I roll my eyes and can't help but smile. He's such a drama queen.

"It's already set to heat, Mr.George, but I can get warm blankets and make a nice hot coffee!" I shout to him even though I'm kneeling next to his recliner, cleaning up the puzzle we finished together. His full name is Harvey George Hadrian. I tease him about having two first names, and he teases me back about being a teenager. I always remind him gently that I'm twenty-four, not seventeen like he insists I am.

Many of my clients mistake me for a high schooler, but it never bothers me.

It works to my advantage. They treat me more like a granddaughter than a nurse, maid, or housekeeper, as my older coworkers experience.

Mr. George twists his mustache as I put away our puzzle, squinting at me. He's going blind, and these days he's deaf as a doornail but twice as sharp.

"Two sugars, please, hun. And a splash of milk. Don't forget the milk!" he growls in good fun.

"I'd never!" I shout with false outrage and laugh. He gives me a warm, lopsided smile. My first time as his aide, I forgot the milk, and he hasn't let me live it down. I slip out of the drawing room and walk down the long marble hall.

Mr. George hasn't told me what he used to do for a living, but he must have been good at it because his home is exquisite.

The long hallways swirl with creamy latte-colored marble floors. They're framed by old dark woods and tall pillars of stone. Statues of haloed, tranquil saints and horned, snarling demons locked in cosmic battles guard two dining rooms and the massive kitchen.

Frank Sinatra's muffled tenor voice floats through the door behind me. The upbeat tune turns haunting as it bounces off the high ceilings of the halls. I haven't had the chance to explore since I typically stay close to Mr. George in his drawing room since he had his stroke in February. I don't think I could forgive myself if he had an episode while I was exploring his vast home.

I've been a caregiver for the elderly since I graduated from college last spring. The salary isn't great, but I got a signing bonus, chose my hours, and love what I do.

Mr. George is a consistent client. I see him every other day, and I take other random assignments the rest of the week. I love all of my clients, but Mr. George has a special place in my heart.

I fix his coffee with milk and grab an armful of freshly tossed blankets from the dryer to swaddle him with. I gently kick the dryer door behind me and hum to myself as I make my way back.

A door in the manor opens and closes with a loud bang. I stop in my tracks. We aren't expecting anyone today. My scrubs swish between my thighs as I hustle to make my way back to the drawing room, careful not to spill the hot drink in my fist.

I wrap the widower's shaky, weathered hands around the cup of coffee with mine, careful not to spill. He brings the cup to his thin mouth and takes a deep sip. He smacks his lips appreciatively.

"Perfect."

I give him a pleased smile, and he returns the gesture.

"Okay, Mr. George," I announce with my hands on my hips and my voice loud, "it's time for me to go home. Your insulin is in the mini fridge. I set a water glass to your right on the table next to your radio. When I come by next, that better be empty," I teasingly shake my finger at him, "or else I won't bring you a new cassette on Friday." He grunts in agreement.

"Oh, doll, have you met my grandson?" He gestures behind me. My brows raise in surprise, and my cheeks heat. I hadn't even noticed anyone else in the room.

I turn my head slowly and see a familiar young man leaning against the massive fireplace. My blood freezes.

Oh. My. God.

"Pleasure to meet you. Cato Hadrian. Thank you so much for your service to my grandfather. He's fond of you."

Cato extends a reluctant hand to me, his face polite and impassive. I make a choking noise out loud. Thank Christ, Mr. George is almost deaf. I've been the caregiver for my nemesis' grandparent for over a year.

I narrow my eyes at him. The nerve. His dark eyes bore into mine. I shake his stupid hand and turn my back to him.

"Pleasure to meet you, too."

I place a quick peck on Mr. George's scratchy cheek and give his warm hand a tight squeeze. "I'll be back on Tuesday. Stay out of trouble, my friend."

"Where's my kiss?" a low voice behind me taunts.

"Go check up your ass," I hiss at him, quiet enough to slip past Mr. George's poor hearing. I snatch up my purse and keys, desperate to make a getaway. I click my key fob to remotely start my car outside, walking so fast I'm close to running.

"Nice scrubs. Pink? Classy."

"Fuck off."

"Oh, come on, that's not nice. I saved your life once. Let's chat about that."

He's enjoying himself. Saved my life? He's one of the reasons I was in danger of losing it in the first place! I whirl around and stick my finger in his pretty face. I take a short breath because I forgot how unfairly dazzling he is.

"Stay away from me, or I promise you'll regret it."

Not my deadliest threat, hardly a threat at all, but it's all I can think of now in my panic. His perfect, tailored pants and soft-looking mouth are distracting.

"You're much nicer to my grandfather than you are to me," he says. He folds his arms across his ample chest.

"Well, that's because your grandfather is patient and kind. Too bad you couldn't pick up those traits."

I step out into the cool night air and march to my car without looking back. My clinical clogs crunch the gravel of the driveway, and I have to focus on not twisting an ankle in front of him. Is nothing sacred?

My favorite patient is his grandpa.

He has the freedom to show up at my workplace anytime he pleases. There is no escaping this pest. He catches up with ease and steps in front of me again.

"This will be a whole lot easier if you would give me a moment to explain-"

"Out of my way, jerk." I steel my frayed nerves and dare myself to look him square in the eyes. He looks down at me with a raised eyebrow.

"I don't owe you anything. Move."

I step around him again, and this time he lets me pass, only to sweep his foot across my ankle and trip me. My purse goes flying. My blood pressure cuffs tumble away. My notes scatter. My extra-strength caffeine pills spill. My cards and coins merrily bounce away. I take a deep, deep breath and squeeze my eyes closed.

"Shit," I whisper. When I panic, sparks can fly from my fingertips. I *cannot* melt another debit card this year. A crunch of gravel close by startles me.

My eyes pop open, and I see him standing with his hand extended, offering to help me up. He managed to clean up all my items and put them back in my bag, which is now neatly sitting beside me.

I swat his hand away and snatch my purse back.

He beats me to my car with his ridiculously long legs and opens my door for me.

I ignore him and get in, slamming my car door and throwing my bag into the back seat like a child throwing a tantrum.

On my drive home, I glare at the blood-orange sun as it dives behind the dark clouds of twilight. As the celestial orb sinks behind purple walls, I curse the cosmos for dealing me such a crappy hand.

4

"Good morning, Violet. How was your weekend?" I toss over my shoulder at my favorite secretary while organizing my reports. I have to start this week off right. I stop into headquarters occasionally to review patient charts and pick up supplies. My senior care agency is run by an older couple, their menace of a son, and a few loyal staff. Violet is my favorite scheduler.

"Not long enough," she grumbles. Violet Beverd is the meanest old fart in the building, and I adore her for it. She's unapologetically herself. I take immense pride that I am the only person under thirty she will spare a word for.

"All partied out?" I flip my hair and tease her with a brow wiggle. She glares at me over her chunky spectacles and throws me a stink eye pungent enough to clear a room, and I beam. Her glare softens into a cheeky barely-there grin, well hidden in her saggy jowls. She turns back to her outdated computer monitor and mumbles.

"Muffins in the break room," she says. My ears perk up.

"No way. Chocolate chip?" I ask.

"Double chocolate chip."

"Violet, you're an angel! I could kiss you," I squeal.

"Well, don't do that," she shakes her head quickly, "but grab one before the other mongrels get to them first."

Her baking is legendary. I would commit international crimes for a pan of her fudge brownies. I spin around to finish my task with haste so I can snag a warm treat of gooey chocolatey goodness before they are all claimed by other hungry staff.

"Did someone say muffins?"

I suck a calming breath through my nose, but my heart still pounds a clear warning song. *Danger, danger, danger.* The hair on the back of my neck stands up.

Howard. His hot breath makes my skin itch. His wrinkled polo shirt. His lanky hair. His patchy mustache. Always too close. Never far enough away.

The way I catch him staring at my hands. My neck. My hips.

The sound of his voice alone inspires a migraine behind my eyes. The others fawn over him because he's the son of the company owner, and he knows how to tie a tie.

Gag me.

Nobody shares my malice for him except my loyal Violet, who, to her credit, doesn't particularly like anyone. Our frowns mirror each other when he enters a room. He's *insufferable.* Howard Jenkins Smith. His name is plain and unassuming, but I know the truth.

"Oh, sweeten up, Ruby!" Peg, a fellow caregiver, commented once after she caught me glaring at his back. If he had a fan club, she'd be the president.

"It's gotta be hard for him to be around us ladies all day. Give him a break. He's harmless." She winked at me like we were sharing a silly little secret. Before *the incident*, I thought his cheap cologne made his presence nauseating, or maybe I was acting like a bitch and wasn't used to working with odd men.

After *the incident* happened, my feelings were validated in the worst way.

I always change at home, but Violet had called to ask if I could stay with a client overnight to provide comfort and company. The client's husband had died that afternoon, and she needed companionship. So, of course, I accepted the assignment.

My first mistake was my decision to swap clothes at the office before driving over to my assignment. My second mistake was that I didn't know Howard popped into the office late at night. How could I have known that?

Whenever he looks at me, I can feel him undress me with hungry eyes. I've stopped complaining to my sister about him because she nags me to quit. I can't. This is the only reputable senior care service in over a hundred miles. I love my clientele. I love my work. His role is accounts receivable and backup management, so I'll suffer through my weekly yet brief interactions with Howard Jenkins Smith to do what I love even if I hate him.

"You look comfy this morning, Violet! I'm such a boring guy. I always wear work clothes to work." I can hear the smarmy smile in his nasal voice as he says his backhanded compliment. Violet is rocking a pair of zany purple leggings and a green sweater today like a comfy queen. She sports a worn pair of yellow clogs under her desk. I turn casually and pretend to scribble a note while waiting for the delicious fallout. Violet's baking is almost as satisfying as her comebacks.

"Yes," she agrees coolly, "you are boring." Her hooded eyes narrow into slits. Howard swallows, the stupid smile wiped from his face. I value her ability to see right through his steaming pile of bullshit. He gives her a tight smile and shoves his empty travel mug into my hands as he walks past.

The movement reveals the pink crescent scar on his palm.

"Wash that for me. Thanks, kitten," he calls over his shoulder.

I chew on my lower lip and say nothing. A useless coil of rage stabs my gut. I'm a coward, but if I do what he wants and keep my head down, he leaves me alone.

The more I rebel or question his asinine management skills, the more attention he gives me.

"Get in there and get yourself a muffin before that weasel finds them first and touches them all." Violet's voice breaks me out of my internal temper tantrum.

"Yes, ma'am!" I chirp and rush to sign off on my hours so I can *finally* snag my breakfast treat.

"Can I help you, sir?" Violet's tone switches back to an impatient growl. I smirk to myself. She's more of a guard dog than a front desk coordinator.

"Ah, yes, could I speak to Miss Ruby Auclair?" I turn around at the sound of my full name. A young man stands at the front desk, holding the most elaborate bouquet of lilies I've ever seen. A thick bandage covers the bridge of his nose.

You've got to be shitting me.

"Happy birthday, Ruby." The glass vase meets the wood of the front desk with a clink as he places it before me.

It is *not* my birthday.

I blink hard and wonder if I'm trapped in a realistic fever dream brought on by extreme stress. I stare daggers at Cato as I remove the heavy arrangement from Violet's desk. What. The. Fuck. What is happening? Violet's eyes slide over to me. She also knows it is not my birthday.

Should I have her call security?

Should I quit my job, change my name, and flee to the wilds of Montana to milk buffalos?

My female coworkers whisper and giggle at him behind their hands. One takes a picture on her phone from around the corners of her cubicle. Naturally, they think he's trying to get into my pants. I want to toss the lush lilies in his smug face, but they are too beautiful to be ruined so quickly in the name of vengeance.

"That was so sweet of you. Thank you so much! They're lovely," I gush and give him my brightest commercial smile. The one I reserve for my most challenging clients.

He can tell I'm faking it and returns my fake smile. He reaches out and tilts my chin up with his index finger. An intrusive thought of chomping down on his finger tempts me.

"Anything for you," he says with an unreadable expression. My traitorous stomach does a little flip. My logic can't seem to fight back our history. I jerk away from him with the heavy vase in my trembling hands.

"I'll go get water for these. Thank you again! Bye!" I dismiss him and retreat to the employee kitchen and slam the door behind me. I set the flowers on the staff lunch table and lean against the metallic sink, trying to take deep, calming breaths through my nose.

While I hyperventilate, I focus on the workplace safety poster taped to the cabinet above the sink. The laminated poster reminds me to wash my hands with a bright yellow happy face and clip art bubbles.

What should I do? Is he obsessed with me?

In high school, Trish and I would bark at cat callers when we went on gas station iced coffee runs after school. Worked every time and made for a good laugh.

Maybe I should make a drastic gesture like that to scare him off.

I don't consider myself a violent person. I've had my fair amount of rough tussles with my siblings growing up, but I usually pulled the younger two apart. I'm not a fighter. But he doesn't know that.

I glance down at my pink crocs and pink scrubs. A shiny gold pin on my chest says *Happy to help!* My name tag has Harry Potter stickers on every space that isn't covering my name.

I'm so fucked.

The kitchen door behind me squeaks open, and he walks up behind me without a word. Then, with a surge of adrenaline, I spin around, grab him by his collar, and shove him as hard as I can into the opposite wall.

I'm not strong, but his back hits the wall hard with surprise on my side. He has a good foot on me in height, so I stand on my tiptoes to get closer to looking him directly in the eye. His brown eyes are blown wide in surprise, but a deep, annoyed frown turns the corners of his mouth. Did he think I would giggle and curtsy when he brought me fake birthday flowers?

The audacity of it all turns my rage up to ten.

"Listen up, Cato. If you and your ugly friends don't leave me alone, I will boil your eyeballs from the inside and make you eat them." My threats are meaningless, but he doesn't know that. He throws his hands up in surrender.

"Relax. If you wanted to hurt me, you and I both know you would have done that by now," he says.

"Bullshit!" I spit at him, trying to press him harder into the wall, but he's solid. I hope he's too distracted to feel my hands tremble on his collar.

"I would appreciate it if you took your grubby little hands off of me. I'm here to talk."

I begrudgingly let him go and cross my arms to keep from reaching out and throttling him. "You want to talk? Let's talk. Who are you? What do you want? Why was I kidnapped?"

"Calm down. I'm not your enemy. Why do you think your car was down the block when you escaped? It's because I put it there," he says. I stutter for words. I thought that was sheer luck.

"You're insane if you think I'm going to trust you because you parked my car."

"You're the one who shoved me into the wall," he says. We lock eyes for a moment, silently gauging our trust in each other.

"Why are you here?" I ask.

"I need to speak to you about a life-changing offer, so I made a plan to see you again."

I blink at him.

Jesus Christ, these multi-level marketing guys are bold.

"I'm calling security."

It was a brilliant plan, I'll give him that. By cornering me at my workplace, he knows I can't make a scene, and I can't leave. He thought he trapped me. But unfortunately for him, I'm not interested in his ' life-changing offer.'

I turn to follow through with my threat, but he snatches my wrist.

I'm shocked that he's not afraid to touch me, despite knowing I can incinerate him in seconds.

"Let go, or I'll scream."

His grip on my wrist tightens when I try to pull away.

"Stop. Listen." He lets me go and steps back. He reaches into his coat pocket and pulls out the fattest stack of cash I have ever seen in my life. It's *at least* two years of my salary. My eyes bug out of my head.

"Flee the state. Better yet, flee the country. Take this and never look back." He firmly shoves the cash at me, and I step back with a frown, eyes jumping from his face to the thick stack of money.

"Uproot your life, run away, and disappear, or find the cure to your…predicament. The first option is a lot easier for both of us." He reaches into another pocket and produces an even fatter stack of bills.

"If you take this right now, I'll throw in an annual allowance of a couple hundred."

"Dollars?"

"A couple hundred *grand*."

My fingers twitch to grab the money. The opportunity he's offering is invaluable. Would it be so terrible to live out the rest of my days in the Italian sunshine? I could own an isolated little cottage by the seaside. Read books all day and walk the beaches of the Amalfi Coast all night like a lonely sea witch searching for her drowned lover.

I'd never hurt anyone or anything again. And no one could hurt me. I ball my hand into a fist and lower it to my side. No. My sister. Trish. Her baby. My clients. Tyrion. I'm comfortable with my life, except for this one little blemish.

"Wait. There's a cure?!" I whisper-shout. My pulse thrums greedily at the hope of a normal life. Fuck the cash.

"That's what I said." He rolls his eyes at my eagerness.

"Why? Why are you trying to help me?"

"You need to make a decision. Take the money and run or remove your power. Choose," he says. He huffs out an annoyed sigh right in my face.

"How do I remove my power?"

"I don't know; that's for you to figure out. But it is possible."

"How could you know that?"

"Stop being difficult and listen to me. I can't let you continue with a normal life. You're going to kill someone. You don't have any other choices. Either you take my money and leave on your own, or I stuff you in a suitcase and drop your ass off on a remote island in Japan. Choose."

Trish's baby is coming so soon. My patients, my sister, my life. I can't leave them. I won't.

"Make a deal with me," I blurt. "If I fail to remove the curse by Halloween, I'll leave. I'll take your disgusting pile of cash and go to a place where no one will ever find me. Ever. I'll change my name, disown my family, dye my hair."

He frowns down at me as he contemplates my offer. He pockets the money and runs a hand through his dark hair.

"If you succeed?"

"If I succeed, I'll be normal again, and you'll have nothing to worry about," I say.

"If you fail, you won't be tempted to come back? You'll stay away?" His eyes narrow in doubt.

"I never break my promises."

"Good, because I will have to kill you if you come back. I don't want to do that," he says. The sincerity of his statement sends a chill up my spine.

"Right, I'm sure that will be *so difficult* for you," I try to snarl, but it comes out of my throat as a squeaky statement. I notice he's clamped down on my wrist again, and I try to yank it away.

"Let go, or I promise I will bite you."

"Don't threaten me with a good time." A new expression crosses his face. One that makes me blush furiously. I shove him again, and he stumbles back. His broad frame bumps the fridge, creating a loud slamming noise as it rocks into the wall. Violet bursts into the kitchen.

We both stare at her, frozen in our positions.

My fingers are curled around his collar. His back is against the employee refrigerator. Improvising, I give him a quick kiss on his cheek and step back, unsure what to do with my hands now that they aren't at his throat. I tell myself I had no other choice, like a cornered animal.

"Sorry, Violet. We got a bit, uh, heated."

I'm so embarrassed I could die. I wish I could tell her the truth was that I pushed around my kidnapper by proxy around the kitchen. The first cover-up I thought of was to kiss him to hide the fact that we were in a not-so-romantic physical altercation. Sue me.

"You cheeky kids," Violet gently chastises, "get out. Shoo!"

He looks back at me on his way out. I make a rude hand gesture at him, and he snickers. I nearly crack a smile, but I remember how damn weird and dangerous this situation is.

A strange young man I made out with months ago rejected me. We reunited at my kidnapping. He helped me escape after I injured him, and now he's brought lilies to my work for the chance to talk and offer me money to get out of his sight forever. A modern romance.

"Think about your choices and have a great day. Enjoy your flowers." He waves at me and leaves.

Good riddance. The vice around my lungs loosens, and I take a deep breath, running a hand through my dark tresses. A sharp migraine pain flickers behind my eyes. I give my sore scalp a soothing scratch.

"What have you gotten yourself into, love?" Violet frowns at me, shaking her head.

"I don't know, Violet. I don't know."

After an uneventful six-hour shift cleaning and reading murder mysteries for my sleepiest client, Miss Hazel Partridge, I pull up to my favorite cafe to treat myself to a warm blueberry scone and hot chocolate.

I'm also trying to avoid being home alone for too long until my sister gets back from her trip tomorrow. I stare into my cup and consider my life's current problems. I was kidnapped but unharmed. Unlike Kazak, Cato has a warmth in his eyes that keeps drawing me in. I won't lie and say a thrill didn't rush through me when I saw him with a bouquet in hand in my office. Or when I shoved him around in the staff kitchen. Or when I kissed the soft corner of his mouth.

My mind wanders back to everything he said and didn't say. He was so vague. Even more pressing is the possibility that I could be rid of my curse. I should have wrung more information out of him instead of losing my temper so quickly.

I rub my tired cheeks and pinch the bridge of my nose, squeezing my eyes shut.

"Another pastry, sweets?" Jaime, my flamboyant waiter, chirps over his shoulder as he wipes down a neighboring table.

"No thanks, hun. I better put the brakes on the carbs. What do I owe you?" I turn to dig cash out of my bag. He puts a hand on his hip and sweeps his cotton candy pink hair out of his eyes.

"Not a penny, babydoll. Already paid for," he says. I blink up at him in surprise. Then, with an impish wink, he tilts his head towards a man lurking in the corner of the cafe before flouncing away.

Of course. Of course, he's here. I was so focused that I didn't even notice him slither in. The cafe is so close to the office, I should have known. I feel my nails dig into my palm. Tension spiders across my back. He has a knack for showing up in places he doesn't belong.

He sticks out like a sore thumb in the charming ambiance of my cafe. His hair looks extra greasy, and his green jacket grossly mismatches his bright red polo shirt.

Howard. The bane of my existence.

Swallowing my irritation, I give the slimeball a tight-lipped smile and adjust my laptop, so it's hiding my face from his view. I can afford my pastries and coffees, thank you very much. However, I realize hiding from him isn't going to nullify that he's sitting right over there. I peek over my laptop again, and he's gone. I do a double take before I finish my cup and glance over my shoulder. How did I miss him?

You need to be more aware of your surroundings, especially around him.

It feels awkward to leave after only twenty minutes when I usually stay a few hours, but I can't enjoy myself with that creep lurking nearby.

Outside the cafe, I reach my arms up to the darkening sky in an indulgent stretch. I dig in my purse to find my car keys when I'm spooked by a loud noise to my left. I whip around, half-expecting to see a thug shove a gun in my face. But instead, a tiny old lady is doubled over beside her car.

She clutches her chest, obviously having a medical emergency. Swollen, arthritic fingers pop open a button on her periwinkle peacoat. Her shoulders bob up and down as she struggles to find her breath.

"Are you okay?" I shout to her.

She turns to me and shakes her head, her face scrunched up in pain. Then, she waddles towards the building next door and stumbles into the side entrance.

"Wait, no! Shit! Dammit! Where is she going?" I shove my keys back into my bag and jog to follow her into the neighboring building. It's a dimly lit office, nearly identical to my headquarters. I swivel my head around, looking for the sneaky old lady in blue. She's disappeared. A bad feeling lurches in my stomach, but I can't just leave her.

"Ma'am?" I call down the hall. Silence answers me. I clear my throat, urged on by the worry that she may have collapsed nearby.

"Ma'am? Hello?" I yell louder this time. A sound between a wheeze and a choking cough from around the corner answers me. I break into a run. I nearly had a medical incident myself by running into a leather chair in the reception area where I finally find her.

She clutches the front desk with one hand and her chest with the other, breathing erratically.

"Ma'am, I'm trained in CPR. Please let me help!" I place a gentle hand on her thin shoulder. "Try to control your breathing. Stay calm for me. We should get you an ambulance-"

I don't have time to block.

The bitch swings a lamp and nails me in the temple with its brass leg. My surprised yelp echoes throughout the empty building. Burning pain throbs in my head, and I fall to my knees, gripping the front desk for support on my way down.

The pain is so intense that my vision is red. Or is it the blood in my eyes? Where in the world is my hunky stalker when I need him? The room spins like a top.

My eyelashes flutter as I blink my blood out of them and try to return to my senses. The lamp she whacked me with wasn't a flimsy modern lamp. Instead, it's a weighted brass antique with golden angels adorning the base. Ironic.

I've never seen a rabid pig before, but what I see now is close enough. This woman is enormous and getting larger before my eyes. She's bulging out of her clothes, transforming into something unnatural. Her previously white face is a nasty shade of purple.

The seams of her peacoat burst, rippling underneath with newly formed muscles. Steam puffs out of the flared nostrils of her snout. She reaches into her dirty carpet bag while I shuffle backward in fear. I grab a tissue box off a bookshelf and frantically try to wipe the blood out of my sight. Thank God she missed my mouth when she struck me, or I'd be picking up shards of my teeth from the floor.

A silvery glimmer in the corner of my stained vision makes my heart stutter. That better not be what I think it is. I squint through the blood in my burning eyes, and my worst fear is confirmed. A knife is drawn out of her bag.

"You should be put down like an animal!" she spits at me. Ouch. That sentiment hurts because I used to agree with it. She's so mad, she foams at the mouth, sweat stains crescent under her massive arms, and I realize she means to do the job herself.

I grab a hefty stack of printer paper from a desk, engulf it in flames, and chuck it with both hands at her fat head. I'll be damned if I let this crazy hag slice me up after all I've been through in the past few days. I miss my target dismally, but it scares her several feet backward.

I take this opportunity to brace my back against the wall and kick the bookshelf on top of her.

If I ate a magic cookie and got fire powers, did she eat a magic pork rind and end up like this? Maybe omnipotent fire powers aren't so bad. Then again, if I were normal and never swallowed that cookie a decade ago, I wouldn't be in this fucking mess. A terrible gurgling noise erupts from her throat as the bookcase slams into her. I jump up on a table and bust ass through the dark rows of cubicles.

I don't know if you've ever been chased through a dark office by a knife-wielding demon pig lady, but I can't say I recommend it. Great cardio, though. My face slams right into a large chest as I turn a corner. The smell of pine stops my pulse. An electric sensation prickles my spine, a memory of our last meeting.

Kazak grins down at me like he's greeting an old friend. His smile doesn't reach his eyes. Cold. Calculated. Reptilian. Like the eyes of a killer.

"Hello, Miss Auclair. Nice to see you again. May I call you Ruby?" He politely smiles, and I hate him for it. Once again, I've found myself trapped by a man.

The only man I want to be alone with is Mr. George. We would build a puzzle together on a lazy fall afternoon with chocolate chip oatmeal cookies baking in the oven, a coffee-scented candle on the mantle, and insulin ready in his fridge.

"I see you've run into my colleague. This is Annabelle. She is a creation of my late father."

He gestures behind me. Pig lady has caught up. She pants like a champion bull about to gore a puny matador. My lower lip trembles.

"Either come with me quietly, or I'm afraid I'll have to ask Annabelle to escort you. The choice is yours. Although, if you choose to run, I'll reward you with a five-second head start." His sharp canines glint menacingly in the low light as he flashes an entertained smile.

"I love a good chase," he whispers with excitement.

The choice to run is an easy one. I'm not a fast runner, but adrenaline and fear pump energized blood into my legs. I fly down the hall. I can hear him loudly count to five over the pounding of my feet. I slam into a door with a bright red exit sign glowing above it. Locked. I sprint over to another on the opposite side. Locked.

I finally see a set of double doors around a corner with small window slots revealing the outside world. My wrists slam so hard into the bar handle I'm sure I've broken one.

It doesn't budge. I scream an expletive in frustration as I hear Annabelle thunder closer.

I try the other door, and it blessedly gives way. I run down the front steps as fast as I can, skipping two at a time.

Before I reach the last step, a hand darts out from the bushes and grabs my wrist. The momentum of my run and the pull of the hand flips me over the railing and into the bushes. My scrubs protect me from the sharp branches as I tumble into a space between the hedge and the brick of the building.

A large hand slaps over my mouth, pulling me into a hard body. Mulch skitters everywhere as I kick and twist, and a scream in my throat escapes through his fingers as a muffled squeak.

Not like this. I can't die like this. I haven't told Rain I'm sorry yet. I won't be able to protect new girls at work from Howard. I haven't met Trish's baby yet. I—

"Shut up and be still if you want to live," a voice commands in my ear. I stopped struggling, not out of obedience but out of fear. The pig lady is thundering down the steps beside us. She looks right at me. A terrified breath puffs out of my nose. I'm certain I'm about to be gored alive. But, instead, she turns and stomps away, as if she didn't see me. Her deep breathing grows faint and disappears.

"Can't see us. That's my power," the voice in my ear explains in a low whisper, "it's called Poltergeist."

He's saved me again.

Cato removes his hand from my mouth but grabs hold of my elbow instead. I look down to find my body missing.

Where my thighs should be, is mulch and dead leaves. Cato must have to be touching me to branch out his ability. God, I wish I had a helpful power. A safe power.

The hand on my elbow disappears, and my body reappears. I welcome back my body by flexing and wiggling my fingers.

"That's pretty neat." I turn and smile at him. He's kneeling in the mulch with his hands on his thighs, watching me.

"Neat?" he mocks me, eyes hard with disgust as if I told him I wear a diaper to bed. I grind my molars and swallow the knot of embarrassment in my throat. We vanished and reappeared like magic.

That's neat as fuck.

I frown at him and finally notice that I'm practically in his lap and quickly shift away, face hot, putting distance between us.

I keep finding myself way too close to him. From our first encounter playing drunken tonsil hockey to dressing his bloody nose to shoving him into a refrigerator, it's all been too close. Every touch is like a burn under my skin.

"Yes, neat. Anyways...bye." I turn a tiny piece of mulch in my palm into ash and blow it into his eyes before he can react. He reels back and bursts into a coughing fit as I vault the hedge and make a run for my car without looking back. Do I feel bad? No. No, I don't feel bad.

Why should I feel bad? He might have saved me, but he's still a jerk. I run to my car, and suddenly I can't breathe. My keys are missing. I dropped my keys and—

"Looking for these?" Cato appears beside me and shoves them in my hand. His eyes are bloodshot. His face is tear streaked. He looks so mad that he might kill me himself.

"Listen to me, you little demon," he growls in my face, "I'm trying to help you."

Now, I feel bad.

"I'm sorry, that was...an overreaction on my part. Thank you for your help. Please don't kill me."

"Look for my note," he says and vanishes.

I arrive home with a splitting headache and a new fear of pigs. A white Mazda is in the driveway when I pull up to the townhouse. My sister is back early from her trip. I use a spare water bottle from my backseat to rinse the blood off my face before going inside the house.

She's washing fresh fruit at the kitchen sink when I enter the room.

"Hey, slut." I pop a sour blueberry into my mouth, greeting my little sister. I recite a prayer in my head that she doesn't see the dark bruise forming near my eye.

"Hello, dumb whore. How's your day been?" Rain barely looks up from her chore.

"Boring." *I almost died a couple times, made some new friends, and got dumped. The usual.*

"And you? How was the trip?" I boink a berry off her forehead when she finally looks up, earning me a scary glare. She zings the berry back across the counter, hitting my shoulder.

"It was great, but nice try. Where were you? You're never out this late."

"I stopped by Jaime's for a snack, lost track of time." I shrug and suck up another blueberry. She gives me an odd look when I shrug and try to pass her before she sees my whole face. "Oh, my God,

Ruby!" She grabs my arm hard, and I know she saw my temple.

"What happened?! That's huge!" she shouts and gapes at my wound. I wince. I can't believe I was dumb enough to think she wouldn't notice.

"Did Seth hit you?"

"No! A client at work tripped over her stupid cat, pulling me down with her. My head bumped her counter. It was worth it, though. Thankfully nobody was injured. Well, except me."

"'Bumped'? It looks like you got smashed over the head!"

Damn her and her creepily accurate intuition.

"It looks a lot worse than it is. I'm fine. Drop it. You're making my head hurt worse. Grab a bag of frozen peas for me and tell me about your trip."

5

The next day at Mr. George's manor, I'm relieved to find he has no familial visitors. He snoozes in his leather armchair, a crisp newspaper in his hands and a warm blanket on his lap. I make his bed, fluff his pillows, and spritz his shower with cleaner.

While it fizzes away the scum, I tiptoe to the massive kitchen. The coolness of the alabaster countertop chills my skin as I lean onto it to write up a quick grocery list. I peek into the fridge to check if we need anything.

A neon sticky note attached to the bottom of the milk jug catches my eye. I peel it off with caution, half-expecting an explosion.

Anything can happen after the week I've endured. It pops as it detaches from the jug. Thin, neat, and unfamiliar handwriting fills the paper square.

Greenhouse. 5 PM.

-C

C for creep, I think, with a scowl. *When did that weasel sneak in here?* I almost bang my head on the fridge door. I can't escape him.

After a quiet day with Mr. George and two miserably lost chess games, I make myself a cup of tea to calm my nerves before heading into the greenhouse. I've been watching reruns of black and white cowboy dramas and worrying about this little meeting all day as Mr. George indulged in cyclical naps.

With my steaming cup in hand, my nursing clogs squeak as I make my way across the soggy back lawn. I pass the large glass structure each morning when I enter the house, but I've never gone inside.

It's a bit spooky for my taste. Dead vines curl around rows of shriveled-up plants, left for dead years ago. An entire shelf in the back is filled with ceramic fairy folk and big-eyed gnomes, blanketed in cobwebs and hollow carcasses of long-dead bugs.

Many years ago, it was bursting with green life. It feels haunted now. In the center of the dilapidated greenhouse, a life-size sculpture of Athena stands guarding a barren fountain.

I sip my creamy tea and study her.

Her expression is proud, and her head of curls is adorned with an olive branch crown. In one hand, she holds a rose, and in the other, she clutches a book to her chest. As I stare at the goddess of wisdom and war, I wonder what she would do. Would she meet her enemy alone to pursue a crazy quest for freedom? Would she call me foolish or brave?

She would look down her Roman nose at me and scoff at the human with the powers of a goddess without the balls to even use them.

A waste. A danger. A terrible accident waiting to happen—

"I can't stand you."

My tea drips down the wrong pipe in the back of my throat.

"Excuse me?" I wheeze at him, trying to hack the tea out of my lungs.

He appears out of nowhere. His arms are crossed over his large chest, and he's staring at me like he regrets having ever crossed my path.

I can't stand you. A "good afternoon" or even "hey" couldn't have been so hard. Rude.

"Look at you. Pink, manicured nails. Your job is to babysit old people. Barely over five feet tall. I bet you read to orphaned puppies in your spare time."

"I do not *babysit* them! I assist with activities of daily living and medication-"

"Whatever," he says, "you should be grateful I even offered to help you. I don't want you to get the wrong idea that I'm doing this because I have nothing better to do."

"And what exactly are you *doing?* Did you leave a note on the milk so you could get me out here to bully me?" I down the last of my cup as if it were a shot of whiskey.

His hostility is edging me towards a panic attack. Who pissed in his coffee?

I don't think there's enough chamomile tea in the whole state to calm me down.

I *hate* arrogance. Cato's arrogance is different from Howard's. Howard *thinks* he's smarter than me. Cato *knows* he's smarter than me. Any regrets I've had about punching or kicking him have subsided.

"I'll tell you what *we're* doing. You and I are about to have a calm, adult conversation," he pauses and looks down at me as if I'm the one being difficult. My ears heat at his patronization. "No tricks, no flowers, and no running away. Do you think we can manage that, Auclair?"

The night we met in the bar, he called me Ruby. He sounds like a different person when he calls me by my surname. I suppose he is a different person.

The Cato from the bar seemed to like me. The one in this haunted greenhouse looks at me like he smells shit.

"I can have an 'adult conversation.' My only issue is that I have to partake in it with a guy like you," I reply. Artificial sweetness drips from my lips.

"A guy like me?" He raises an amused brow, intrigued by my venom. My ears heat.

The anger I've been holding back rushes against my mental dam like a mudslide.

"Yes. A jerk and a criminal with a superiority complex."

"Why would you think that?" He shakes his head as if trying to reason with an upset child. It's unfair how long his lashes are and how clear his ivory skin is.

I bet he washes his face with dish soap and wakes up with a glowing complexion. He probably wipes his face with the same towel he uses to wipe his ass.

You pushed me down a garbage chute so your nutty brother didn't pick me apart, and you expected me to quietly take your shit. Fuck you.

He sighs a long-suffering sigh when I don't respond. I interrupt his dramatics with a question that's been burning to get out.

"Will you help me?"

"What?"

"Will you help me remove the Dotion? I can't do it alone." I'm begging at this point. I need at least one ally on my side, even if it's him. I'm sick of being alone. He stares at me for a moment and sighs heavily again.

"You're so much more trouble than I thought you would be. But, yes, I will help you. On my terms."

"What does that mean?" It's my turn to raise a doubtful brow.

"I tell you where and what to look for, and you do it. No questions asked. No complaints. And don't forget, the deadline is Halloween. If we fail, you bear the consequences and disappear."

"Fine, deal." I can't hide the desperation in my voice as I agree with his terms. Unfortunately, I don't have another choice. He sits on the edge of Athena's empty fountain and leans forward with his elbows on his knees.

"Listen," he sighs, "my father created it. The food you ate gave you your powers."

"What? The cookie? *Your dad?* How did he do that?" I blurt. The corners of his mouth shift into an annoyed frown, and I wince at myself.

"Shut up and listen. Please."

"Sorry," I sheepishly mumble. I've waited over a decade for answers. I can't help being a little giddy. Cato inhales a calming breath through his nose before continuing.

"As I was saying, my father created Dotions. He was a terrible man, but also a terrible genius."

"Neat," I croak, my throat tight as worrying thoughts about how long he's been watching me, following me, circle around my brain.

"My brother wants to kill you for yours."

"What?" I choke again, this time on nothing but air, "The? Fuck?" I hack out in between coughs. He scowls at me and offers me a handkerchief from his pocket. I snatch it and try to quickly collect myself.

"Charming," he says, raising a brow at my curses. How big of a rich asshole do you have to be to still carry around a handkerchief?

"Father died before my brother could get one, so he wants yours. We didn't know our father had created yours until my brother got a letter last year from our long-dead father. It revealed he had given a child his last and most powerful Dotion. So powerful, it could wash the world in fire."

I gulp, trying to fight a strong wave of nausea as the reality of my situation seeps in. Ever since I destroyed that poor owl over a decade ago, I've known how dangerous my power is, but I didn't realize it was designed by an evil genius for destruction.

"The letter contained a code with the locations of his notes for transfer of the power to another user. He challenged him to find the child and reclaim it—"

"Why would anyone do that?" I blurt out, unable to listen quietly any longer. What kind of father implants a super weapon in an unsuspecting child and challenges his son to find it and take it for himself? Like a sick scavenger hunt. I watch a muscle in his jaw clench, and his Adam's apple bobs up and down before he speaks.

"I can't explain to you the motivations of a long-dead lunatic, but I can tell you for certain that my brother is hellbent on taking it from you."

Dumb luck and minimal use of the Dotion have gotten me this far. How can I beat a well-funded and meticulous villain in a race for the key to my shackles?

I could bring hellfire upon him and his minions with a wave of my hand, but I'd rather die than lose control and hurt people. Or have my own family be afraid of me.

"My brother is a cold-blooded opportunist. A snake in the grass. Do *not* underestimate him. You have the power he needs, and he won't hesitate to kill you for it."

It's a truth as cold as the breeze against our faces. He took me hostage once and let me live. I doubt he'll make the same mistake twice. He steps in close, pulling me in by the collar of my scrubs, and leans down. I swallow, eyes wide.

"I need you to grasp the gravity of this. If you aren't serious about this, stay upstairs and play patty-cake with grandfather or scrub a toilet because I don't need you screwing this up. As I explained before, I don't care if you win. I need Kazak to lose. Clear?"

My nails dig into my palms, and I grind my jaw.

"Crystal."

"And by the way..."

I cut him off by exhaling a dark puff of smoke, allowing it to escape through my clenched teeth and past my lips in a way I hope appears threatening and not like a goofy teenager vaping for the first time.

He stares at my mouth, and I wonder if it's in fascination or disgust.

"I'm also dead serious. I don't know if you have a job or not, but your new job is going to be searching for those removal instructions and to keep me alive. Keep me safe, and I'll do what you say to ensure Kazak doesn't get my Dotion. I can't have your brother's mutant pig demons chasing me around."

He shakes his head, seemingly torn between shoving me in a box with packing peanuts addressed to Europe and helping me.

"Why does he want it?" I ask.

"Jealousy."

I scoff and roll my eyes.

"If he had watched me close enough, he'd realize it's not worth it." Fear is a part of my daily routine. Anxiety sits under my skin. Who would want this?

"He's a bad person, Ruby. He stabbed me when I got higher grades in middle school." His fingers ghost over a spot near his left rib cage. "You should back out now, leave the country, change your name, and leave everything behind. It's the safest option."

"I told you I can't," I say, fighting to keep my voice steady, "and since when do you care about my wellbeing?" I think back to when he commented on my bloody hair after I punched him in the nose. I know I shouldn't be metaphorically poking the bear, but I can't stand being babied by men who don't even know me.

"I don't, but you've made it my job. Do what I say, and I'll ensure your curse is broken."

My teeth dig into my lower lip as I fight back a sassy retort.

I need him. He can set me free. I pull my arm back, reach into a pocket on my scrub pants, pull out a key, and press it into his hand. Attached to it is a Lego figure keychain of Darth Vader. He twists its toy helmet in between his large fingers.

"This is the key to the townhome I share with my sister. Her name is Rain, and her girlfriend is Sydney."

I'm not worried about Sydney, but my pesky little sister may be an issue. Even if Cato can be invisible, he'll need to be extra careful to slip past her keen eye.

"She comes and goes frequently. They are the only two people besides myself who have access to the apartment by key. I have an ex-boyfriend who has a key, but I've had all the locks changed," I clear my throat awkwardly, realizing that detail wasn't necessary to add, and continue to note, "as for my parents, they live out of state and won't be visiting this month, so there's no need to worry about them."

"Anyways, this goes without saying, but don't let them see you. Don't lose this key, and don't come into my bedroom without messaging me first."

"Do you currently have a boyfriend?" he asks me blankly.

"Uh, what?" I blush so hard I can feel the skin of my neck throb with heat.

"I need to know if you have a boyfriend, so I don't accidentally put him in the hospital if I catch him sneaking around your place."

He stares at me emotionlessly as if he were talking to a wall. He's turned off his emotions.

"No, I've been a little preoccupied lately. You won't have to worry about that."

"Good."

"Good." I bob my head in an awkward nod and reach into my bag again.

"This is my work schedule, address, and cell number. Memorize this. Burn or shred it when you're done," I say. He looks at me like he's never seen me before. Or maybe like I've grown another head. It's a pleasant change from his dark and brooding stare.

"You planned this."

"I like to be a few steps ahead." I shrug and pull my jacket tighter around myself. I'm lying, of course, but he doesn't need to know that. I just happened to print out my monthly work schedule this morning, with my address and cell on it.

"You play an interesting game." His eyes narrow at me but not in suspicion. He might be impressed.

"I play to win."

I'm bullshitting this conversation, and I'm praying that he can't see through me. The building excitement inside my chest is doused by a sudden cold rush of doubt and suspicion.

"Alright, is there anyone else you need to tell me about? Any enemies?"

I immediately think of Howard. Given a chance, I think he would ruin my life. But if I tell Cato about Howard, I'll have to tell him about *the incident*, and I'm not ready to do that yet.

"No enemies. Just Kazak. How do I know I can trust you? That you won't take it for yourself?"

"You don't. You have to take a chance and put your faith in me if you want that Dotion gone for good."

He steps around me, eyes on the ground, to exit the greenhouse. He pauses in the doorway to drop a tiny piece of paper. It bounces off his shoe and rolls towards me.

"Sleep on what I've told you. Call this number when you're ready."

I wait a moment for him to fully exit before throwing up a middle finger at the back of his head.

"Helpful, Cato, thank you for that," I say aloud to the plant graveyard. It makes perfect sense that the same man who cursed me also sired that vexatious man. He's infuriating and callous, but he's vital to my freedom.

No more nightmares. No more paralyzing fear when I hold a baby, or sneeze, or clap my hands together. I crack my knuckles, allowing little sparks to fly.

Soon, they'll be gone for good. Keep your chin up, work hard, and you'll be free in no time.

Dots connect in my head, and I run out of the greenhouse, into the manor, and down the hall. I skid to a halt in front of the library and look into The Blue Man's painted eyes. I've passed the painting countless times without a second glance. He is the only portrait in the house. It's hard to miss him. This time his charming smirk mocks me. The warlock who cursed me. My oppressor. A mad man. Forcing omnipotent power on a child. He looks like his eldest son, down to the icy blue eyes. I fight the temptation to flick my wrist and watch him burn and shrivel up as if burning his image will take back all of his sins.

I decided to make the call later that night.

My fingers find his number in my purse as hope blooms in my chest. I sit on our porch and stare at the little piece of paper with thin, angular writing. What will my life be like once I remove my curse? It's been so long. I think back to what my life was like before age thirteen.

I buried that version of myself on the top of a faraway hill.

Her biggest secrets were her middle-school crushes hidden in a pink diary with a tiny heart-shaped lock. Her biggest worry was that her little sister would find out that she was the sticky-fingered little thief who snatched the milk chocolate coins from her Easter basket. Her favorite game was hide and seek with her little brother. Her most ambitious dream was to save the world with love, hearts, butterflies, and rainbows. I try not to mourn for her. It hurts too much.

I dial the number with trembling fingers, and he answers after one ring.

"That was fast." His deep voice is slow and casual as if he had been expecting me to call at this second. I suck a quick breath in through my nose. "I've decided. How do we begin?"

A noise that sounds like a laugh. Cynical and low.

"It'll be dangerous."

"I'm more dangerous," I quip back.

"You must truly be desperate. Are you sure?" The light taunt of his voice in my ear turns a knob in my brain. I switch from nervous to furious at lightspeed. This isn't a game of chess. This is my actual life.

"Let me be clear, you insufferable meat-head," I hiss into the speaker. My cheeks are hot enough to cook an egg, and I'm gripping my poor phone so hard I'm surprised it hasn't melted.

"I would cut off my arm and toss it to you if it meant getting rid of this. Do. You. Understand. Me?"

A pause. For a moment, I think he hung up on me…

"Good. That's exactly what I wanted to hear. See you Monday."

My Monday starts with a boiling mocha in my hand and my pink leather purse on my elbow. I frown at Howard's puke-green Kia Soul as I think about what Cato said.

See you Monday.

He had said it like a promise. Like a threat. So far, no sign of him. But alas, the day is young.

I speed walk to the copier in my rush to avoid Howard. In my hurry, I almost slam into someone when I turn the corner.

"Slow down, Ruby! Where's the fire?" Meredith smiles down at me good-naturedly.

"Oh, shoot! I'm sorry, Meredith. I was distracted!"

"Anything bothering you, jelly bean?" Her pristine brows elevate. My throat tightens at the genuine concern in her eyes.

Meredith Clineman is the epitome of my dream self. She's ten years my senior, and the woman has her shit together. She's the district nurse manager, oversees a fifty-mile radius of patient care, and is the proud mother of toddler twin boys.

She's tall and radiant. With flawless skin and a neat little bob of brown hair, most of the older ladies in the office avoid her like the plague. Jealousy can make insecure people unkind. I, however, thrive off her electrifying energy and make a point to visit her whenever she's around the office, which is unfortunately rare.

A busy powerhouse of a woman like Meredith is rarely confined to a desk. She's also a professional at putting Howard in his place.

Meredith is the first person I should have told about Howard. I almost told her about *the incident*. I've wanted to tell her since the moment it happened. But I can't do it. Howard has his own little piece of dirt on me, and I'd lose the best job I've ever had as a consequence. So now I'm left to give subtle yet strong warnings about him to any new hires.

"Um–" I nervously tug on a loose piece of my hair, "do you have any advice on setting boundaries?" I weakly smile. I noticed a poster she put up last week in the break room on the topic, and I know she's been dying for a team member to ask. It's an easy scapegoat.

"Define the boundary, communicate it clearly, and outline the consequences of breaking it. It's *such* an important skill for anyone, especially people like us, to learn."

I nod and give her a tight smile. "Thanks. I'll keep that in mind."

"Anything else on your mind, hun?" She can see right through me. I have *a lot* on my mind. Howard happens to turn the corner behind Meredith's shoulder, and our eyes meet.

Keep your mouth shut, or I will ruin your life.

"Nope. I'm fine. Thanks for asking, though, Meredith. You're the best. I'm heading out for the day." She gives my arm a comforting squeeze as I pass her and wishes me good luck.

Thanks, Meredith. I'm going to need it.

My morning assignment is an easy one. I sit with a non-verbal client for a few hours, make her lunch, adjust her pillows, and read Jane Austen to her. Her daughter told me last week that it was her favorite. I catch her smile when I read the first chapter of *Pride and Prejudice*. My second and final client of the day is much more engaging. Monday nights with Rosetta Sutton keep me on my toes.

"Baby, Imma need you to pick me up more of that sweet wine at the store next time you come 'round. It's the pink one. Real cheap. Big ole bottle. Zinfa-sumthin. Zinnfanny, maybe!" she shouts at me from her bed, a raunchy romance novel in her lap and an oxygen cannula in her nose. I wonder if she forgets which of us is almost deaf. This is the fourth time tonight she's made such a request.

"I'll bring your zinfandel next week, Mrs. Sutton," I reply loudly, matching her volume so she can hear me.

She has half of her liver. There's no goddamn way I'm bringing her wine next week. I mix cranberry juice with a little water in a carafe, and she doesn't know the difference. So Rosetta gets her "wine," and I get to protect her from a UTI. Win win.

"Oh, good, thank you, baby. You take such good care of this old lady." She takes my hand in her spindly fingers and gives it a loving smack. A slight pang of guilt tweaks my gut, but everything I do is for her own good.

"I'll bring Lil' Bastard inside for the night before I go home." I squeeze her hand and pull away. She nods and turns back to her huge TV to finish avidly watching a television judge tell a divorcing couple to get their act together.

I step outside onto her splintering deck and call out into the dark to the tiny dog. Lil' Bastard is a one-eyed, temperamental devil of a dog.

This dog looks like an abomination. A cross breed between a squirrel and a half-dead wolverine.

I love him.

He used to try to bite me, but his teeth were long gone. His conquest for my blood has been fruitless. After a few weeks of sneaky peanut butter spoon licks and chin scratches, I eventually won his heart.

I make kissing noises into the night to summon the mischievous chihuahua. He's always sneaking off to terrorize the chipmunks deep in the backyard.

"Lil' Bastard! Here, boy!" I make kissing noises again and snap my fingers.

"You called?" Cato snickers, lounging in an old deck chair in the dark, long legs stretched out over a wicker table.

"Jesus. You're such a creep," I hiss at him, "and you're going to scare the dog! I don't have all night." I turn back to the dark yard.

"It's. Bedtime." I command with two claps, "Bastard, come here!"

A tiny sneeze to my right startles me. Cato opens his jacket to reveal Lil' Bastard, as snug as a bug against his chest. I can't help but giggle as I take the minuscule, shivering dog out from the warmth of his jacket.

"Come on, rascal. Time for bed." I nuzzle his little walnut of a head. He smells like expensive cologne.

I can feel Cato's eyes on me until I slam the door shut, leaving my stalker/bodyguard out in the cold. I was starting to hope he'd forgotten to meet me. I kiss the mutt before placing him gently into Rosetta's lap. He sneezes, curls into a circle, and falls asleep before my eyes. I slip fluffy socks on Rosetta's feet before grabbing my purse and locking her doors.

Cato meets me on the stoop outside. He's wearing black cargo pants, combat boots, and a gray, form-fitting jacket that stretches over his muscled shoulders. A reminder that he could break me in half before I had the time to snap my fingers.

He rubs his hand on the back of his neck and twists his head to the side. His neck cracks loudly, and I wince out of habit. When a patient produces a crack that loud, we usually end up in the emergency room.

"Is there a problem?" He raises a dark brow at me.

I should have known he would pounce on the awkwardness

between us and weaponize it.

"Nope. No problems here. How are you? How was your day?" As soon as I finish my question, I see him shift from nonchalant to annoyed.

What does he even do all day? Rub his fingers together maniacally? Brainstorm insults about my job and my hair? Work out? My nervous fingers don't know what to do with themselves, so they tug on a loose piece of hair from my bun. I'm lucky they aren't smoldering yet.

"How was...my *day*?" He looks at me like an extra hand has sprouted from my armpit.

"Mm hmm," I nod, "it's a standard question asked in greeting an acquaintance...or whatever the hell we are."

He doesn't need to be an asshole about it.

"My day is getting worse. How about you, princess? Did you have a nice day making flower crowns with little old ladies? Tell me, Auclair, how many pink bunnies can you sew onto a quilt in an hour?" The hostility in his voice is strange and harsh. He's testing me. I pat his large deltoid with feigned sympathy.

"Jealousy doesn't suit you," I tut. His chocolate eyes glint in the dark.

"A few rules. Don't touch me. Don't talk to anyone about me. Don't defer from your normal daily routine unless I tell you to."

My mouth tightens. He's never had a problem with me touching him in the past.

"Fine."

"Follow me. We're going to my grandfather's house."

I follow him through the dark halls of the manor, a guilty feeling flopping around in my gut like a goldfish on carpet. I *hate* being in Mr. George's house without his knowledge or permission. After the end of our shift, we're supposed to leave the premises immediately. I might be a dirty liar, but I hate rule-breaking.

We pass the painting of The Blue Man, and I can't help but stare. I still can't believe he's the cause of all my problems. Cato glances back and notices me staring at it.

I clear my throat. "He's quite a character. His eyes seem to follow."

"I painted this one," he says plainly. He watches me look from the painting to him, to the painting, and back to him.

"You?" I point at him. He nods once. "You painted that?"

"Why the surprise?"

I've always thought of painters as sensitive and dreamy people who can capture compelling images of starlight, bright eyes, and emotion and transfer them onto a canvas.

Cato Hadrian is the opposite of sensitive and dreamy.

He's mean and cold and a bad team player. He needs stringent therapy and an appointment with a skilled proctologist to remove the huge stick up his ass.

The notion that he's a brilliant artist heats my cheeks, and my head aches. I refuse to believe it, but his words are honest.

"It's...it's a masterpiece."

"Thanks, I hate it. I would have burned it years ago if it weren't for my mother. It was her favorite."

Without another word, he leads me through the silent halls. Finally, when we reach the cellar door, I can't stand it anymore.

"Alright, Cato. I'm gonna need you to drop the suave and mysterious act. It's getting old. Why are we here?"

He sighs, annoyed as if I've asked a great deal from him and not a simple explanation.

"The plan is to find my father's removal instructions, remove your power, and destroy it before my brother can claim it as his own. I know something my brother doesn't." He has a devious glint in his eyes, and now I can see the resemblance in the brothers where I didn't before. They're both bastards.

"What?"

"The removal instructions are in three possible places. One is the basement of this house."

"Oh my God! Are you serious?" I bounce on my heels in excitement, peeking over his shoulder at the door.

Countless times I've walked these halls, washing clothes, making Mr.George's bed, preparing his breakfasts, and little did I know the secret to my freedom was under my feet the whole time. It's almost poetic.

"It's not going to be that easy." He rolls his eyes at me. Of course not.

We step into the dark, dusty basement.

Cato continues into the blackness, but I stop and reach up on my tip toes and yank on a light bulb's string. My heart sinks into my butt. Hundreds of boxes line the mildew-spotted walls, bursting with papers, books, and folders. From what I can see, none of them have labels.

Not one.

"Oh, my God," I whisper in despair. This is going to take forever. "You better not have made this shit up so I can organize your grandpa's basement."

"After my dad died, his personal documents were put down here. There's at least a decade of paperwork down here. We better get started."

He instructs me to look through the documents for anything with my name or birthdate. We work in silence for two hours straight. My eyes sting as I search through the stacks of paperwork with Cato.

"This is impossible! The two of us are up against ridiculous odds! On top of that, this mess is a serious fire hazard! All this dust and paper is waiting for one little spark," I say.

He blurts out a mean laugh. "That's the pot calling the kettle black. You. Calling this a fire hazard."

I shove my hands up into the deep pockets of my sweatshirt, a dead giveaway that I'm upset. I've trained myself to hide my hands in case sparks fly from my fingertips.

"Does that creep know you're helping me?" I ask. He huffs at me like a parent on the cusp of a breaking point after answering their toddler's hundredth question.

"*Which* creep, Auclair? I happen to know more than a few." His frown deepens. I frown back. He's so annoyed with me for asking a question.

"*Your brother.* There's no way he's cool with you teaming up with me. I can't imagine it comes up over dinner."

"He doesn't know, and he won't find out. But that's not for you to worry about. Do as I say and keep your questions to yourself. They aren't worth my time." He turns back to his current book without another look at me.

"Are you calling me stupid?"

"Did I call you stupid?" he snarls back mockingly, dark eyes snapping back up to me, cruel and judgemental.

"I have questions about your father-"

"I don't talk about my father," he cuts me off. I blink at him incredulously. We've talked about him before.

"Well, you do now. Why would he choose me to experiment on?" I ask.

He steps close to me, leaning down to meet my eye level. It's a patronizing gesture, a power move. But I don't flinch.

"Didn't you hear me? Or are you deaf and dumb? Honestly," he scrubs a hand over his eyes, "I can't believe you ended up being the Morningstar Dotion wielder."

My eyes narrow. What an asshole. There it is. A truth shoved in my face again. A truth I already know. A truth on my mind every day I wake up and remember I'm not normal anymore. I force my eyes to roll, even as my cheeks heat in humiliation.

"Are you done? Did that feel good?" My face burns hotter, and my pulse pounds. I'm not used to confrontation. He straightens his back to loom over me, and a severe emotion flashes in his chocolate eyes. He has at least a foot on me. The thought of making oneself bigger to scare away a charging black bear pops into my mind. Is he afraid of me?

"You really don't want it?"

"Why would I *like* being a stick of dynamite? I haven't held a baby since I was ten. I sleep with my hands in oven mitts. I hate it."

As soon as I ate that cookie of the damned, power embedded in my bones. It swims through my blood like an infection. One I'll never be cured of. He runs a hand through his hair, pondering my statement for a moment. What a rollercoaster of a conversation. I should have crumpled up the milk note and thrown it in the trash. That's it. I've had enough growling for one night. If he scowls at me one more time, I may burst into tears, and I'll melt his eyeballs before I ever let him see that. The hefty tome on my lap tumbles to the floor as I stand, grab my bag and rush up the stairs without a glance back.

"Jerk wad," I mumble to myself as I push through the bushes to my car, "I'm not stupid. He's stupid."

6

I try to elicit a reaction out of him on Wednesday night. I swallow my pride and defy him by bringing him a coffee, but he barely acknowledges me when I hand him the steamy drink.

No 'thank you.' Nothing. What I would give to be searching these piles with anyone else. Even Kazak would be more of a kindred companion than the sour and silent prince I'm trapped with. He clears his throat suddenly, startling me so much I nearly fall off of my stool.

"Your fake attempts at kindness are degrading."

"Excuse me?"

Frankly, I'm offended. I've put a lot of effort into overcoming our shaky beginnings and his shitty attitude. He turns towards me, dark eyes alive with simmering anger.

"Coffee. Questions about my personal life. Compliments."

He points this out like it pains him to even speak to me. My hands shake as I form an angry fist.

"Forgive me," I say through gritted teeth, my cheeks on fire, "but I'm failing to see the issue here."

What is he talking about? Is he as nuts as his elder brother? What's the problem?

"I'm not your friend. I never will be. I'll never kiss you again, so if you're hoping for a replay of last year's mistake, you can forget about it. Tell me that I've made myself clear."

His expression is complex and unkind. He's being petty and cruel for no apparent reason that I can decipher. Angry tears threaten to sting my eyes, but I clear my throat and square my shoulders. My intentions are genuine; if he can't figure that out for himself, it's his loss.

"Crystal."

"Good," he says, turning on his heel and climbing the cellar stairs, unable to look at me a moment longer. I follow behind, keeping my distance. He turns back to me when we step out the side door to walk the drive back to our cars.

"We will have to infiltrate Hadrian Pharma and destroy files to stall my brother for a few weeks. It'll be dangerous."

"Okay." I roll my eyes at him. It can't be more dangerous than being a living flame-thrower for a decade.

"Can't you burn it down and spare us some competition?" he deadpans. I scoff at his suggestion of arson.

"Are you insane? Absolutely not. Are you okay? Have you been drinking enough water? Are you in therapy?" I think this was a bad call because the crease between his brows deepens sharply.

His eyes drop to my scrubs, and his mouth turns into a sneer. Today I'm wearing my favorite set. The top and bottoms are plain and black, but the torso pocket has a graphic of a fat, little mouse sitting in it.

"Aren't you adorable?" he mocks me, "I swear, it's like you want us to fail. You don't use your power in any useful way. Instead, you pretend to be powerless and then bitch at me when situations go wrong."

Be the bigger person, Ruby. He's had a rough night. Hurt people hurt other people–

While calming myself down, he glares at me like I'm stupid. It strikes a match on my skin, and my anger flares to life. I've had enough.

"Oh, Cato, please forgive me for avoiding mass casualties–" I beg sarcastically. He stomps off ahead of me, and I kick off a foam clog and throw it at his back.

Thwack. It nails him directly in the back of his head. He stops.

"Don't walk away from me when I'm speaking!" I can barely feel the sharp rocks of the driveway dig into my unprotected foot.

He turns and looks directly into my eyes. He vanishes, and I'm so screwed.

An unseen force sweeps my feet from under me, and I land hard on the rocky drive. I shriek and blindly throw a fist full of gravel into the night as I scramble to stand.

"I would say nice try, but it wasn't," a whisper in my ear taunts me. I blow a hot puff of smoke to the right. A hand grips my hip hard, and another snakes around my throat.

The invisible man flips me and drops me on my back, knocking the air out of my lungs. He appears over me, looming, face blank. For a moment, I think he might kill me and put an end to my pain.

Pieces of my past life before power flash behind my eyelids. Before, I kept my hands folded. Or in pockets. Or hidden.

Late springs on my knees in dark, lush earth, helping my grandma plant her flower garden with benign hands. On tiptoes in the kitchen, stirring a pot of gooey macaroni and cheese with a wooden spoon while my mom changed my baby brother's diaper. Late summer games of catch with my father in scratchy, dry grass. Pinching the cheeks of little cousins to make them laugh at family gatherings.

No fear. No chaos. No danger.

The good old days.

Every touch is a risk, every movement a threat. The benign bliss of carefree life had been stripped away. We stare at each other for a few intense moments. Finally, he sighs and pulls me up by a pocket on the front of my scrubs. I drop the gravel in my fists and sigh in defeat.

"Just...just talk to me. You leave me in the dark, and I need a partner in all this, not an enemy," I say.

"If I speak, you have to let me finish," he raises a doubtful brow as he looks down at me, "got it, Matchstick?"

I nod fervently, pleased with his willingness to talk.

"To answer your most burning question, three."

He holds up three fingers, and I want to snap that I'm not a child, but instead, I dig my teeth into my bottom lip and wait for him to continue. He almost smirks. He tested me to see if I'd blurt out a question or curse at him.

"We have three areas to search. This cellar is the first. I have coordinates to the other locations memorized. Luckily for us, they're fairly local. If we're going to cure you by Halloween, we need to search one site per week." *What if we don't find it? What if Kazak gets it first? Why can't we split up and search? What the hell does 'fairly local' mean?*

"Come back inside, and let's draw up a concrete plan. Please."

To my surprise, he obliges without further complaint.

After an embarrassingly long verbal fight over Mr. George's colossal kitchen table, we scrounge up an official plan.

Our deal was to remove it by Halloween, so we have less than six weeks to pull this shit off.

   i.   Search every nook and cranny in the cellar.

   ii.   Search a creek in the orchard where his parents met on a clear, moonlit night for best visibility and optimum stealth.

iii. Search a secret location unrevealed by Cato because he is an asshole.

iv. Don't die or, worse, get caught.

v. Remove Ruby's power by Halloween night.

I don't know how he knows where we need to search and how pertinent they are to our mission. I casually asked for an explanation, a map, a clue, but he ignored me.

I have to trust that he knows what he's doing and follow his lead. Yet, as I read the vague plan for the tenth time, a nervous little knot in my gut aches, and I can't help but feel like a lamb being led to slaughter.

"We can do this. Easy. No sweat. Go, team!" I'm talking to myself more than to him, but I catch him nod out of the corner of my eye.

"And no need for bloodshed," I smile with relief, "it's more of a scavenger hunt than anything else."

At this moment, I realize I should have kept this calming thought to myself instead of voicing it out loud to my sarcastic and moody companion.

"Oh, sure," he rolls his eyes, " we can have a fucking pizza party to celebrate the winner."

"You're not nice," I say.

"I never claimed to be nice."

I sweep my pile of freshly chopped onions into the salsa bowl and rush to the sink to wash the stink of them from my hands. Rain's partner, Sydney, giggles at me as tears stream down my cheeks. Rain simply shakes her head and opens another bag of shredded cheese to add to the enchiladas.

After I dry my hands, I collapse onto the couch. I tug my phone out of my pocket. A message from twenty minutes ago greets me on the screen.

Cato: Don't leave the house tonight.

I roll my eyes. Always so cryptic. I don't plan on going anywhere, anyways. A patient punched me in the face today. It was my fault for being careless. The client is nicknamed Black-Eye Beth for a reason. Also, it's Taco Tuesday in the Auclair household.

"Ruby! What the hell is this?"

I peek over the couch at my irate sister, a sauce can clutched in her fist.

"This is red enchilada sauce. We need green enchilada sauce. Are you colorblind?"

"No," I scowl at my sister, "make it with the red sauce. It'll be fine."

"*No.* Go get the right sauce. Now. And hurry up! We're hungry!"

The grocery store is only a block away, but I still drive to make as much haste as possible. The hungrier Rain gets, the bitchier she gets. I find the sauce aisle and squat down to find the green enchilada sauce.

Red enchilada sauce.

Hot sauce.

Mild salsa.

Aha! Green enchilada sauce. A shadow passes over me when I wrap my hand around the can. I look up and squint at whoever entered my personal bubble.

"Need any help this evening, little lady?"

Fuck.

Howard smiles widely, thighs too close to my head. His usual work attire. Ugly pants and wrinkled polo. Over-gelled combover hairdo. Cheap after-shave burns my nose. It's become too familiar.

It wafts through my nightmares.

"Uh, hi, Howard. How are you?" I stand and shift away. My sneakers squeak as I step with haste to the left to exit the aisle, the prized can held tightly in my fist.

"I'm wonderful now that I've seen you," his grin widens so I can see his straw-colored teeth, "I was in the neighborhood. In need of a few *essentials.*" He emphasizes the last word. I scan him with great apprehension. We're in a grocery store, and he doesn't have a single item. No cart. No basket. Not even a coupon. Freaking weirdo.

"Cool. Well, have a nice night, Howard." I give him a strained smile and an awkward nod. I jog to the cash register, pay for the sauce, and step out into the night. I check my phone. Only seven minutes since I left the house.

Rain can't be too mad. I cross the barren lot quickly, open my car door, and toss the can into the passenger seat.

A loud pop startles me.

A sting in my elbow joint. I jump and whirl around.

Howard stands there with a handgun. It's such an odd sight to see such a dork brandish a deadly weapon. He has the tip aimed at me, a smug smile on his chapped lips.

"Put your hands up and come with me. I won't hurt you again if you comply."

I clutch my arm close to my stomach and wince as the warm sensation of blood dampens the inside of my jacket. Oh, well. That's what scrubs are made for, although it's usually another person's blood, not mine.

"Did you...did you *shoot* me, Howard?" I ask, voice cracking. My thoughts are clouded with shock.

"It's a pellet gun, Ruby. You'll be fine. I have strict orders to keep you alive. Now, come on." He waves his hand at me as if beckoning a stray kitten to him. I weigh my options. No weapons and limited advantages.

Even if I could wrestle the gun off of him, I don't know how to use it and would probably end up shot again. I've received way too many boo-boos in the last month. An evil little voice in my head suggests I roast him alive.

I slowly stand, and I raise both hands in the air. My blood tickles my elbow as it slinks downwards. Howard's lanky frame struts towards me like a cat that got the cream.

"Excellent. I knew you would come to your senses. Kazak's gonna flip. Here, let me see your arm." He steps forward and gingerly touches my arm. Thin fingers survey the damage he deliberately caused. He shot me with my back turned.

How very...Howard.

He always takes advantage when I'm defenseless. Like when he followed me into that dark changing room. I want to smash a white-hot first right in his hooked nose. Or spit boiling saliva into his face. My eyes sting with angry tears that threaten to make an unwelcome appearance. I backpedal into the side of my car, and a sharp object pokes my butt. A mechanical pencil is still in my pocket from this morning. It's the lucky purple one I use to update patient charts on Friday mornings.

Reliable and sharp.

An evil plan forms like a dark cloud in my mind. A stupid, desperate, excellent plan. I force my jaw to loosen and my expression to soften. My mouth morphs into a demure frown. Showtime.

"It hurts," I whine in a high voice and grip my injured arm.

"My apologies, but I had to do what I could to catch you. Kazak will pay me handsomely for you, kitten," he breathes low and steps closer. I flutter my lashes to lay it on thick.

"It's okay, I understand," I whisper as flirtatiously as I can manage without throwing up. He's so close I can smell his cheap hair gel again.

It's noxious. While he continues to assess the damage he did to my numb arm, I reach my back pocket with my other.

"It will need ice, but you're okay. I would never hurt you."

As soon as this lie slips from his lips, my inhibitions about my evil plan disappear. He hurt me so badly during *the incident* I bled for days. I deserve an Oscar for this performance.

"Oh, thank goodness," I sigh and hold his lustful gaze as I slowly slip the pencil out of my pocket.

"Remember our little run-in a few months back?"

My heartbeat stops.

"I watched you for a while...Did you know that? Pinkest nipples I've ever seen...." A snakelike grin spreads across his face at the memory of *the incident*. When he attacked me. My brain short circuits for a second. The painful knives of vulnerability dig into my back, and I fight the urge to spit boiling saliva in his fucking face. I swallow my shame and try to focus.

"I remember..." I coo at him and touch his chest with my injured hand as my fingers grip the pencil behind my back so hard my fist shakes. His pasty face turns pink, and his mouth gapes. He's a wide-open target.

Vulnerable and distracted, just like I was in that locker room. When he shot me with a pellet gun, that was strike one. The nickname "kitten" was strike two. His comment on *the incident* was strike three. He's out.

I raise my pencil like a poisoned dagger and plunge it into the side of his neck. Blood spurts onto our chests, and he looks between me and my purple plastic instrument of death, dumbfounded for a moment. He lets out a howl, and I twist him around, my chest to his back.

I stabbed a man. In the neck. With hands meant to heal, hold sick patient's hands, play puzzles with lonely clients. My hands. I'm horrified, but I shove my self-deprecating thoughts to the back of my mind and focus. At least I'm in control of this weapon.

In between gasps, he gurgles out misogynistic names at me.

These slurs rhyme with pour, pitch, and punt. I stand on my tippy toes to speak in his ear.

"Based on the amount of blood loss, I may have punctured your carotid artery. That's an important one, you greasy idiot." To emphasize this, I shove it further in. He whimpers.

"Let me leave now, and I won't pull it out. Try anything stupid, and I take back my pencil and leave you to bleed out."

We are interrupted as a sleek black car zooms into the lot. I don't recognize the driver, but he's heading right for us. I shove Howard off of me. He clutches his neck as we watch the car screech to a stop. The driver remains seated, but the back door opens. No one visibly exits the vehicle. Howard fires three rounds into the windshield. The driver doesn't even flinch. The man smiles and moves to get out of the car. Howard now recognizes the man because he turns a pale color and sprints for the woods behind the grocery store.

"Do you trust me?" Cato appears beside me, eyes on Howard's retreating form and hand on my arm.

"No."

"Too bad, matchstick. Bones works for me. He'll take care of you. Behave." He pushes me towards the massive other man and vanishes without further explanation.

"Cato!" I hiss after him, but he's long gone. Cato's employee, Bones, turns to me.

"Are you hurt?" he asks. His kind eyes contrast with his shocking face tattoo.

The word FUCK underlines his right eye. The K in the design is dangerously close to his tear duct. I dazedly wonder how badly the procedure hurt, why he picked FUCK, and why he chose such a unique placement. The curse word disappears into the folds of his face as he squints at me. He looks concerned as his eyes jump from my face to my clothes.

"Are you hurt, kid?" he repeats himself more emphatically. Dazed, I look down at the blood spray across the happy faces on my scrubs.

"Not mine. I'm okay," I say.

I'm as okay as you can be after you stab a guy you work with and discover he does part-time work for the man desperate to squeeze your superpower out of you. The large man tilts his head towards me.

"Folks call me Bones."

Of course, they do. I stick out my hand, nonetheless. "I'm Ruby. Nice to meet you."

His brows surge upwards in surprise, but he shakes my hand.

"You aren't going to give me any trouble, are you, Ruby?" he asks and opens the back door for me.

"Me? Never." I smile at him and slip into the back seat, welcoming friendly banter. Anything to get my mind off of what happened. I get the sense that he isn't used to being around civil people. His eyes avoid contact with mine, and the apples of his cheeks are bright red.

He gets in the driver's seat, and we quietly wait for Cato to return.

"Any requests?" His huge hand hovers over the car radio. I shake my head and smile politely.

"Surprise me."

Bones chooses a smooth jazz station and quietly watches out the window as I nervously pick at my cuticles. The music is comically appropriate. Then, the passenger door opens and slams shut with such force it rocks the car. Bones doesn't flinch, but I nearly piss myself.

"What happened?" I squeak.

"He got away. Get out." Cato reappears, royally pissed, dark eyes alight with fury. I've never seen him so emotional before.

"What?"

"I said get out!"

I scramble out of the backseat, confused and a little embarrassed he had to tell me twice, like a child who can't understand instructions. I'm trying to process what happened. What I did. *I stabbed Howard. I'm a stabber.* My phone buzzes in my pocket. I snatch it up and answer, knowing damn well it's Rain.

"Hello?"

"Where are you? We needed a sauce, not a couch!"

"I got into a car accident."

"What?!" she shrieks right in my ear.

"I'm fine, just a fender bender. Let me finish up with the police, and I'll be home in...." I glance over at Cato. He holds up two long fingers.

"Twenty minutes. Love you, buh-bye." I hang up promptly to avoid further drama.

"You should have listened to me!" he shouts. This guy has some nerve.

"I needed to go to the *grocery store*! Jesus, you aren't my babysitter!" I shout back in his face.

"Yes, I am! You're a wanted woman, and you need to act like it, or you're going to die before we even make it to..." he trails off, finally noticing the blood all over me.

His eyes drop to my arm. I squeeze it to keep pressure on the small wound.

"What happened? Are you hurt? I thought I saw something sticking out of that guy's neck when we pulled up."

"I gave him the ol' razzle dazzle."

"You stabbed him."

"He shot me first!"

"He shot you?!"

"I mean, yeah. He shot me, but he said it was a pellet gun." I shrug and rub my arm. His eyes narrow.

"*What*?!"

He looks at me like I'm the one who shot myself. I ignore him and turn to Bones, who has been watching us joust while he puffs on a cigarette.

"Do you have a band-aid?" I ask. Bones pulls out a well-stocked first aid kit from the trunk of his car and helps me with my arm. He tells me he has military medicine experience as he gingerly helps my arm out of my sleeve.

It doesn't hurt too much, but I'm concerned that the pellet has embedded itself too deep in my skin. He sprays an antiseptic mist on my arm while Cato paces. Bones and I make small conversation as he easily removes the pellet with tweezers.

"You're handling this well, little bird," he compliments me. A sharp pain pinches my skin, then the metal pellet bounces away on the blacktop with a tink.

"I think I'm still in shock, but thanks, Bones."

"Either way, you're tough as hell. I'd be whimperin' like a bitch."

Cato rolls his eyes at this. Tough is the last word he'd pick to describe me.

"Ignore him. He's a dickhead." Bones winks at me conspiratorially. The curse under his eye disappears and reappears with the gesture. I smile at that. He finishes the job with a pink bandaid, and I slip my arm back into the sleeve of my jacket.

Now to plant corroborating evidence.

"You heard me, Poltergeist. I told my sister I was in a car accident. Hit my car," I order him. He stalks over to my vehicle.

"My name isn't Poltergeist. My Dotion is called Poltergeist." He kicks my car so hard that it feels personal. I wince even though I'm the one who told him to do it. A decent dent mars my front bumper.

"Don't care," I shrug, "but I do care that my coworker tried to kidnap me for your brother. He saw you. He's going to tell Kazak that you're working with me."

"My brother is a psycho like my dad. He won't care. Makes it more of a game to him."

"That doesn't make any sense." I shake my head.

"He sees you as an opponent. A weak one. With me on your side, the game changes. Like cat and mouse."

"This isn't a game. It's my life."

"It is a game. One that we're currently losing. Don't be late tomorrow night and do as I say. Don't make me regret our deal." He looks down at me as if I'm a stain on a new shirt. Like a clump of cat litter in his cereal bowl. Good.

"We're *not* losing because he hasn't found the next clue. Annabelle only gave me a mild concussion, and Howard has my pencil stuck in my neck. So the game is tied." I poke him in the chest with my last word. A muscle in his jaw jumps. I can practically see him swallow down an argument. He can't stand my determination. He's allergic to optimism. He shakes his head at me and looks away like he can't bear it a second longer.

"Go home, idiot."

"Thanks for stopping by. See you tomorrow." I wiggle my fingers at him and strut over to my car. Tonight may have been a shit show, but at least I got the green sauce.

7

Cato is supposed to meet me shortly at the Hadrian Manor after I change out of my work scrubs. I never know what to wear. Part of me wants to look cute because I think he is cute; therefore, I want to look cute. As I lift the mascara wand to swipe the black goop over my stumpy lashes, another part of me screams that this is stupid and dangerous and that he is a jerk with aesthetically pleasing genes. I swear under my breath and put the tube away, settling for a more natural look tonight.

I tug on a tight pair of jeans and a soft, red long sleeve. I step outside into the cool October air. As I turn to lock the door, my foot kicks a heavy object on our door mat. I yank out an earbud and look down, expecting to see that a porch pumpkin rolled out of place.

A decapitated pig head stares up at me with black eyes. Its tongue is stuck out and covered in squirming maggots. My hand covers my mouth. I'm glad I found it and not my sister. I'm not sure how her poor vegan heart will handle it.

Our charming Mickey Mouse doormat is ruined. Poor Mickey's face is smeared with the gore that slid out of the head.

"Oh God, oh God." I inhale and exhale quickly. I need to think of somewhere to hide it before Rain sees it. This is retribution for the Howard incident from Kazak. I just know it. I sob as I set my purse on a pumpkin and shrugged off my rain jacket, ready to sacrifice it to hide the decapitated head. A loud wretch accidentally escapes me. I smack my hand over my loud mouth, but it's too late. On cue, Rain bursts out of the front door. "What's wrong?! What-"

She looks down and sees the head. She runs back inside the house, and I can hear her throw up her dinner, hopefully into our kitchen sink.

Once she's done, my sister helps me lift the wet and heavy pig head into a trash bag. I double bag it and tie it tight with frantic fingers as she grabs the garden hose to wash away the crime scene. I'm so freaked out that I lose focus and melt a small part of the bag with smoking fingertips. It's a threat. He wants to get in my head. And it worked. Fucking asshole.

I toss the head and the doormat in the trash bin and hurry back to the house to wash my hands.

"Should we call the police?" She picks at the skin of her lower lip in worry, pacing around the kitchen as I scrub my hands with vigor.

"No," I say too quickly. Rain looks at me as if I'm the one who put the head on our porch.

"Ruby. It was *a pig head*! That's like Texas Chainsaw Massacre type shit. Aren't you freaked out?"

"I mean, I guess. It's not that big of a deal."

I dry my hands and throw the towel down on the counter. Her baby blue eyes narrow.

"You know."

"Know what?"

"You know who did it!"

"How would I know that, Rain?" My temper flares as she corners me.

"You lie like a rug, bitch. What happened?"

I lean against the counter and cross my arms. A white lie comes to me quickly. A good lie is fluffed with pockets of truth.

"You know the bad kid down the block? Tyler?"

"Tyler?" My sister scrunches her nose at the name.

"The little gremlin who smashed our pumpkins last Halloween?" she asks.

"Yep, I ran over his skateboard last week while you were gone. It was an accident, but he was pretty mad."

"That doesn't mean he can put dead animals on the porch! How did he even get access to a pig head?! Shouldn't we tell someone?"

"No, let's give him a break. He has issues. And parents who don't love him. You've seen his haircut."

She snorts, and I crack a smile. I'm doing fine. I can hide my kidnapping and stalkers and my powers while I figure out how to get rid of them with a grumpy asshole. Easy peasy.

"You're too nice, Rue," she says and shakes her head.

When I park at our meeting spot, Bones is waiting for me. He informs me Cato will arrive shortly.

He lights up a cigarette as I step closer to him and zip my jacket up to my throat. The nearby pond has frozen over tonight. I hope Bones hasn't been waiting long.

Bones turns his face when he exhales so that his cigarette smoke doesn't waft into my face. I sniffle to break the silence.

"Where are you from, Bones?" He taps the cigarette's base with his thumb. Cinders fall like bright orange snowflakes onto the road. He turns to me with a thoughtful look in his eyes. "Why do you ask?"

I tilt my head and smile. "We should get to know each other better if we hang out so often."

"People usually don't wanna talk with a guy like me."

"Nonsense. Tell me about yourself." I lean against the abandoned farm house's garden gate and cross my legs, ready for a good tale. He's hesitant, so I give him a prompt.

"Any kids, Bones?"

He lights up immediately.

"I'm a single dad. The kiddo is ten. Sweet boy. Smart, too. Smarter than me. Future astronaut, no doubt about it. Cato's already paid for a full ride to Princeton for him. The gift was anonymous, but I knew it was him. He's a generous guy."

"That's amazing. You must be so excited."

"My kid is going to the stars, Ruby." The warmth in his eyes as he talks about his son makes me smile so big my cheeks ache. It reminds me of the glow Trish gets when she talks about her baby.

"Stop flirting with Bones. Let's go." Cato appears at Bones' side and cracks his neck. I ignore him. "Why are you here tonight, anyways, Bones?" I ask.

He stomps out his cigarette and opens his mouth to speak. Cato speaks for him.

"His job was to babysit you because I was running late-"

"I was talking to Bones, not you. He can speak for himself," I snap. Cato's brow creases, and he stalks off towards the house. I don't think he's used to people talking back to him. Too bad. He better get used to it. Fate has tied us together for better or for worse.

"Go easy on him, little bird. The kid's been to hell and back," Bones explains with an exhale of gray smoke.

"Ugh! So have I!" I run a hand through my hair and scratch at my scalp in frustration. "Maybe if he'd open up a bit to me, we could-"

Bones cuts me off with a quick shake of his head.

"Try not to take his cruel act personally. Life hasn't been kind to him. His mother died when he was just a kid. Shortly after that, his dad was found dead. He may not have liked his pops, but his mother was a saint."

"Jesus," I exhale softly. I can't even imagine losing a parent, let alone both. I bite my lip, feeling oddly guilty. I quickly say goodbye to Bones before I jog to catch up with my moody companion.

"God, you're annoying," he grumbles when I catch up.

"What? I can't be nice to our security guard?" The pang of guilt I felt earlier is long gone, replaced quickly with annoyance.

"*My security guard*. You're distracting. Leave him alone."

I wrinkle my nose at his back, but I say nothing. We don't speak as we hike the long driveway and sneak into the house.

Before we settle into our designated sides of the basement, I pull a little bag of popcorn and an energy drink from my work tote and set them on a crate next to him. He frowns down at his drink and snack.

"We aren't friends, Ruby." He looks back up at me. The central organ in my chest aches. *Focus on removing your curse. Toughen up. Not everyone is going to like you.*

But I notice his eyes aren't as cold as usual, a tangible warmth hidden there, but the frown remains firm. Embarrassment threatens to color my cheeks, but I refuse to feel it. He called me Ruby. He never calls me Ruby.

We work silently for an hour, with no noise except for the shuffle of paper. I wait another thirty minutes before I allow myself to speak and ask a question that's been burning in my brain for days.

I drop another box in front of me and look at my partner. His focus is on a thick folder of documents in his lap.

I rub the spot between my eyes with my thumb and index finger and sit down.

"There is a 33.3% chance it's down here," I say. He doesn't even bother to look up.

"Why won't you tell me exactly where else we need to look? We could split up and widen our search instead of hyper-focusing on one area. And when can we start the orchard search?" I ask.

"We'll do that when I say so. I don't trust you," he says icily and turns a page.

"Excuse me?" I stand up and make my way through the maze of yellowed papers and scattered documents to hand-deliver a piece of my mind to him.

"You tell your sister where you'll be. She tells her girlfriend. Who mentions it in the grocery store where a spy overhears. Boom. We're compromised."

"You're ridiculous. I'm not going to tell anyone! I've kept a pretty big secret for a decade, and no one has caught me."

"I caught you." He breaks out of his unsympathetic character to show a signature cocky smirk.

"You only caught me because you can turn into a ghost. That's cheating."

He snorts. "A ghost?"

"Can we at least switch it up? Can we move onto the orchard soon?"

"If that's what it takes to stop your whining, fine."

"Fine."

"Fine."

"How do you have so much free time to help me?"

"If you can't tell already, my family is pretty well-off. I don't need a job, so I don't have one."

I must not have been able to stop the apparent look of disdain on my face, and he sees it before I can turn my head because a scoff escapes his lips. It takes all of my self-restraint to not mutter, "must be nice."

"Don't act so high and mighty because not all of us have to wipe the drool off other people's chins to get by," he sneers. That's it.

I slam the binder in my lap closed and throw it on the dusty floor, puffing up a cloud of debris.

"If you must know, I love my job. Even if I were a billionaire, I would do it daily with no complaints. But, unlike you, I am cursed with hands that can kill. I wish I had power as simple and mundane as invisibility, but I don't."

We fall into annoyed silence. I've found a soft-covered journal to flip through, and he looks like he's checking a fat textbook for notes in the margins. I carefully glance over at him every ten minutes to ensure he hasn't bailed on me or fallen asleep.

The basement light turns off by itself, and we're plunged into darkness. Before I can even yelp in surprise, a deep voice whispers a warning in my ear.

"He's here. Hide. Now." He grabs my arm and pulls me into a closet I hadn't even noticed was down here.

The door creaks as he quickly closes it. Footsteps on the old staircase send a shiver of fear down my back. Low voices from outside the door send my already frantic pulse into overdrive.

"Goddamn it," he whispers into my hair. His large hands grip my hips tight, holding me in place. I'd blush if I wasn't so scared. But instead, I lean my head closer to the door and listen.

"Someone was down here. This lightbulb is still hot."

"She can't be far, boss."

"Don't be stupid. There are no cars in the driveway, and the old man is asleep. She's long gone."

"Prickle, what do you smell?"

A creepy laugh echoes through the basement. A jolt of fear shoots down my back from my neck to my butt. Who the *fuck* is Prickle? I try to focus on a happy place in my mind, my lake with still waters, but I can't conjure it as a raspy male voice speaks again.

"She was here recently," he jovially announces to the room, "the scent is all over."

Don't freak out. I am calm. Don't freak out. I am calm. I chant the mantra in my head to fight back an oncoming panic attack. I clasp onto Cato's shirt for dear life, trying to ground myself with his lean form. He settles his warm hands on my shoulders.

"And there's another scent here, Kazak."

"Another?"

A pause. A sinister giggle.

"Your older brother has been here. His scent is almost as strong as hers." A longer and more sinister giggle starts but is cut off by a choking noise. My heart pounds so hard I can't hear my shaky breaths.

"You're certain? You can smell both of them? Together?" Kazak sounds royally pissed.

"Y-yes!" the goblin-like voice chokes out. Silence. A few piles topple over and crash as something, or someone hits the ground.

"Fuck. *Fuck!*" Kazak yells and thunders up the stairs.

My father was a soft-spoken man. Never once heard him raise his voice. Because of this, I had a safe and loving childhood.

An unforeseen consequence is that whenever men yell, I sometimes spiral into a panic attack. It doesn't always happen. The worst time was when I was a sixteen-year-old grocery store clerk. I had to hide in a bathroom when a man lost his temper at check-out, and I turned into a puddle of tremors when a male customer loudly cussed me out when I caught him stealing a six-pack of light beer.

I left that job shortly after.

Here in this closet, the long familiar hand of panic seized me by my throat. I hear Cato say my name as he grips my arms to hold me up, but it sounds like he's underwater. Or maybe I'm underwater.

When I finally come to my senses, he's still holding me. His dark eyes are pools of night, wide and still. I squeeze the muscle of his arm softly.

He looks down at my fingers twisted in his shirt.

He startles like a skittish horse and backs away so quickly I almost tumble forward. I clutch my hand to my chest. My cheeks heat in shame. I shouldn't have done that. That was inappropriate. He told me not to touch him. Bones told me about his past. What is wrong with me?

He rubs the back of his neck.

"Sorry about that," I apologize.

"'Bout what?" he asks, avoiding my eyes.

It reminds me of how my little brother looked at Trish when she'd come over for sleepovers. We'd giggle, make popcorn, and talk about school with my mother while my brother watched from his bedroom door. Trish would notice him and call out a hello. He'd stutter and say a dumb greeting and couldn't elevate his eyes higher than her chin. I don't blame him. Trish is a knockout.

"I broke your rule. I touched you. Sorry about that."

"Whatever, let's wrap up for the night. I need to go check out a few concerns with Bones. And forget that stupid rule." He turns and exits the closet before he can see me gawk. *Forget that stupid rule?! He made that stupid rule!*

I don't even bother to ask if I can join him and Bones. I'm emotionally spent and want to go home, crawl under my covers and pretend everything is okay.

"Oh, wait." He stops at the top of the stairs and reaches into the breast pocket of his black wool jacket. He pulls out a delicate gold necklace and places it in my hand.

"I had my tech assistant make this for you. Press the pendant if you need me to come to your location in an emergency. *Only* for emergencies. Got it?"

I hold it up to the old lightbulb near his head. A small, red gemstone pendant dangles from the chain and sparkles in the light. A ruby.

"There's a GPS in there?" I squint at the tiny pendant.

"Yes. I don't want to waste my time following you around anymore." He climbs the rest of the way up and disappears down the hall without speaking to me.

I count to ten as I listen to him stalk away down the hall.

My thumb clicks the little gem. His footsteps stop. Start again, coming back my way. I press my lips together to hold back a childish giggle. He reappears. Chocolate eyes were on fire from holding back repressed indignation.

"Just checking." I grin innocently. He doesn't smile back. I climb the final steps but don't realize he hasn't moved, so we nearly collide. I grip the railing, and he grabs my sweatshirt pocket.

"Last chance to take the money and run. It's the best option for both of us," he whispers. My eyes widen as he crowds my personal space.

"No way, rich boy," I whisper back, meaning every word. I'm not taking any money.

I'm taking my life back.

We walk down the driveway in less tense silence than we arrived in. He clears his throat and looks down at me as we reach our hidden vehicles.

"I will train you to protect yourself. You can't be left defenseless if I can't get to you fast enough."

"Isn't our agenda a bit tight already?" I ask in a clipped voice. My teeth dig into my lower lip. Work, hunting for the Dotion notes, and now self-defense classes?

I'm overbooked.

"Take time off work, call out sick, do what you have to do. Thursday night. Nine. Don't be late. I'll text you the address."

He's already stalking away, his long black coat flaring out behind him like a dark prince. I flip off his retreating form.

After waiting for him to pull away first, I turn off my car and go back to the dark house and into the cold cellar alone. Without him hovering nearby, my head is clear and my focus unbreakable. I stay an extra hour on the hunt for my destiny in the dust. A cure in the chaos.

I crawl under my duvet shortly after midnight. I snuggle my face into the sweetly scented sheets. My shoulder pops as my body sinks into the memory foam top of my bed. My phone vibrates in my back pocket. I groan and pull it out. It's an address to a building downtown and a message.

Cato: Thursday. 9PM. Don't be late.

8

The gym we train at sucks. It's not even a real "gym." The first floor is a laundromat. The second floor is our training space. When I followed my phone's directions, it led me to an ominous dark hallway. It hosted a lone, dented door with a keypad lock around the handle. I double-checked my phone for the address. It was correct. I entered the code he texted into the keypad, and it unlocked with a loud beep.

Two treadmills, a barbell, and three rolled mats line the opposite wall. The carpet of the ample space is marred by deep indentations every other square foot, where heavy office desks once sat. I unrolled the mats, sat, and played on my phone to wait for him.

He arrives late. I stand as he enters, eyes avoiding me as usual. Instead of his typical formal wear, he wears a flattering pair of gray sweats and a thin black tee. His hair is wet, like he just stepped out of a shower. He passes me, and notes of mint and eucalyptus cloud my senses.

"You're late," I say with my hands on my hips. Tardiness is a sign of disrespect. I've accepted that he doesn't like me, but he *will* respect me.

"Sit." He points at one of the unrolled mats.

"I'm sorry, do I look like a dog to you?"

"The laundromat below should drown out any noises," he says and sets down his gym bag, ignoring my previous question.

"'Any noise–?"

He cuts me off with a jab to my throat. My hands are still on my hips when he strikes my voice box. I fall to the floor and clutch my throat. I sputter and cough into the mat. He pulled his punch, but it still took my breath away.

"Your reaction time is poor. We'll need to work on that." I can hear the smugness in his voice.

"You're a psycho–" I croak from my spot on the floor.

"Get up. I don't have all night," he barks.

He thinks I'm a wimp. In some ways, I am. I'm not brave like Trish, smart like Rain, confident like Meredith, or tough like Violet, but I am scrappy. He forgets that at my job, I hoist old ladies from commodes, dodge quick fists of angry seniors, and scrub showers until they shine like the Chrysler building.

I dive for his knee, and he folds like a lawn chair. His back smacks the mat, mouth open in shock, eyes wide. A rush of victorious serotonin celebrates in my brain, but before I can pin him, he disappears.

"That's cheating!" I shout to the empty room. His breath skims my forehead, and I claw at where I think his face might be. One swipe lands before he holds my wrists above my head. A pair of thighs pin mine down. I try to squirm out from under him, but his grip is iron. I rock my hips desperately, trying to escape his weight. An unseen hand squeezes my hip firmly.

"You better stop that. Otherwise, we're about to be in a very different situation."

"You pig. Let me up." My face burns so hotly that I wish I was the one invisible.

He reappears and extends a hand to help me up. I take a page from his book and ignore him. I stand and move away.

"You're a menace." I frown at him and rub my throat.

"Not a bad counterattack. You're stronger than you look. Your left side is weaker."

I roll my eyes at the backhanded compliment, but I accept it's the best I'm going to get.

"You should have burned my hands, or at least blown hot air into my face," he adds, rolling his shoulders. I copy his movement.

"I don't like to do that."

"You did it with no qualms after I saved your life the second time." He stretches his knee and avoids my eyes. I wince as I think about how I blew a smoldering piece of mulch in his face. He has a point, but so do I.

"I did what I had to do to get away. I didn't trust you."

He looks at me strangely. "You trust me now?"

"I don't have the option not to," I say.

We look at each other for an awkward moment, and I have the

feeling he's thinking the same thing as me. *How did we get here?* He clears his throat, and the spell breaks.

"Hit the treadmill. Two miles in under thirty minutes. Go."

After I finish, he hooks up a punching bag and tells me to punch it until I can't feel my knuckles.

"I've been thinking...." I say between punches.

"A dangerous activity for you," he quips as he moves the target up.

"If Kazak has all those resources...his efforts to foil our plans and kidnap me again have been...pretty mundane."

"What do you think I do all day?" he cooly asks. I punch the foam harder.

"No idea. You've never shared," I say.

"Bones and I ensure no one comes within a mile of your townhouse or work assignments. Last week he tackled a man outside one of your client's homes. I think my brother tried to facilitate a hostage situation."

"Damn. How did you meet Bones?" I ask as I continue to hit the bag. His eyes burn a hole in my cheek.

"What?" The T at the end of his word is crisp and impatient.

"Bones. How did you meet him?"

"Ruby."

"Cato."

"I know what you're trying to do, and you're failing at it."

"What am I trying to do?"

"You're trying to worm little ice-breakers into our conversations."

"Oh, fuck off," I snort, "God forbid we spend over twenty hours a week together and act civil towards one another." I punch the bag well past the point where my hands lose sensation.

He thoroughly wears me out for an hour. Planks, squats, planks, squats, run a mile. Finally, I collapse into a sweaty heap on the floor while he impatiently watches.

"You're so mean," I croak as I fight to catch my breath. His eyes soften for a moment.

"How does your power work?"

"What?"

Trying to explain how my power works is like trying to describe the flavor of bubblegum to someone without a sense of taste. I make a face as I try and think of an explanation that would make sense to Cato.

"It's like...." I blush and clear my throat when a perfect analogy comes to mind. I'm unsure if I can say it out loud, especially to him.

"It doesn't matter how it works," I blurt.

"It does," the corners of his mouth turn down even more sharply, "I need to know if there are any weaknesses to it in case we fail and my brother gets his hands on it."

I grind my molars together because he's right.

"It's like going to the bathroom. Or sneezing. Or swallowing. You just do it. Nobody taught you how to do it. It's ingrained in your DNA. So once I swallowed that thing, I knew how to use it. But like peeing your pants or sneezing, it slips out and causes chaos."

"Peeing your pants?" he asks, and I can tell he's holding in a laugh.

"No! Well, yes...but no!" I can't help but laugh that he picked out the most embarrassing part. "Fine. How does *yours* work, smartass?"

He smirks up at me. "It doesn't matter how it works. Don't worry about it. Show me yours."

"What? No! No, I'm not a show pig." I frown and cross my arms like an angry child. He can't possibly...

"Show me," he steps closer, "I want to see. Firsthand. I dare you."

My eye twitches. He said the magic word. He *dared* me. Maybe I'm childish, but I loathe to turn down a dare. I look up at the moldy ceiling and decide on a small demonstration. As satisfying as it would be to make a big fireworks show right in his face, it's not ideal in this space.

"Fine." I hold my hand in front of me, fingers spread out as if non-verbally telling him to stop. I light the tip of each of my fingers like birthday candles. The five little flames that crown my fingertips flicker. Cato stares at my hand, transfixed at my power. My tummy flips.

"Can you feel it?"

"It's a gentle sensation," I shrug. He nods in understanding. A spark in his eyes allows me to open up. There's a new warmth in them.

"My younger sister had a hamster named Onion when we were little, and he could fit in the palm of my hand." I cup my hand like I'm holding the fat little ghost of Onion.

"It feels the same as holding fire to me. Soft, warm, light."

He almost smiles. Then, I see it. Dimples. Dammit. He has fucking dimples. I bite the inside of my cheek to ground myself.

"Did you have pets growing up?"

With that stupid question, my window of opportunity slams shut on my fingers. His shoulders tense, and his eyes turn cold. I'm such an idiot. I brought up his traumatic childhood to bolster some friendly conversation. Bad call.

"Goodnight."

He leaves before my brain even has a chance to process what happened. I recognize his behavior because I did it myself for years. Avoidance and denial.

The weak wicker handles of this dirty laundry basket creak in my hands as I lug it down the hall. An old country song my mom used to sing on long car rides has been on repeat in my head for the last two days, growing louder and louder until I find myself singing it softly as I open the dryer door. Cato even gave me a dirty look over his shoulder when I hummed it aloud as we walked down the driveway last night. He texted me not to go anywhere besides work today. Kazak's cockroaches are out and about.

Cato: I mean it. Go to work, go home, don't go out, even to the grocery store. If you need food, tell me, and Bones will take care of it.

He better pay Bones well to take care of stupid tasks like picking up milk for me.

Thump. I turn around to see if I knocked over the detergent. Thump.

I freeze and listen carefully to find the source. Silence.Thump. It's from the cellar. I drop the dirty laundry hamper and tiptoe to the cellar door.

Thump. *Okay, Ruby, calm down… Maybe a neighbor cat snuck in. Or a giant mouse.*

I wouldn't do this if I wasn't on assignment, but Mr. George's safety is my priority.

I descend the steps slowly, one hand on the wall and the other at my throat to press my emergency necklace from Cato. I don't want to press it in case it's only a small animal, not a murderer. *Lake with still waters, a crane glides above the glossy, dark water.*

I peek around the corner, feet planted on the bottom step. Nothing catches my eye. I see my familiar dusty stacks and a few snack wrappers I forgot last night. I step down and take a few long strides into the basement.

"Hello?" I squeak.

Famous last words.

A rustle from behind a metal support column startles me. I cover my own mouth to stop a scream. A man steps out from his hiding place in the back of the basement. I press the ruby around my neck and pray

Cato disregards the speed limit.

At first glance, he looks like an ordinary, bald, middle-aged man. There is, however, one glaring difference that makes him stand out. His eyelashes, eyebrows, and soul patch are long, sharp, porcupine quills. It's the freakiest face I've ever seen.

They sway as he curiously moves closer to me, like palm branches in a breeze.

"You must be Prickles," I surmise as calmly as I can as if I've been expecting him.

"Heh. Yes." He grins impishly at me, and I don't like it.

The quills on his chin bounce as he speaks. His voice matches the strange one I heard in Mr.George's cellar while I was pressed into Cato's chest. His eyes are too close together. His teeth are too big for his mouth. My temple throbs as I try to perceive him. He's terrifying and working for Kazak, but I can't help but feel immensely sorry for him.

He's like me, pulled into a mess against his will by goddamned Perseus Hadrian.

"Pleasure to meet you, Ruby. You are as sweet as Kazak said."

He bows to me, his quills nearly brushing the dirt floor. My stomach rolls at the thought of Kazak talking about me.

"How can I help you today, Prickles?" I mimic Cato's trademark air of cool boredom to trick Prickles into thinking I'm not terrified of him. I clasp my shaky hands behind my back.

"The nice lady can call me Prick," he says cheerily. He waves a purple notebook in my designated search pile for later tonight. His long fingernails dig into the cover.

"Give me this? Please? Kazak would be so happy if I was the one to bring it to him," he begs in a sing-song voice.

My fear of him morphs into anger. He thought he could bang around the basement, draw me down here, and ask me to hand over a potential key to my freedom. My heartbeat thunders in my brain.

"Well, Prick, I'd give it to you, but it's not mine to give. Sorry. I think it's time you went on your way." I force myself to maintain eye contact with him as I retreat back to the stairs, despite every muscle in my body encouraging me to run out of here screaming. I'm going to need therapy after this interaction. He steps closer to me, feet shuffling on the cellar floor.

"We'll see how you feel after I stab my spikes into the eye socket of your old man upstairs-"

I lunge, grab his thorny soul patch, and pull hard, so we're eye to eye. I heat my hand to the temperature of a scalding hot shower. With my other hand, I rip the notebook away. His beady eyes are blown as wide as they can stretch. He screeches and whines through his big teeth but doesn't pull away. He must be uncomfortable. Good.

"If you lay a single crusty quill on Mr. George, I will roast you. Like. A. Pepper." I enunciate each word for him. He whimpers.

"Do we understand each other, Prick?"

"Yesss! Yessss!" he hisses at me. I let go of him, and he cowers. I feel bad. Less bad than I did before he threatened to hurt Mr. George.

"Get out of this house and never come back," I say. My cruelty is pretended, but the emphasis I put behind it is enough to scare him shitless. He runs up the stairs, through the house, and out the back door as soon as I release him.

"That was scary," a dry voice comments.

I whirl around. Cato stands behind me like he's been here the whole time. He pulls an apple out of his pocket and takes a bite.

"Back up would have been nice, asshole," I say through clenched teeth, but I'm secretly glad to see him. I don't feel like being alone after my short showdown with that creature.

"You clearly had it handled." He wipes apple juice from his chin with a thumb and sucks it clean. He watches me watch him wrap his lips around the top of his thumb. Milk chocolate eyes darken, and my throat tightens. The room is sweltering all of a sudden.

"He tried to steal this." I hold up the book for him to see.

"Hold onto that. We'll look through it later."

"Go be invisible and make sure he's gone. He gave me the creeps." In dismissal, I wave my hand at him and turn to hide my face. When I look back, Cato has vanished. I open the notebook I won from the porcupine man.

Lab notes, quotients, and factorial figures fill the lined pages and bleed into the margins. It looks like intense math homework. I take it upstairs with me and shove it into my bag. If Prick was willing to fight me for it, it must have some unknown value.

Before I start an evening of training and bickering with his grandson, I squeeze Mr. George's hand and pull his covers up to his chin.

A long hour of gym time with Cato wipes me out. My shoulders burn. My arms tremble. My only respite from his torture is the sweet rush of water down my throat that he allows me to take only once and the coolness of the brick wall on my forehead when I slump against it. He is a relentless trainer and an even more impatient teacher. His hatred for me shines through in our sessions.

Not fast enough. Too much time around old ladies. Are you fluffing a pillow or trying to hit me, Auclair? Two laps around the gym for weak-ass punches.

It takes a significant amount of inner strength to not call him a little rich Victorian ghost boy.

After a punishment of planks, he lets me go for the evening. As he rolls up the mats, I exit the backdoor of the gym. My legs burn with every step to my car, only a short walk away.

A force shoulder checks me out of nowhere and knocks me to the ground with an *oof.* The tip of my nose scrapes the ground, but I'm otherwise unharmed. I scramble to stand and whip around. A shadowy figure stands over me with the purple notebook in its hand. The shadows around them wiggle and swallow the book.

"No!" I squeak helplessly. The first promising lead I had after hours spent in a dank cellar with a jerk was swallowed by a shadow demon. Son of a bitch.

Three more black, misshapen figures emerge from the alley's shadows like smoke. My eyes widen as they form into more humanoid shapes. Three large males and a smaller, more feminine shape approach. As they move closer, I realize they are human. Almost. White, milky pupils and dark clothing, guns at their hips, headed straight for me.

Oh, Hell no. No. No. No. No.

Cato steps out of the gym and glares at me.

"What now?" he growls. His tiny supply of patience for me ran out about two hours ago. My tight throat won't release the words correctly.

"There's–" I stupidly point at the figures behind him, frozen in fear. He whips around and boldly sizes them up. He doesn't flinch while I stand beside him, frozen like a puppy scared of a vacuum.

"Wonderful," he says through his teeth and jerks me backward by the shoulder. Then, as he shoves me behind him, he lands a punch right in the face of the largest attacker. I'm awestruck by him. He's impressive to watch.

Ruthless and fast, I'm confident he'll come out on top. But even with all that muscle, he's outmatched in numbers. The four are a better team than the two of us on a good day.

For every punch he throws, he takes two hits. My chest tightens with worry. Four against one. I have to move and help him, but the anxiety that I'll lose control and turn this alleyway into a cremation chamber renders me useless. So I stand there helplessly and watch the unfair fight. A strike lands on his temple. Another to the back of his knee. Watching him take the hits goes through me like physical pain. The woman throws a punch at his throat, and he dodges and disappears, sending her careening into a wall.

He falters for a moment. His movements have slowed down considerably, his punches less powerful, and his kicks less accurate.

He shoves one man off him while another kicks him in the ribs. My body starts to tremble as I realize I have to either help or watch him get gradually beaten to a pulp.

The sweet smell of fresh rain on the pavement clears my mind. The sting of the scrape on my nose heightens my senses. The chill of the night air cools my hot face. I suck in a breath of it through my nose and splay my fingers wide. Cato's large frame is finally knocked to the ground by the taller man. The woman has recovered from her earlier fall and pulls a gun from her side and points it at Cato while he struggles to get out of a fierce headlock. Her weapon bursts into flames as soon as she steadies her hand to take the shot. She drops it with a shriek.

With a wave of my hand, a circular rush of hot air rushes into the eyes of our attackers. They keel backward and claw at their eyes. I snap my fingers and jerk my wrists upwards. A thin wave of fire rushes under their rubber boots and melts them to the cement. They trip over themselves like cartoon villains. I grab my colleague by his collar and yank him to his feet.

"Are you okay?"

"You ditz! They're still alive!" he yells as I shove him into my backseat.

"Of course, they're still alive, you asshole!" I scream back at him, "Put your seatbelt on!"

He grumpily pulls on his seatbelt with a dramatic sigh worthy of an angry teenager denied a trip to the mall. I burn rubber as I drive away.

"Where am I driving?" I ask him, meeting his dark eyes in my rearview mirror.

"I don't care." He closes his eyes and leans his head back. His left eye darkens to a nasty purple hue, and his lip is split open. My own lip trembles at the sight of it. My fingers tighten on the wheel.

"They took it, didn't they?" he asks. His eyes in the mirror burn me, a disappointed yet unsurprised expression on his face. My cheeks heat with shame and guilt.

"I'm so sorry. The lady stole it. Grabbed it right out of my bag."

"Let's hope the book was a useless red herring. But, on the other hand, it might be to our benefit."

He looks like he's about to make a nasty comment, maybe about how stupid I was and how useless the Dotion is in my hands, and I flinch preemptively. But instead, he shuts his mouth and turns away from me without a word. It hurts almost as much as a verbal assault.

We walk into my dark home, and he immediately collapses on my couch like he lives here. I don't mind, though. His face is busted because of me. His ribs are cracked because I can't help my idiotic curiosity. I'm so pathetic. Damn Perseus Hadrian. He chose an altruistic bimbo to wield this power to watch it tear me apart. And he isn't even alive to see the show.

Pathetic, pathetic, Ruby.

I swallow the lump in my throat and busy myself in the kitchen. I make us both cups of oolong tea, prepare a cold compress, and wash his blood off my hands and wrists. The crimson mess mixes with soapy water to create a pink foam as it swirls down the drain. I lean on the sink and allow myself a quiet sniffle.

"Ruby. Stop it," he snaps from the couch. His eyes are dark chocolate and pissed. Embarrassed, I clear my throat. I bring the ice pack, gauze, a water bottle, and some ibuprofen to him on the couch. I hand him the items and guiltily turn away, unable to look at his busted face, but he snatches my hand with a solid grip to hold me in place.

"I didn't get my ass beat to watch you blubber, understand? We still have a mission to complete. Get it together." The kind look in his eyes contacts with the harshness of his words. I nod, but he still doesn't let go. In a rare moment of vulnerability between us, I squeeze his hand. It's grubby and blood smeared from the fight, but it's also large and warm, so I don't mind. I don't mind at all.

A sudden knock on my front door startles us apart. I pull on a long cardigan and check the peephole.

Mother of God.

I lean against the door and utter a few low curses to the wood.

With great reluctance, I slowly open the door a couple inches and peek out.

"Hi, Seth."

My ex-boyfriend stands before me in the glow of my porch lamp.

"Rue! Can I come in?" He grins that sweet boyish grin at me and puts his hands in his pockets. Months ago, it would have charmed me. I might have even blushed. But, at the moment, I want him to get the fuck off my porch.

"Now is a bad time, Seth."

"Let me in, Ruby. We should talk. I miss you." He steps forward, and I move subtly to block him.

"Seth," I strengthen my tone, "*I said* it's a bad time. Go home."

"Babe, come on–"

I open my mouth to lie out of it like I always do. *I'm sick. Very contagious. My sister's here. I have an injured hot guy on my couch. My parents are in town. I have to be up early.*

"She's preoccupied," a low voice above my head says smoothly. I feel his front against my back. Heat rises to my face faster than I can process what's happening. My ass is flush against him. He puts a hand on my shoulder. Seth's eyes bounce between Cato's hand on my shoulder and the face above my head.

"Oh, I-I was–" Seth stutters weakly. He openly stares wide-eyed at my houseguest.

"Have a nice night, man," Cato says, gently pulling me backward with him by my ponytail and slamming the front door shut in Seth's gobsmacked face.

He turns and walks back to the couch. I can't help but let a naughty little smile curl my mouth up. An odd thought blooms in the back of my mind. *Maybe he doesn't hate me after all.*

I mindlessly ramble to him and clean his wounds. If it bothers him, he doesn't say anything. I do this with my clients too. I'll jabber on about the weather, about a funny story, about my gecko Tyrion, about how my best friend has a baby on the way, anything to keep the uncomfortable task at hand off their mind.

I'm terrified, but my fear isn't as strong as my courage.

"Goodnight, Cato."

"Goodnight, Auclair." I can't see him, but I can hear a smirk in his voice.

9

As I lie in my bed and stare at my popcorn ceiling, I can't help but feel like a lovestruck idiot. Like a little girl with a crush on her best friend's big brother. A young camper awestruck by the hot new counselor. I raise my hand up and wiggle my fingers. I let a tiny spark shoot like a miniature firework out of my pinky. It pops and dissipates into a little puff of gray smoke.

I need to focus and remove my curse before the baby gets here. I can't have sparks shoot out of my hands around a newborn.

Rolling over, I press my face into my pillow and reach for another to cover the back of my head to stifle all noise. I scream for a few seconds and come up for air. I refill Tyrion's water dish and play around on my phone until a sudden phone call startles me. Trish has a knack for calling when I need her the most. I pick up the phone and answer in a phony Cockney British accent.

"Whot do ya need, love?"

A sob on the other side of the line moves my ass faster than any alarm could. I jump out of bed and shove my feet into a pair of my boots by the time she takes a breath to respond.

"I…need french fries," she stammers out before choking on another pathetic sob.

"Be there in ten. Anything else, babycakes?" I switch my phone to speaker while pulling a sweatshirt over my head. "An Oreo milkshake, if it's not…too m-much trouble," she squeaks.

If I have to arm wrestle the cashier at Dairy Queen to get her that milkshake, I will.

"Done. Be there soon, babe."

I peek into the living room, where Cato is supposedly asleep. The soft glow of a tiny night light in the kitchen provides a dim path for me to tiptoe my way over to the couch. The pillow and blanket I brought him are mussed up and moved, but it looks unoccupied. I suppose he sleeps with his invisibility activated. Weirdo.

"Hi, Cato. I, uh, I'm leaving for a few hours. Be back later. Um, bye, I say to the empty couch.

"Who the fuck are you talking to?" a voice asks behind me.

I smack my own hand over my mouth to stifle a scream and whip around. He's shirtless in my kitchen with my favorite mug in hand. He smiles, amused at surprising me or maybe at my conversation with the couch cushions. Seeing his Adonis belt above the waistband of his plaid flannel sleep pants tightens my throat.

Did he bring an overnight bag?

"I thought you were–never mind. I'm leaving and will be back in the morning. G'night." I move towards the door to leave, and he blocks me. I scowl at his massive chest in my face.

"Where do you think you're going at one in the morning, Miss Auclair?"

"My pregnant best friend is having a breakdown. You have seconds to get the fuck out of my way."

A dark brow raises, and he looks...concerned? I think? I'm not used to his face showing this emotion. Any obvious feeling from him throws me off. Except for maybe hatred and annoyance. Those he has in full supply for me.

"The plan was to start our comb of the cellar at 8. Are you sure—"

"Cato, I appreciate the concern, but you are not my father, and I will meet you at the house at 8 AM sharp. Goodnight. Please move."

He obliges slowly. I grab my keys and sprint out to my car.

I enter Trish's swanky home with the edge of a brown bag between my teeth. It's packed with hot, salty food. My arms are full of a heated blanket, my box of nail polish, and a pillowcase full of all the chocolate I could carry from my secret stash. The Oreo milkshake of her dreams is icy cold in my hand.

My very emotional and very pregnant best friend deserves all the options I can offer. I find her stretched out on her white leather couch with a red, blotchy face and a runny nose. Her dark eyes are shiny and full of tears. Her black hair is twisted into a perfect knot at the top of her head.

Her swollen tummy pokes out from her fluffy blue robe as she waddles over to me, and I pull her into a hug as soon as she is within arms reach. We collapse onto the couch, and she sobs onto my shoulder.

At first, nothing she says makes sense amongst the snot, tears, and shaky breaths. She calms down a bit and explains that her baby's father apparently texted her to never contact him again. I rub her back as she cries on me. We talk shit about him and other exes until our tummies hurt from too much junk food and chocolate. Finally, she goes upstairs to wash her face while I flip through movies. After almost an hour of waiting, I tiptoe upstairs to check on her.

I know she has an extensive skincare routine, but I'm starting to worry. I find her curled up in a plush pregnancy pillow in her bed, fast asleep. I pull a blanket over her and turn out the light before heading downstairs. I turn on her obscenely large television and flick my pinky to create a small fire in her fireplace.

I turn to some trashy reality TV channel, one with big-lipped ladies on the East coast throwing wine glasses and Prada bags at each other's heads at tacky parties. I fall asleep to the sound of vapid gossip and wish my biggest problem was having to find a new dog groomer.

Warm fingers stroke my hair and gently pull me from my sleep. The nails of the hand are short, but they still give my tired head a pleasurable scratch. My breath stutters in my chest as I realize who it must be. The bastard must have snuck into my car when I was rushing out.

Why he's touching me now is beyond me. I pretend to still be asleep. The leather of Trish's sofa is stuck to my sweaty cheek, and my eyelids feel as heavy as wet sandbags, so it's not hard to pretend to be sleeping. I want to see what he does. Need to. He's such an enigma to me.

A cold, glass wall, twelve inches thick. I can't melt it nor break through.

Kind gestures piss him off. Friendly conversation makes him slam doors in my face. Logic tells me he's a poorly raised asshole that hates me. Classic daddy issues. If that's all true, why is he stroking my hair right now?

A warm body slowly sinks beside me on the couch near my head. That almost breaks me out of my fake slumber. But, I stay in character and lie as still as a corpse. Soft lips kiss my hairline softly. At first, I think I imagine it, but the weight beside me shifts off the couch, and after a moment, I hear the backdoor open and close softly.

Trish yawns widely.

"Thought I heard the door open. Thought you left." She sniffles.

"No, I stepped outside to make sure I locked my car," I lie quickly.

"Okay. I'm gonna stay down here with you." We lie on her couch head to head and fall back asleep, hand in hand.

Despite the tender moment on Tee's couch, our forced partnership is going worse than I thought. When Cato's not scowling at me, he's brooding silently. My anxiety sky-rockets when he does this.

At least when he's speaking, I can guess where his thoughts are, but his silence is heavy and vague. *Is he going to abandon me to find it myself? Is he going to trap me and let his brother do what he wants? What did I do to make him hate me so thoroughly?*

When I meet a client who initially doesn't like me or is resistant to having a nurse at their bedside, I bring them their favorite snack or find out their favorite hobby or movie or song from their younger years and bring it up to slice cleanly through the thick ice. Works like a charm every time. Cato reminds me of a grumpy old man, so it shouldn't be too hard for me to butter him up. We meet at our spot at exactly ten and walk down the gravel driveway together. The only sound is the crunch of our shoes against the small rocks. He only greeted me with a slight nod when he said hello, and now he walks ahead of me like usual. Never beside me. The clear message doesn't escape me.

"What kind of coffee do you like? Don't want to waste my money on a drink you don't like." When he doesn't answer, I open my mouth to ask again. Maybe he wasn't listening. I step closer to him and glance at his profile. The muscle in his jaw ripples as he grinds his teeth in irritation. I snap my mouth closed and try to push down the feeling of hurt. *What a drama queen. Honestly. I've asked a valid question.*

"What is your issue? Do you have a problem with me?" I stop walking, and he whirls on me.

"I know what people like you want. I don't want your help or your pity. Mind your business and stop trying to be my friend," he spits at me.

"Oh, please. Not this again. Fine," I shrug, "you'll get black coffee."

He steps up to me, and I lean back and cross my arms. I've been through so much already, and I'm not about to let him intimidate me or tell me what I can and can't do.

"You won't give me anything, and from now on, you won't speak to me unless necessary to our goal. Understood?"

Tears threaten to blur my vision, but I fight them back. My cheeks burn in embarrassment at the finality in his tone. I thought maybe I could at least find a friend. A fellow victim in this mess to bond with. Angry heat crawls up the skin of my neck. I lift my chin.

"You're an asshole," my voice cracks.

"Yes, I am," he says, stone-faced and cold as ice.

We don't say another word as we continue our walk up the dark drive to the house.

We worked in sustained silence for a few hours. I turn to the next page of the journal and pop a peanut in my mouth. My eyes narrow to a squint as I try to follow the loopy handwritten entries. I nearly choke on my peanut when I see my name at the top of the page. The tips of my ears burn, and my heartbeat thunders in my head as I read this entry about myself:

I had planned for the chosen child to wreak havoc on this mortal plane, consuming everyone she loves with oceans of fire and pain. I had predicted Miss Auclair would kill her younger brother first, followed by her younger sister within six months of Dotion consumption. But, disappointingly, she hasn't harmed either sibling. The ashen remains of a burned owl have been the only evidence that she has harmed another creature. In fact, our studies have shown her suppression success rates are over 99.45%...

3/4/2010

A young man in Miss Auclair's class stuck a piece of gum in her hair. Miss Auclair defies expectations to a disappointing degree. She did not attack the student nor retaliate. We had estimated she would burn him on at least 75% of his body...

I toss this journal back into the box and snatch another.

6/5/2011

Our pig-human hybrid subject died this morning. Bloody foam coated her mouth when Dr. Weathers checked her cage this morning. No family on file. The subject was incinerated.

Jesus Christ. I swallow thickly and continue reading.

The porcupine hybrid continues to thrive. Two more weeks, and he should be able to breathe without the help of his ventilator. Miss Auclair's mother has once again filled a prescription for allergy medication. Our hypothesis is that she has done this to prevent sneezing and coughing that could result in an ignition-

A loud clap echoes through the basement when I snap the stupid journal shut.

Josef Mengele comes to mind when I picture Catos' father. A long-passed client was a vet and told me all about him. Mengele was Nazi officer and scientist from WW II who performed the cruelest human experiments. His nickname was the Angel of Death. Pink fingernails scratch my inner wrist as if my curse is an infected vein buried under my skin. My phone alarm blares to life. It's 2AM. Time to go home.

"I'm sor-" I cut myself off, trembling fingers digging into the cover of this awful book in my hands.

The sting of his harshness from earlier tonight has softened my voice. Why am I apologizing? I have nothing to be sorry for. And I have nothing to be afraid of. I clear my throat and try again.

"Could you take a look at this?" I ask. I reach my arm out to pass a journal to Cato. He hesitates before taking the book from me, careful not to touch nor look at me, and opens it up.

Cato chews on his lip thoughtfully as he reads over the text. *I'd like to bite his lip for him.* My intrusive thought echoes through my mind like a sneeze in church. This isn't the time for naughty thoughts. This is serious. I tear my eyes away from his distracting mouth and pull yet another old box towards me, kick up my feet and wait for him to finish. After a few moments, he snaps it shut and hands it back to me.

"Well?"

"Creepy, but insignificant." He shrugs and reaches for a novel.

"It's not insignificant! This changes everything! He tried to get me to kill my siblings! My privacy has been violated for years by your psycho dad! He has a whole journal analyzing my grades in middle school." I throw the book in question at him. "I was a lab rat for him."

A flawed lab rat, based on the content of these journals. Perseus Hadrian *hated* me. I never did what he wanted. That gives me a small reprieve.

"There's not a word in these that I don't already know," Cato says, a strange look on his face.

"I hate your dad," I mumble, my lower lip quivering. I've never hated anyone before in my life, but the revulsion and rage I feel are frighteningly strong.

"I hated him, too," he admits bitterly.

I rest my chin on my knee and regard him thoughtfully. There are a million questions I want to ask, but I resist the urge to interrogate him for fear of pushing him away. He's the only person I can trust right now, and he's already saved me from dying twice. He sees me as the real monster I am, a land mine waiting to be stepped on by a poor unsuspecting soul.

If my family, Trish, coworkers, or future partner ever found out about what I'm capable of, they'd turn me away. Run away screaming if they were smart.

Who could ever love a monster? A vessel for effortless and total destruction.

"How? How did he have so much time to follow me?" I ask.

"My father wasn't around much. Too busy with his work."

I stare at him, horrified. The unspoken truth is as loud as a thunderclap.

He was too busy stalking me. Studying me. He was too busy to spend time with his own children. He was a narcissist unable to comprehend the choices of a teenage girl with a great power thrust into her hands. It's chilling. Now one son is a supervillain, and the other is a moody and misunderstood vigilante trying to stop a disaster from occurring.

My chest tightens as feelings of guilt and anger wash over me. Both emotions are as heavy as they are useless. "I'm-" I stop myself from saying I'm sorry. The last thing Cato Hadrian wants is my pity.

"I wish things were different. For both of us," I say this to him before turning and leaving the cold cellar without another word.

The short October days burn up quickly, like a votive in a jack o lantern. Cato's height and big shoulders are distracting. However, they don't distract me from the fact he is an asshole. We've been at each other's throats for days after following the same routine all week. I thought we had some meaningful moments to thaw the ice, but I was wrong. Sometimes he makes me so mad that I want to punt him into the sun. He's rude, abrasive, and a terrible communicator.

I work all day, come home to shower and change, check in with my sister, drive to the woods and hide my car by Mr. George's house. Then, I wait in the cold for a huge jerk who is *always* late and in a bad mood who either doesn't speak to me at all or makes a snarky jab at me or my job or my hair or a minuscule detail about my outfit.

He has a talent for getting under my skin. His power may be invisibility, but he can set my temper on fire faster than I could turn an owl into a pile of ash.

Today he gave me the silent treatment, which is fine since I had an emotional and challenging day at work. A few hours in, I twist, and my back pops. The action sends a bright spark out of my palm. It fizzles out quickly but lights a fuse of panic and impatience in my brain that I've been fighting to control.

For nearly half of my life, I've been fighting down this panic.

The closest I've ever come to getting caught has been by my pesky little sister. After a long night of partying with Trish, I had come home and threw up little fireballs into the toilet like a sick baby dragon. Then, I did the worst possible thing. I sneezed and engulfed my bathrobe in fire.

Despite my inebriated state, I drunkenly shoved the burning garment into my bathtub full of water to quench the flames. The belt of my robe flaked away like croissant crumbs.

Rain knocked on my door a minute later and entered.

"Did you burn something?" she asked me and sniffed the air of my room.

"Yeah, sorry. Knocked a candle over. Burned my robe," I croaked from the spot on my rug where I had curled up in a ball and fallen asleep the night before with a slipper for a pillow. My head was still spinning from the night before. She stared at me for a long time, then made a snarky comment about how I need to be more careful.

I *need* to get this out of me. Or cure it. Get rid of it. I desperately want to pop my back, and nothing happens. I want to hold Trish's baby safely with harmless fingers. He'll be here within one month. A sweet new life with tiny toes and a loud personality like his momma.

Cato and I quietly work the week away, sorting through box after box of laboratory paperwork and handwritten notebooks. We don't speak, except for a polite request to pass an item or a simple greeting and goodbye. Even during these short exchanges, he keeps his eyes down, avoiding my gaze. I hate it.

"Are you really wearing that?" Trish asks. She playfully wrinkles her nose at my scrubs. I pinch her arm as she adjusts a gold earring in the mirror by her front door. It's margarita night, a monthly tradition for us since college (virgin for her nowadays). Cato let me take the night off when I requested it, saying he also had another priority. I'm trying not to think he might have a date himself. Not that it matters, because it doesn't. It doesn't matter.

"Shut up, bitch. They're comfy. I didn't have time to change for your highness." I turn to deliver a teasing glare. She looks like a model with glossy black hair and a perfectly pressed pantsuit. It tastefully shows off her baby bump.

She grabs my face with both hands and forces my head to turn to the left. I gently touch her wrists in confusion before she shrieks.

"Oh, my God! What happened?"

Her brows fight against her Botox, and her glossed mouth hangs open.

"I fell," I say and try to step away, but she holds me tighter. I thought my thick hair was aiding in the concealment of my leftover bruising from Annabelle, but I was too optimistic.

"Don't. Lie. To. Me. What happened?" she asks again. Her dark eyes burn me with a look of betrayal.

"I fell at work, Tee!"

"You're lying! You idiot, do you know how many crime scene photos I've seen at my job? You were hit with a blunt object! What happened to you? Were you jumped?" she asks, and her lower lip quivers. I don't respond. Can't.

"I love you, Ruby, but I hate when you lie to me. What happened?" she asks again.

I shake my head and mumble that I have to go before opening her front door.

"Ruby!" she shouts after me, but I can't turn back now. Steam has already started to waft off of the tears streaking down my face. I walk fast down her street until I come upon a greasy spoon diner.

Oil-infused air hits me in the face as I enter. Every breath feels like a mouthful of salty food. A rusty bell atop the door rings as I shut the door behind me.

No one notices me. As I cry, I slide into a booth in the back and cover my face with my arms. The dim lighting and cigarette smoke from a waitress on break should help hide any wisps of steam.

I'm such an asshole. To my friends. To my sister. I'm a liar and a danger. I should have left while I had the opportunity. Maybe I should call Cato and tell him he was right, we can stop our search a month early, and I'll take the money and leave the country in the morning.

"Can't cry in here, baby. I already mopped," a harsh smoker's voice interrupts my pity party. I look up and see an aging waitress with a hand on her hip. Deep lines fix her wide face into a permanent frown, but her blue eyes sparkle as she stares at me in concern.

"Sorry, I'm almost done." I wipe my face quickly and manage a watery smile. Her messy bun is held together by a decades-old rubber band.

A coffee-stained apron is tied so tightly around her hips that the sides of it are frayed.

"How about a slice of cheesecake, babydoll? On the house." She grins widely at me.

"Stop givin' away my food, woman!" a man shouts from the kitchen. I open my mouth to tell her it's not necessary, but she gives me a look and rolls her eyes.

"Fuck off, Lenny," she barks, "don't mind him. He's a fat ol' penny pincher. I'll get you the biggest slice I've got." She smacks her red-polished fingernails on my table.

"That's very kind of you." I sniffle deeply, and my nose makes a loud, wet noise.

"Be right back, babe." Her wide hips knock over a syrup bottle as she hurries away.

The diner door jingles open. A familiar man bursts in, out of breath and fuming. I try to slink down to hide, but he sees me immediately and stomps over.

Cato's eyes burn with such intensity it almost knocks me out of my booth. What is he mad about now?

"What are you doing here?" I wipe snot on my sleeve and give him a confused frown.

"Get up," he says, with a look that makes me think if I don't, he might strangle me. My waitress sees him and comes over, and I tense. She looks like she's about to beat his ass or slash his tires.

She says, "Are you okay, honey?" but it sounds like *you need me to take care of this fucker?*

"I'm fine, thank you. He's a friend," I say. He flinches at that but otherwise stays silent.

She holds a plate of the most luscious slice of blueberry cheesecake I've ever seen in my life. She slides it in front of me.

"Enjoy, baby. Let me know if you need *anything*," she says with fierce emphasis, glaring at my companion. I thank her as she waddles away. Our eyes finally meet, and I offer a small smile.

"Help me finish this?" I ask.

"Sure."

"What are you doing here?" I unroll the silverware at my elbow and pass him the fork while I take the spoon.

"Your heart rate and blood pressure were elevated. I rushed here with Bones to check on you." He stabs at the cheesecake. Pink speckles color his cheeks. I forgot my necklace can track that.

"Trish and I got into a fight. She saw my forehead." My fingers ghost over the old injury.

"Who?" He pushes the juicy blueberry garnishing the top of our dessert over to my side of the plate. I pop it in my mouth before responding.

"My best friend."

"Oh. You okay?"

"No, but I will be." I shrug and take a bite. It's as good as it looks. I moan. The color on his cheeks intensifies.

We share the cheesecake in silence. He lets me have the last succulent bite.

"Do you have cash on you?"

He nods and pops a piece of gum in his mouth. Before he can shove the pack back in his pocket, I swipe it and take a piece myself. To my shock, he almost smiles as I push the blue mint strip between my lips.

A plan to scoop out a morsel of his character forms in my conniving little brain.

"Could you leave her a tip, please? I'll pay you back."

He's a generous guy.

"Bones is waiting for you in the car. We'll take you back home." He reaches in his wallet and slips some cash under my plate after I stand. Warm hands touch the small of my back before I can peek over my shoulder, urging me towards the door.

"How much do I owe you for her tip?"

"Five bucks."

"Okay," I say. He opens the diner door for me. Bones leans out of the window of a black sedan to greet me.

"Hi, Bones!" I smile. He smiles so wide that I can see a golden molar.

"Hey, you little shit! Scared the boss half to death." I can feel Cato glare at Bones from over my shoulder.

"That's an egregious exaggeration. I was mildly concerned."

Bones throws me a grin and turns up his music. Today he's playing afrobeats. Cato nudges me to get in the car, ushering me with his arm.

"Actually, I forgot my phone. Whoops," I lie and duck under his arm. He exhales a long-suffering sigh so dramatic that it ruffles my hair like a minty breeze.

"Hurry up."

I slow jog back to the entrance and pretend to retrieve the phone I know is safely tucked in my pocket. I spot the evidence.

A crisp $100 peeks out from under an empty plate.

* * *

As soon as I get off work the next day, I call Tee. She picks up after the first ring.

"Hi, sugar tits," she says.

"Hey, hot stuff. I'm really sorry about what happened earlier," I say.

"No, I shouldn't have pried. I know you'll tell me when you can."

"Can I come over?" I ask.

"Please do."

I text Cato that I won't make it tonight. He doesn't reply. We hugged and talked for a long time. Trish organizes new clothes she ordered for the baby while I research cribs. A reality TV show about married couples making bad choices plays in the background. Trish drops a folded onesie onto her floor and scootches closer to me on the bed, a goofy grin on her face. She looks me up and down.

"You're in love!"

"What?! No, I am not!" I say a little too loudly. *No. No way. I'd rather hit him with my car than put my mouth on him again. I need to change the subject.*

I ask her about her mom's upcoming Halloween party.

"So, the event is literary classic themed." Trish pops her gum in thought as her nimble fingers gently French braid my hair. My ears perk up. I've been a bookworm since I learned how to read, especially in those lonely first years with a superpower I didn't want nor understand. I would devour books like Tyrion devours mealworms, cover to cover, one after the other.

"I think I'm going to be either the mad hatter or maybe the lady from Great Gatsby. Ugh, what's her name...pregnancy brain has been driving me nuts."

"Daisy," I remind her gently. She snaps her fingers.

"That's her name! I love a good '20s getup. And you'll borrow my baby blue dress and go as Wendy from Peter Pan. The one from last Spring."

I don't miss the devious smirk on her face as she pops her gum again. My eyes widen as I realize which one she's talking about.

"No, Tee, *no*. That one is too short. I can't—"

"Too bad. You're hot. You're wearing it even if I have to hold you down and shove it over your head."

She pops her gum in emphasis. I can't see her face, but I know she's serious. I swallow the argument bubbling up from my throat. She loves to dress me up, and it's our final hurrah before the baby arrives.

"All done." She strokes my braid and gives it a yank. I swat at her and get up from her fluffy sheepskin rug.

"I'll wear the dress if you do a teensy favor for me."

"Deal, if you wear it with heels."

"Fine," I growl. Trish's knack for investigative journalism is impressive. She uncovered a money laundering scheme at the middle school last year and an affair between a married school board member and a city council representative. Hot local news.

If anyone can find info on the Hadrian family for me, it's her. If Cato doesn't tell me, I'll have to find out for myself. I text her Perseus, Kazak, and Cato's full names. Her phone dings from her bed.

"Use your magic and find out any info on those men. I need dirt."

She wiggles her brows at me. "Interesting."

"It's not like that."

"What *is* it like?" she giggles, and I pinch her leg.

"I can't tell you yet." I don't miss the look of disappointment on her face. It hurts more than when Howard shot me with a pellet gun.

10

Tonight, I don't think I'll be able to sleep with the guilt of my power wearing down my friendships, drying up my prospects for love, and dissolving my happiness.

I rub Tyrion's scaly tummy with my forefinger.

"What are we going to do, buddy?" I absently question him. He blinks at me, not a single thought behind his glossy reptilian eyes. He blinks again, and his black bulbous eyes shift to a space behind me. The only warning I get is a tiny creak of the floor right behind me. A hand claps over my mouth before I can scream. I'm suddenly pulled into a large male torso, and my head bumps against a muscled chest. I throw an elbow back in a vapid attempt to bust his pretty face, but he easily dodges the affront.

"God, are you always so jumpy?" Cato scoffs and lets me go. I shove him in the chest, putting some distance between us. I absently notice his chest is firm. And warm. And also firm.

"Ugh! Are you always a handsy psychopath? How did you get in here?" I quickly pull on a cardigan to cover my bare shoulders.

"Are you always a bitch? The window. You should install better locks. Is that... a gecko?" he asks.

"No, he's a parrot. Yes, I'm always a bitch. Get the fuck out of my house." I scoop up my scaly friend and gently put him back inside his glass enclosure. Cato takes his time looking around, taking in my small bedroom. He's wearing those gray sweatpants again, this time with a black hoodie.

I tilt my head and wonder if he shops at the downtown Big n' Tall store. He has to be 6'4" at least, with broad shoulders and a slim waist, reminiscent of a swimmer's build. So how did he even fit in my window with those shoulders?

His eyes linger on my bed, then his gaze drifts over to my desk where his lilies are arranged in a vase, and he looks back at me. My face heats, and I clear my throat.

"Hello? Get out of my room."

His smirk widens as he picks up a book from my bedside and flips it over to see the cover. My eye twitches. Acting like he fucking lives here.

He steps over to my closed window and gently moves aside my spindly orchid on the sill before he slides the pane up. The sky darkens as twilight approaches.

A light fall breeze wafts into my room. He leans against the window sill.

"We're going to search the orchard tonight. Time isn't on our side."

"You couldn't have sent me a text?" A heads up would have been nice.

"Grab your shit, and let's go."

I scrunch my nose in disdain. "I'm busy tonight."

"Clearly."

The immature thrill of sneaking out and hunting my destiny with my handsome new sidekick pushes me to concede.

"Let me grab my coat."

I consider the man in my window as I tug on a sweatshirt, trying to gauge how much I trust him. He reaches his hand out to me, like an adult Peter Pan, pulling me into the night. My eleven-year-old self would blush and stutter, but I know better.

I swat his hand but step up beside him.

"Let's get this over with."

He shrugs and slips out the window with ease. I climb over the sill shakily and realize too late that this is my own damn house, and I could have used the front door.

Strong hands grip my waist and lift me up into the air and over the tall, thorny hedge under my window. After he sets me down, I rip one of his hands off.

"I was fine! Can you keep your clammy hands off of me for ten minutes?" I snap. He releases me so quickly I nearly fall over.

"If you weren't so clumsy, I wouldn't have to. You're going to trip, fall, and light the place up like a Christmas tree. Watch your step."

"...light you up like a Christmas tree," I childishly mutter.

"You're already covered in bruises. I don't need you covered in scratches too. Makes me look bad."

I lift my wrist up in the dim light to check it. As I thought, it's already a nasty shade of green.

"Side effects?"

I nod.

"My inner wrists always bruise after I create flames larger than a fist. I'm pretty good at hiding it, but if someone sees it, I tell them I'm anemic. Works like a charm." I tighten the bun on top of my head as I reveal this to him. A nervous habit. I've never told anyone this. Thought the secret would die with me someday. It's nice to talk to someone, even if it's Cato.

"You want to give up omnipotent firepower over some light bruising?" he asks. His tone is harsh, but his touch is gentle. I yank my arm back and stomp down to his car. There he goes. Ruining the moment.

"What did you burn recently?"

"Your brother left me a little gift on my porch. Don't worry about it. Let's go."

Out of nowhere, he materializes in front of me, a scowl already glued to his face. He made me wait for him on a log in this orchard while he walked the field perimeter and scanned the area for Kazak's scouts. It's more of a park than an orchard. We had to hike a spindly trail to this spot, and I spotted a few campground sites with grills and flat areas where tents once sat. I thought I saw a public bathroom up on the hill.

"No one's out here except for us, but we need to wait longer for total darkness."

He sits beside me on the wide log. We wait for darkness to fall. The sky is barely lit by a blotchy pink and streaky orange sunset. I glance warily at my stoic companion. His dark hair is neatly combed aside, and his scarf is tied in a complicated knot at his throat. His usually pale cheeks are stained red from braving the icy October winds while he stalked around the field. I press my lips together as the idea of planting my mouth against them again intrudes my thoughts and makes my own face flush.

"What?"

He caught me staring. His dark eyes flash at me with accusation, a skeptical frown on his face.

"Nothing."

He concedes and stops pressing me about lewd thoughts as I pull out my flashlight and play with it, clicking it on and off.

"Put that away!" he hisses. He's in a bad mood tonight.

"Remind me why we have to be so clandestine about searching a creek?" I click my light on and off, on and off, soaking up childish glee at his annoyance.

He stares at me, his eyes flicking between the flashlight and my face. A muscle in his jaw ticks. My mind blanks out. I'm not used to being around such stunningly attractive men.

"You are...the most infuriating woman I've ever met."

"I'm cold."

He shifts and pulls his coat tighter around himself, huffs loudly. "Come here."

At first, I think I heard him wrong, and before I can stutter out an expletive, he does exactly what I feared and pulls me right into his lap. The warmth from his body immediately bleeds through my clothes. A new flame lights low in my pelvis and flickers into my tummy. This is simple survival. A tactical strategy. It's glacial out here.

Bear Grylls would do the same in a heartbeat, surely.

My grumpy companion mumbles words spoken too low for me to hear. His hoodie is pulled up, and it muffles the sound of his deep voice. I wiggle in his lap to hear him better. "What did you say?"

"Stop!"

"What?"

"Stop squirming!" he snaps, almost panicked.

"I'm not! I only moved when you started bitching."

"I said we have to wait until dark to search. No flashlight unless absolutely necessary."

We sit in awkward yet companionable silence until darkness fully envelopes the woods. Night falls incredibly quickly, and before I know it, he gently nudges me off his lap.

"Let's go."

An orange full moon crowns the sky above the field. The wind scurries through the trees. It carries the smoky and sweet scent of burning leaves. I inhale deeply, and it reminds me of autumn nights with my family, cinnamon sugar pumpkin seeds roasting in the oven, and telling ghost stories by the fire. The scent latches onto my thick hair and makes itself at home. It puts a smile on my face.

This is when he chooses to ruin the moment.

"Stop smelling the daisies. Move it." Cato bumps my shoulder hard and stomps ahead of me. I glare at the broad set of shoulders that nearly knocked me on my ass.

The next time he pushes me aside like a rag doll, I will heat my thumb to a thousand degrees and shove it in his ribs.

He descends the path to our right. The night is quiet except for the crunch of our shoes as we follow the rocky path. I can barely make out my steamy puffs of nervous breath.

"Stay close." I stick my tongue out at his back but obey, falling into step right behind him. I'm determined not to lose him. God knows what happened the last time I lost my way in the woods.

I command my wobbly knees to toughen up as we trek in the dark. Countless jagged rocks poke up from the dirt trail. Unfortunately, I made the wrong choice when I tugged on my light running shoes instead of boots.

I concentrate on a reflective stripe on his jacket. It's close enough to brush my nose. We reach the bottom of the hill, and he guides me to a brick bridge that guards the creek below. I wiggle the flashlight at him, and he nods in permission. I click it on and aim it at the fast-moving water. Hundreds of fallen leaves spin and bob with the current; at first, it's difficult to see the bottom. I lean over the railing bar on my tiptoes to get the light closer to the water.

"There! I can see a briefcase! By that rock!" I whisper-shout in excitement. A rough tug on the hood of my sweatshirt pulls me away from the rail. I stumble into his side.

"Wait here," he huffs.

My heart pounds with fear as he quickly kicks off his shoes and makes a step up on the bar. I grab the hood of his jacket, pull as hard as I can, and jerk his head backward. He twists his torso to deliver a glare as cold as the night wind.

"What?!"

"You can't jump in a freezing creek, moron! We're miles from medical attention. You'll drown! Or freeze!"

"That's why I have you," he says slowly as if I'm too stupid to understand his loony plan.

"I can't swim! And I will not set myself on fire to keep you warm!" I growl and let go of his jacket. "Calm down. It's not going anywhere."

I point the flashlight around our feet. Various pieces of trash litter the bank. I grab a few pieces of garbage. A long, rubber exercise band with streaks of mold. A rusted hanger. Tangled fishing line. An empty Coors can. This could work. I can work with this.

"I'll go into the park bathroom up the hill and use the light in there to make a hook. Then, we'll fish it out. Give me a few minutes."

"Fine," he mumbles in a tone that says *You're right, but also fuck you.*

I gather my garbage and lead the way back up the hill like a little trash goblin with a fresh hoard. I slowly open the women's bathroom door with my foot and flick on a light with my shoulder. Yellow ceiling lights above the stalls hum and click in a patterned rhythm. I place my pile on the floor and shove open the curtains of the two shower stalls.

No one except for a dead stink bug stares back. Quickly, I check for murderers and demonic pig ladies in the other stalls. I plop myself cross-legged in the middle of the dirty bathroom floor. The achy protest of my bruised fingers and arms is ignored as I work.

"Why did you do that?" he asks with one raised eyebrow, arms crossed, assuming his usual position of nonchalance by leaning on the doorway. My face heats. I thought he was waiting outside. He nods at the showers.

"Axe murderers," I mumble, focused on untangling the fishing line first.

"Axe murderers?"

He laughs, *a real laugh,* for the first time since I kissed him in the office kitchen. Head thrown back and perfect teeth on display. I scrunch my lips together defensively.

"I can't work without making sure there isn't a maniac hiding in the showers! You ass!" I toss the empty beer can at him, and it bounces off his knee and clatters to the floor.

"You know what?" I huff, "Get lost for a few minutes until I finish making this...this retrieval device. You're distracting me."

"Retrieval device..." he scoffs as he exits. I roll my eyes and get back to work.

After I untangle the fishing line, I melt a spot on the latex band and break it into two long pieces. I grab the hanger and get to work. I fashion it into a hook big enough to catch a briefcase handle. The hanger is caked in grime.

My pretty pink nails are sacrificed to scrape the grime off of the part where the wire is twisted around itself. I shift uncomfortably, taking a break from my work to push my heavy mess of hair out of my face. My butt aches from the unforgiving and cold bathroom tile, but I'm almost finished. My once pretty fingers are ruined. The top gloss is marred with deep scratches. My lower lip juts out in regret.

A sudden adrenaline boost rushes through me as I refocus. The key to freedom could be a hundred feet away, stuck in the thick mud of an icy river. The bathroom door creaks open and closes with a click. Another metallic click a moment later.

"You don't have to lock it. It's only the two of us," I say without looking up from my handiwork. I bend the hook into a more useful shape. I cheat, heating my fingers a few hundred degrees to make the metal more pliable. I managed to fashion a wonky line and mediocre hook out of the few items we found.

"Not too bad, huh?" I turn to smile at him and hold up my invention, expecting a pair of chocolate eyes to sparkle back at me.

Cold blue eyes stare back. Crinkles form at the corners to form a wicked smile. Kazak's frame fills the doorway of the bathroom. I jump back and drop my project.

"Not bad at all, Ruby."

I stammer a few words before scrambling backward on my hands and knees, trying to get as much space away from him as possible.

"Were you expecting someone else?" he asks me with a coy smile. He's as handsome as his younger brother but not as tall. He still towers over me, nonetheless. It contributes to the heavy feeling of vulnerability building in my chest. My fingers tingle with the memory of electrocution.

"Listen, I love to play cat and mouse with you, I do, but I have an agenda."

He seems more focused this time, less unhinged, as he looks down at me. Predatorial.

My sweaty palm slides out from underneath me on the floor, and I nearly bust my chin on the hard tile. He lunges at me. I squeeze my eyes shut and open my mouth to scream, expecting him to plunge a knife into my chest.

A large hand smacks over my mouth, muffling my scream and shoving my head into the wall behind me. His other hand pins my wrist onto the grimy floor at a painful angle. I swing to punch him with my left hand, but I'm weak and tired from late nights and little sleep. It lands on his hard torso, hurting me more than him. I try to claw at his face with my free hand, but he's too tall.

"Naughty girl," he chastises me, "stay quiet for me for a moment, please."

The Hadrian brothers may be twisted, fucked-up bastards, but damn if they aren't the most polite motherfuckers I've ever met.

"You and my younger brother have become quite the little team. How's the search going?"

Swimmingly. Just peachy. I swallow and clench my fists.

Pop. A tiny spark excitedly bursts from my palm and fizzles right in front of his face. It wasn't close enough to singe his corneas. Unfortunately, if the tickle on my fingertips is any indication, they're about to look like birthday candles if I don't calm down.

"By the way, Ruby," he smirks down at me, " how did you like my gift?"

Even if I could respond, I wouldn't. I knew the pig head was his fault.

"Pig heads are only the beginning. I will bring Hell to your doorstep. But it doesn't need to come to that." He's so close I can see the striations of blue and gray in his irises. The hand over my mouth moves away. He cocks an eyebrow and drops a finger down the apple of my hot cheek.

"Let's make a deal, Ruby. Just between you and I."

He has made a mistake by allowing me to speak freely.

"Fuck you."

"Hush. Let's have a civil conversation." He 'boops' my nose.

"I'll stop the chase. I'll call off all my staff. No more pig heads, no more parking lot fights. You impressed me with the pencil attack, by the way. Well done."

"He had it coming." I mimic Cato's growl, only making myself sound like an idiot with a sore throat.

"I know." His smile widens, and I know he knows about *the incident*. He knows what Howard did to me, and I have to push down the shock and pain to focus on speech.

"What do you want?"

"Your power."

"I can't give it to you if I don't know how to remove it–" I try to say.

"If I find out you removed the Dotion and disposed of it, I will murder my brother and squeeze the life out of you," he says as he softly runs his index finger down my face again.

"Why are you doing this? I don't understand."

His eyes glaze over, and he's somewhere far away from here and years in the past.

"Father never understood."

Twenty points to Slytherin for the creepy-ass answer.

I hate this. I could melt his face off with a hearty sneeze, yet I'm the one frozen in terror. The difference between us is that I have a warm heart, and he has an icy rock behind his ribs. He blinks, and he's back in the here and now.

"I'll kill him, and you'll have no protection from me. And I will take my revenge." He affirms, his eyes flick up to mine. The coldest blue. He releases me and steps back.

"Bring the Dotion to me by the end of the month, or I'll make you wish you were never born. Don't break toys that aren't yours, Ruby. Or you'll suffer the consequences."

"If I give it to you, you won't harm him?"

"You have my solemn word."

A shaky breath escapes my chest. The unsaid truth is he will attempt to kill me, and I'll have to either let him or turn him into a heap of ashes. Neither are palatable options.

"Fine. It's yours." My voice sounds foreign to my own ears. I sound strong and resilient, yet I feel the opposite. His eyes flash with glee. I clench my fists to try and collect myself. While Cato and I aren't best friends, I don't want him to die.

"Good girl."

With that final misogynistic sentiment, he's gone. I catch my breath and slide down the grimy bathroom wall to the floor. Despite everything, I smile. Kazak forgot the most important trait about me when he proposed that stupid deal; I'm a liar to my burning core.

After we fish out the briefcase, we struggle to get it open. I melt the locks, and we pry it open together. I point the beam of my flashlight onto the precious contents inside.

It's an advertisement. A soggy, moldy ad for a furniture store.

"Randy's Rooms! If you've got a room to furnish, Randy can do it for the best price in Northwestern Maine..." a balding cartoon man gushes with a big thumbs up.

"What the hell?" I mutter. I look up at Cato, expecting him to be pissed, but he has a quizzical look.

"This could be something." He pushes his hair out of his face.

"Really?" I look at the ad doubtfully. Did that psycho hide my freedom in a discount furniture store?

"I'll look into it." He throws it in the back of his car when we hop in. He notices me shivering and turns the heat to high.

"Here." I nudge his arm with a bottle of hand sanitizer from my purse. He takes it from me with an attitude, swiping it out of my fingers aggressively.

"Does this—have glitter in it?" he snarls at me, undoubtedly about to berate me about being girly and useless.

"Don't tell me your masculinity is so fragile you can't bear to touch sparkles. Suck it up." My daily store of patience for his ungrateful ass has run bone dry. I expect him to toss it in the trash can beside us, but he quickly squirts a glob in his large hands.

11

"Ready, Bones?" I asked.

"Prepare to get smoked, kid."

"In your dreams, tough guy."

I feel bad that Bones has to babysit me on grocery runs, so we make it a game. We chat and shop until my list is down to six items.

We pick three things each and race to find them. Whoever gets all three and touches the ATM in the store's back corner first wins. The loser has to buy the winner whatever candy bar they want. No running allowed. No pushing allowed.

Bones' strength is strategy. Mine is panicked speed.

I think Bones lets me win.

After a hard-fought victory, Bones and I leave the grocery store, a prize milk chocolate bar in my hand. He pops a quarter of my bar in his mouth before loading the groceries into his sedan.

I like to share my winnings with the less fortunate.

"I can hold the bananas in my lap. We don't want the almond milk to crush them," I say and turn to my shopping partner. He's glaring into the woods beside the store.

A chill runs down my spine. I'm not over my previous parking lot trauma. Howard called out of work for the week. The rumor around the office is that he got mugged and survived a stab wound to his neck. I don't have to see his stupid face, but I can't fully relax without knowing where he is during the workday.

"What's wrong?" I nervously question Bones.

"Nuthin. Please get in the car."

I might have argued with Cato, but when Bones tells me to do something, I do it.

I hurry into the passenger seat with the bundle of bananas. Bones turns down random side streets and alleyways. His hard eyes stay glued to the side mirrors. Is Howard back for round two? What did Bones see? Bones notices my worried frown and sighs.

"I'm real sorry, Ruby," he scrubs a hand over his mouth, "but we're being followed."

"Yeah, I figured," I shrug—nothing new for me.

"There's a new guy today. He's bad news. Cato says he has poison skin and a long tongue to catch you."

"Ugh," I shiver, "like a frog?"

"Yeah," he shakes his head, "fuckin' gross. Anyways, we gotta be extra careful because sometimes new guys try to show off and do something stupid for Kazak's attention or money, like that guy you stabbed. Howard? Was that his name?"

I swallow tightly.

"Yeah. That's his name."

My phone vibrates in my pocket.

Rain: I need pads ASAP. Thx. Love u :p

Dammit.

"Bones, I am so sorry, but I need you to stop at a pharmacy right now."

He turns to me, an unfamiliar look of confusion and mild panic on his face.

"Ruby, I can't-"

"Lady problems. I'll be in and out in three minutes. You can time me."

He cracks his knuckles against his chin, brow creased with stress.

"You'll be quick?"

"I swear," I say. No poison man is going to get me. I need pads for my sister.

"Dammit, Ruby. I'm busting in and carrying your slow ass out if you take longer than three minutes."

"Deal."

He pulls up to the pharmacy and pulls out his phone to start a timer. He nods at me, and I nod at him.

"Go."

I toss the bananas into his lap and jog through the pharmacy's automatic doors to the back. A pink box of pads on an end aisle calls my name. I snag it and spin around, slamming right into a fellow customer. My forehead almost bumps into his collarbone and I steady myself on a display case of athlete's foot creams.

"Sorry! Excuse me!" I look up and a pizza-faced teenager grins down at me. He can't be a day over eighteen. I politely smile back and step away. For just a moment, everything is fine. Until I feel something wet on my ankle. I look down. A slick, pink rope wraps around my legs and jerks me to the floor.

The frog fucker got me.

"Ruby Auclair? I can't wait to see your guts when Kazak slices you open." The pink rope trails up to the corner of his mouth.

"Shouldn't you be in gym class?" I stomp on his tongue and wriggle free. But before I can move any farther away, I'm stopped by a hand in front of my face.

"Ah, ah, ah. Don't move. Come with me, and I won't touch you. If you fight me, I'll turn your pretty face into a mass of boils," he threatens with a grin. Thick droplets of purple goop bubble on his palm and slide down his wrist. It smells like ammonia and burnt toast. Does nobody work in this pharmacy?

Bones is probably jamming to jazz. Cato will murder me if I press my emergency necklace for a frog boy. I desperately glance around for someone, anyone, to help me.

"I don't have all day, lady. Let's go," the boy snaps. A dark shadow moves behind him, and a wicked smile crosses my face.

Bones forces the young man into a chokehold.

His arm is covered with a thick gauntlet, protecting his skin from the man's poisonous touch. I stand, brush myself off, and pick up my dropped pad box.

"If you come within a mile of her, I will hang you with your own tongue," Bones growls in his ear. The teen tears up and swears he'll leave me alone forever. Bones tosses him outside, and the kid runs off. We hop in the car and speed away.

"I owe you a whole warehouse of candy bars, Bones," I sigh and sink into the leather seat.

"Don't mention it. Glad you got your, uh, supplies."

"On that note, let's not mention this to Cato," I say.

"Agreed."

"These people are wild," Tee says.

"Spill, I'm listening."

"Perseus Hadrian had a clean criminal background, and before his death, he owned a pharmaceutical company, Hadrian Pharma. Huge building downtown. Lots of protests at that address over the past fifteen years about their animal testing labs. He died about eight years ago after a nasty fall down the stairs. He died at only fifty-five. His wife passed the year before of an apparent suicide. I couldn't access the autopsy reports, but I managed to get into an old web forum where housewives were gossiping about her jumping off the top of her husband's building after she saw the nature of his experiments and animal testing subjects."

"Jesus..." I whisper in shock. Cato's mom killed herself. Mr.George's daughter-in-law jumped off a building.

"I know, right? I haven't even started on the sons. The older one is Kazak Hadrian. In high school, he was detained at a juvenile corrections center *twice* over several months for *the attempted murder* of another student!"

No surprises there, but I quietly feign surprise to Trish over the phone.

"Get this: he's the current president of Hadrian Pharma. The younger brother is much less interesting. Cato Hadrian has a clean record. Honors after graduating high school. Master's degree in physics."

"You're incredible, Tee. Thanks so much."

"Are you gonna tell me why I had to do all that impeccable research?"

"Can't tell you yet. I have to go. Love ya."

"Love you too, Rue. Call me later.

"I will, jelly bean. Bye."

"Goodnight, Mr. George! Sleep tight, and I'll see you in the morning." I squeeze his hand tightly. He squeezes back and makes me promise to drive safely. I always lie to everyone around me, even if it is for the best, but I hate lying to him.

I say goodbye, knowing I'm about to walk to my car, park down the block, and sneak back here with the lesser evil of his grandsons. I'll never lie again when I finally get rid of my curse. No more excuses or sneaking around. No more hiding. Although, I think he'd understand if he knew the whole story.

I waited twenty minutes for him before walking the dark drive and slipping into the cellar alone. A thick document in French sits in my lap while I skim it for my name. I warily glance over at my phone on a stack of papers. No notifications. *Is he mad at me? Did something happen to him? Has he given up? Did he find trouble?*

At midnight I walk back alone to my waiting car in the woods. The night is surprisingly warm, and a pleasant breeze ruffles my hair, but I'm too anxious to fully enjoy it. A stupid jerk and his evil, creepy brother consume my thoughts.

A yawn escapes me as I stretch and twist in my chair. The clock atop Tyrion's cage reads **12:47 AM** in bold red numbers. I rush to finish my grocery list for the week.

A curl of smoke rises into my eyesight, and I drop my pen. The tip bubbles, its body now twisted into an S shape after being held between my infernal fingers.

"Oh, God."

I look at my hands. My fingertips and palms are glowing blue with intense heat. I extend my arms away from myself as far as possible to spare my eyebrows.

I race into my bathroom, kicking the door with my hands held high in surrender. As if they were covered in blood. Contaminated.

I maneuver the bathtub nozzle with my elbow and stomp the drain plug closed with my heel. I bounce nervously as I wait for the tub to fill with cool water.

I plunge my hands into the water as I pray out loud.

"Please, baby Jesus, make it stop. Please, please, please! I *cannot* call out of work again this year! Shit, shit, shit…." I stare at my submerged hands and wait. A moment passes like molasses in a freezer.

A lone bubble rises from the bottom of the tub and pops at the surface. Another. A dozen more rise up.

"No. No, no, no!" I chant and wrench my hands out of the now boiling water. The alarm necklace over my heart bounces against my skin from jerky movements.

I need Cato. No. He won't come. He ditched me tonight. He's either occupied or doesn't want to be around me. Who else do I have?

I sink to my knees beside the still steaming bath, arms outstretched like a zombie with locked elbows. I slowly bow, use the counter corner to press the button against my chest, and sink onto the blue memory foam mat in front of my tub. I glare tearily at my glowing appendages.

This is so stupid. I ate a cookie on a leaf in the woods when I was twelve, not knowing I signed up for a cage match with destiny. I'm burdened with insurmountable power. Don't want it. Don't need it. I think it's punishing me for not using it.

Why couldn't I have a useful power? Super strength? Super speed? Even Cato's invisibility would have been better than this shit. Unfortunately, I drew the short straw, and now I have to pay for it. A shaky grasp of pyrokinesis.

It feels like I've been waiting for years on the bathroom floor. But then, the click of my window outside the bathroom startles me. A sliding window pane.

"Cato?" I call out, followed by a hiccup.

"Auclair?" He enters the bathroom and looks at me, undoubtedly looking pathetic and tear-streaked on the bathroom floor with glowing hands and messy hair. Concern knits across his brow. He bites the tip of his left leather glove and yanks it off when he notices my glowing hands. He drops to my level for a better look. A whoosh of the cool night air ruffles my hair.

"It won't stop," I squeak. A sob escapes me. I hyperventilate again, spiraling thoughts pulling me under.

I can't work. I can't eat. I can't use my phone. I couldn't even wipe my ass if I wanted to.

"Has this ever happened before?"

"A few times. Never this bad," I choke out.

He gently pokes my nose and rolls his eyes.

"You need to calm down. Stop that," Cato hushes me, "Jesus, what are you so stressed about?"

"The whole kidnapping was—like—a lot. To deal with. And the Howard issue. I don't sleep well, and I'm constantly stressed about hurting anyone–I want to be normal. And boring. And not shoot two-thousand degree sparks out of my nose every time I sneeze," my voice quivers as Trish's unborn son crosses my mind, "I want to hold a baby without horrible, anxious thoughts racing through my mind. So I-" I have to take a deep breath before continuing.

"I'm so tired," I admit.

He looks at me for a moment and lets my confessions wash over him. He stands.

"Where are you going?"

"Stay there. I'll be right back."

He leaves, and I cry again. I rest my head on the cool surface of the tub rim, staring at a fluffy cluster of my dark hair on the bathmat.

Damn, I wish I had a moment to clean before he got here. I sniffle and cough. What a silly thought. *Why do I care what he thinks of me? He's a dangerous criminal I'm temporarily tied to.*

He comes back with an armful of oven mitts. He slips my favorite pair on my hands in a way that reminds me of an adult dressing a small child. I stare at my covered hands. A print of Winnie the Pooh slurping honey giddily covers the mitt. He pulls out his phone, fiddles with it, and shoves it in his pocket before pulling on our backup pair of oven mitts. These are sage green and heavily stained with pasta sauce and burns.

"I don't think this is going to–" I huff at him.

"Shut up," he harshly cuts me off, "stop crying and stop thinking. Turn it all off." He roughly grabs my mitted hands with his own mitted hands and pulls me up off of the floor.

The Girl from Ipanema, sung by Frank Sinatra and Antônio Carlos Jobim, softly plays from his pocket. I meet his eyes, expression as unreadable as always. *He's a dangerous criminal. Dangerous criminals don't know the Girl from Ipanema.*

He leads me out of my bathroom and into the middle of my bedroom. Cautiously we move side to side. He pulls me closer as I quietly sing the words to the song.

I keep my eyes trained on my Winnie the Pooh mitt on his shoulder. If I meet his eyes, I'm afraid my whole body will burst into flames. His large, mitted hands both find my waist, and he pulls me even closer. Heat blooms on my face as I realize this is the first time since our rendezvous in the bar that he's touched me without disgust or disdain.

I give in and close my eyes and lean onto his shoulder. He smells like clean, warm laundry and spice.

I break out of my trance when I catch him watching my mouth as I sing, and our eyes meet. "How did you know I love this song?"

"I've heard you sing it to my Grandfather," he quietly answers, "you seemed to enjoy it." *Dangerous criminals aren't thoughtful.*

My hands aren't burning anymore, but I don't say a word for fear of breaking this strange spell. I let him twirl me around my room until I didn't remember why I was crying in the first place.

A soft shuffling noise from the bathroom wakes me up. I tiptoe in and peek around the corner of the bathroom door. Cato is asleep in my bathtub. His head rests against the side of the tub, and his long legs are stretched up the shower wall. My white fluffy blanket covers his top half.

He's so handsome when he's not scowling at me. He must have picked me up, carried me to my bed, and made himself comfortable in my bathroom. I frown down at his snoozing form.

That's an interesting favor for a woman you claim to hate. He's in serious denial. Or he has mommy issues AND daddy issues. That would explain why he has such a hard time trusting me.

This Cato Hadrian asleep in my bathtub, who danced with me in oven mitts, had a ruby necklace made for me, and paid off Bones' son's tuition in secret, will be gone in the morning. He'll be replaced by a bitter man who sees me as more of an inconvenience than a companion. He's the first one I've been able to tell my secrets, true fears, and shortcomings.

One time I told him about the owl, and it felt like an elephant taking a foot off my chest. Maybe this is why his scrutiny and unfriendly manner cut so deep. Yet, when he shows his kind side, it hurts even more.

My lip quivers when I spare a glance at myself in the mirror. I look the most well-rested I've been in months. My shoulders are relaxed. My head isn't pounding, and my pulse is slow. The recent dullness in my eyes is replaced with a new spark, and the dark rims under my eyes have vanished. I look like a new woman. *He did that.*

I tiptoe out of the bathroom and crawl back under my covers. When I finally wake up, he's gone. Tyrion's food bowl is full of protein pellets. The blankets I kicked off last night are neatly folded at my feet. A full glass of water is on the table beside my head. A small smile tips my mouth up. *Guess I'm not the only caregiver between the two of us.*

It takes weeks of consistent teamwork, patience, and snacks until he tells me about his mother, Annette. So far, he's told me she was Canadian. She was visiting a cousin in America the summer she met his father in the orchard.

"She was an artist too, but she preferred sketching landscapes. She used to say she found nature more interesting than people," he says.

Sounds like someone I know. I keep this to myself.

"Self-taught?" I ask.

"Not at first. My mom trained at an art school in Paris but dropped out when a professor spat on a colored pencil drawing of a pond that he disagreed with. She came back to Maine and met my father shortly after."

"She's beautiful. And talented. I wish I had the chance to meet her," I say.

He nods in response.

"She would have liked you."

I can't stop the laugh of disbelief from bubbling up.

"What? You hardly like me. Why would she?"

He doesn't answer.

"I need to know what happened to your father." I blurt. It's been keeping me awake at night, amongst other things.

"I told you, my father died before he could create a Dotion for my brother," he says.

The deep emotion in his molten chocolate eyes contrasts with his expressionless face. The accusation weighing on my mind for weeks finally slips out into the air between us.

"You killed him."

He makes no motion to deny nor confirm my accusation, simply turns a page. He killed his father to stop the cycle. To prevent his deranged brother from destroying the world, he made himself a killer to save lives.

Unfortunately for us all, it didn't work. Perseus Hadrian still had wicked post-mortem plans up his sleeve. Because I exist, his brother still has a chance to cause chaos. I swallow as another dark thought plumes like a mushroom cloud in my head.

If he killed his father to stop Kazak from getting a Dotion, maybe he'll kill you too.

I thought we'd had a breakthrough from our little dance session the other night, but apparently, I was wrong. I've never seen him in such a crappy mood. He slams his car door when he arrives, and a wave of his menacing aura hits me right in the face when I turn to greet him, and he shoves past me.

An old piece of advice from my father floats across my mind. *There's nothing a bully hates more than being ignored. Drives them crazy.* A wicked little smile forms on my lips. I ignore him easily when he makes a mean quip about my shoes as we walk the driveway. My mind is light years away and ten feet under my lake of peace. Calm, cold, holding my breath under dark waters.

I will not engage.

Tuning him out is easier than I thought. I've had plenty of practice muffling out my siblings' squabbles and sports team discussions. This is the best idea I've had since last week when I came up with the plan to stab Howard.

When we reach the cellar, I flick on a tiny glass lamp in my corner and busy myself with organizing my pile to dig through for the next four hours.

Another snarky remark from him on the other side, but I stay quiet. He says my name. I hear him go up the stairs, thinking he may have left. The old wood alerts me to his return a few minutes later.

I look up to see him place a coffee in front of me. I'm too stunned to speak. My eyes flick from the cup back up to him. His Adam's apple bobs, but he doesn't say anything. I turn back to my book silently. A stupid cup of joe isn't enough to break me.

"Look at me, dammit!"

He rips the book from my hands and flings it across the cellar. I raise my eyes and give him a bored stare.

"Mr. George is trying to sleep. Could you at least try to wait to have your temper tantrum outside?" I ask, deadpan.

"You little-" he snarls but quiets his voice, "what is your problem? Why are you ignoring me?"

"You know why," I calmly reply, brushing off the dust clinging to my black jeans.

"We always fight. Why was the last one any goddamn different?"

"You don't like me. We aren't friends, remember? So get lost," I say.

My voice is colorless, but my pulse is pumping. I calmly reach to pick up another book. He takes a deep breath through his nose. His wide chest rises and falls; at first, I think he's about to shout at me. My shoulders tighten as I prepare for the fallout.

"I'm sorry if I came off as...." he rolls his shoulders before continuing, "...as abrasive. We may not be friends, but we are teammates, so I owe you a level of respect. I apologize for offending you." He presses his lips together, and his eyes jump away from my gobsmacked stare.

Did he apologize? To me?

"Um. Thanks." That's all I can think of to say.

We settle back into our routine, searching through dusty piles.

When I return from a bathroom break, he quickly shoves a paper in his pocket, discreetly but not discreetly enough.

"What's that?"

"What?" he snaps at me.

"Don't bullshit me. The paper you stuffed in your pocket, what was that?"

"Honestly, you swear like a sailor. Do you ever listen to yourself?" he snarls at me. Unfortunately for him, his attempt at provocation isn't going to work this time.

"Don't change the subject. What do you have?"

"It's only a note…from my mother. There's nothing important on it. But…I know it's her's based on the handwriting."

"May I?" I hold my hand out. He pulls the small piece of paper from his pocket and hands it to me. It's a simple grocery list, but it represents so much more. Grief. Loss. Vulnerability.

"She had pretty handwriting," is all I can think to say as I smooth out the folded edges.

He shrugs and moves on to the next box of papers, shutting me out and getting back to business. Walls up. *We're not friends, Ruby.*

We don't share sorrows or losses, or pain. I gently fold it back up and place it by his hip before moving to search the back shelves. When my grandmother died, I saved every scrap she'd written on I could find. It was comforting to hold her words in my hands, immortalized, lasting longer than her final breath. Even a little reminder to pick up the dry cleaning or a card with an 'I love you' scrawled at the bottom patched up a few holes in my heart. So I'll let him quietly heal on his own with tiny paper memories.

He only walks slightly ahead of me tonight as we trek the long, dark drive.

"Before you know it, we'll be done, and I'll be relieved of this exhausting babysitting job." I hear the smug smile in his voice.

"Privileged asswipe," I snarl with playful disdain at his well-defined shoulders.

"Strawberry shortcake," he tosses back.

"Poltergeist."

"Matchstick."

"Daddy issues." I regret it as soon as I say it, fearing I went too far, but he surprises me by throwing his head back and laughing. He runs a hand through his dark hair and looks back at me with a rare smile. Not a smug grin or a smirk. A genuine smile.

"Too true. And you don't even know half of it." I fall silent, torn between asking for him to divulge more and dropping the subject altogether. He waits for me to come to his side before walking again.

It's minuscule progress that I'm incredibly grateful for. I try to quell the feeling of pride bursting in my chest. Small steps towards victory are still in the right direction.

"You may ask me one extra question tonight."

"What's your favorite color?" I smirk at his profile. He's going to say black. It's the only color he wears. He cracks a grin so amused and sincere that it's like a slap to my face.

"A deep, dark red. Ruby," he says and vanishes into the night like an infuriating, moody, flirtatious ghost. As I go about my bedtime routine and refill Tyrion's little beach ball-shaped food bowl, I can't think of anything else for the rest of the evening. I swaddle myself in a well-loved throw and crack open my window two inches to allow the cool night air to slither in. I fall asleep thinking of milk chocolate eyes.

12

Mr. Dan Puntzel occupies my morning. I carve a happy jack o' lantern for him as he tells me about a summer long ago in Vietnam. He's a grizzled war vet with decades of stories and stage three colon cancer. Storytelling is cathartic for him. He always slips into a deep nap when he finishes a tale. A note under my windshield wiper catches my eye when I step out onto his stoop. Child-like handwriting fills the piece of paper.

Meat at Hadley Park for info-2 pm. Aloan.
Prickle

I crinkle the note up and toss it in my backseat. I do not want to resort to accepting help from Prickle, but Halloween is only one week away. I bite my lip and check my watch. I have fifteen minutes to make a decision. Prickle stands by the park pond when I pull up. Initially, I didn't recognize him. His needles are retracted. I approach him with caution. Our last meeting was less than friendly.

"Hello," I say.

"Hello. Happy you came." He smiles and gestures for me to walk with him. Prickle and I sit on a bench by the murky duck pond. A bonded duck pair squawks and splashes the dark water, caught in a public lovers' quarrel.

"Prickle thinks he can help Miss Ruby. Want to help. It's the right thing to do. But he is afraid of his boss," Prickle sighs and swings his short legs on the bench.

"That's ok, Prickle. I'm afraid of my boss too." Howard is the last person I want to think about, but if he helps me get Prickle to open up, it'll be worth it. His eyes widen.

"You? You're afraid?"

"I'm always afraid." I smile sadly. It's not a lie. We sit quietly before I decide it's time to get to business.

"What was in the notebook you tried to take?"

"A riddle to help Kazak."

"Can you tell me?"

"Can't tell. Not allowed to tell."

"Oh. Can you maybe write it down?"

"I can write down the riddle for you!" His eyes brighten, and his pointed teeth appear in his wide smile. My eye twitches, but I can't help it. My revulsion toward him makes me feel guilty. It's not his fault he's a monster.

"Sure, Prickle. That would be useful. Thank you."

He digs in the junk of a park trash can until he finds a pencil and paper. He scribbles a few lines and hands the paper to me. I stuff it in my pocket without looking. Cato and I can review it later. What I want to do is get away from Prickle.

"Thanks so much, Prickle. See you around." I spin to leave, but he grabs my wrist and makes a whining noise.

"Please, Ruby, please don't leave yet. Something terrible is coming, Miss Ruby."

I bite my lip and think back to what Meredith said about boundaries. *Define, communicate clearly, and outline consequences.*

"I have to leave, Prickle. Please let me go. Do not grab me again, or I will stop meeting with you." To my surprise, he lets go when I outline the consequence, and my gut flips with guilt again. He must be truly desperate for companionship, and I can relate more than I'd like to admit.

I immediately call Cato about the clue. When he asks where I got it from, I don't lie. He's initially pissed that I went without him, but I explain that I wanted to make up for my blunder of losing the purple notebook. His temper fizzles out before I arrive home. He follows me to my room, and I open the note for us to read. It's a rhyme.

Headboards and tables
 Seek out the gold labels
 Among beds beyond measure
 Your mother's greatest treasure
 Shall reveal the secret to you.

He frowns and rubs his chin. The twisty sinews of his muscled forearms appear with the movement, and my eyes glaze over.

"My father had shares in that place on the ad we found in the creek. Randy's Rooms. It's a furniture store. Most of the pieces in my grandfather's house are from that place. So we'll forgo our cellar search tonight and head there now." At his words, I snap myself out of a debaucherous daydream.

"Oh, fun. A side quest." I roll my eyes, using sarcasm to hide that I'm angry he's so hot without even trying. It's disgusting. *He doesn't like you. He will never like you, and you shouldn't like him either. Grow up. After this is over, you'll never see him again.*

"Grab your ugly purse. We're going shopping."

His eyes are honey brown in the light of day. It's a rare treat to see him before nightfall. He catches me staring almost immediately because I'm a dork.

"See anything you like?"

"Nope." I pop the P in the word and scramble to get out of the car.

Randy's Rooms is in a strip mall so old that not one shop still has all of its letters on its signs. Randy's R oms is next to Valu illage. As I enter, Cato holds the door for me, and I know it's not out of chivalry. If we are attacked upon entry, my powers provide the best defense.

The squeaking air conditioner above blows my hair out of my face upon entry, and I'm met with a huge furniture showroom. The riddle is spot on. This place does have beds beyond measure.

High-end pieces fill every square foot of the vast space. Antiques mix with modern models. A stunning King bed with an equally stunning $16,000 price tag catches my eye. Silver foil highlights the carved vines on the footboard.

Randy must be on lunch break because there's not a soul in sight.

"I'll search this section. You search the other. Gold label, got it?"

"Got it, good luck," I say.

"Speak for yourself." He winks at me, and it's so surprising that I choke on the dusty air.

An hour later, I'm on my knees searching for any sign of gold on a velvet upholstered loveseat. When I attempt to stand, I whack my head on the corner of an exquisite dresser.

"Ouch."

I turn to glare at it as if the dresser hit me on purpose. A shiny gold label glints from the corner of a drawer. My mouth falls open, and I scramble up.

"Cato!" I shout to the huge room.

"What?" he calls back.

"Found it!"

"You liar."

"I'm not kidding!"

I wait for him to find me before touching the dresser. Knowing my luck, it would burst into flames before he saw it. The only other tag on it states that it was previously owned. It has beautiful stained dark wood with bronze knobs.

We kneel down together to look closer at the gold tag. It says nothing. No price. No details. No clue. I open the drawers and run my fingers over the dark wood. Nothing of interest at all. Just an old dresser.

His breath brushes my neck before I realize how close we are. I meet his chocolate eyes cautiously.

"This is a dead end," he growls.

"'This is a dead end,'" I mimic him, "it's not! There is something here we aren't seeing." His impatience and pessimism are killing my spirit.

"You wasted our time by making a deal with a lab rat. You're so naive. I honestly can't believe you haven't gotten us killed yet."

"You're such a jerk! I only met with him to give us an advantage, so fuck off! I'm doing the best I can with what I have."

"…An asinine scavenger hunt with the most annoying woman I've ever met…."

"Shut up! This has hardly been a damn picnic for me, too! You think I like being bullied by the man who rejected me?"

There it is out in the open. One of my biggest insecurities has been spoken out loud. I feel like I painted a bullseye over my heart.

"Do you know why I'm such a jerk to you?" he asks, voice low and eyes glazed.

"Be-because you're not nice?" I stutter. He smells like peppermint. He's too close. He's not close enough.

"I love getting a rise out of you. Pink cheeks. Heavy breath. Big eyes. So sensitive."

I think I might have a heart attack. Is he…? Are we…?

But then he remembers he's an asshole who hates me. He moves back so fast that, at first, I think I burned him. He stands and crosses his arms, gaze avoiding mine. An ache in my throat warns me of oncoming tears. But I refuse to let him ever see me cry again. It's not my fault he's an emotionally stunted crap sack.

"It's a dead end. Let's go."

Mr. George yawns widely, and the golden molars in the back of his mouth glint in the lamp light. We've had a quiet October afternoon together. Down the hall, the dryer hums as it warms his bathroom towels. On his ancient television screen, a handsome male newscaster tells us to expect lots of rain in the days ahead. My lower lip juts out. I could use sunshine this week.

I sigh and open a chocolate pudding cup and fold in a tiny atorvastatin pill before handing it to him. He's been having a hard time swallowing pills lately.

"My grandson is downstairs. Lookin' for something," he comments as I carefully press a large spoon in his palm. My brows raise, and I glance at the mahogany grandfather clock across the room. Cato's not supposed to be here for another hour. My heart skips as I remember how close we were last night before he pulled away.

"I love getting a rise out of you. Pink cheeks. Heavy breath. Big eyes. So sensitive."

"Oh, I'll go see if I can help. Be back soon." I adjust the blanket around his shoulders, and he nods, eyelids heavy with sleep. I blow out the candle on his mantle, pop a lemon drop into my mouth, and make my way to the red cellar door. I flick on the light like I've done dozens of times before. Nothing happens.

After mere weeks of use, the old lightbulb has finally failed. Suffocating darkness, so deep my pupils ache, fills the basement to the brim like a swimming pool of black ink. My upper teeth sink into my bottom lip. God, I hate the dark.

I picture the lake in my mind to calm my pulse. Lush green trees line the shore, and tiny waves lap at the roots.

My worry for Cato sitting alone in the dark cellar overwhelms my childish fears.

Maybe finding his mother's grocery list put him in a dark place. Or our almost-kiss. He saved me when I couldn't control my power; I can't let him wallow here alone.

A high-pitched crack breaks the silence when I make a tiny flame ball in my palm before slowly descending the stairs. I vanish it as soon as I reach the bottom step. By now, I could make my way through the familiar basement stacks and narrow paths blindfolded. I navigate my way over to his usual workspace. My nervous tongue turns over the lemon drop in my mouth and accidentally makes a loud pop. A shuffle from the back of the room answers it.

"Cato? You down here?" I call into the dark. Thankfully, my voice isn't trembling like my hands. A warm body meets my back. The pull between us has been undeniably strong. Even with an empty stomach and a bloody scalp, I felt a spark. When we scream in each other's faces, when we don't speak, when we walk side by side, when I make him laugh. It's undeniable. I think about the hundred-dollar bill he left for an underpaid, protective waitress. Dancing with oven mitts on our hands.

With a surge of courage, I spin, step up on my tip toes and kiss his mouth softly. And then I do it again, more firmly. Before I can retreat, he grabs my upper arms, pulls me to his body, and takes control of the kiss, dominating my mouth with his own. The butterflies in my stomach erupt in a jubilee of fluttering. He steals my lemon drop and bites through it with a crunch.

Rude, I was enjoying that. His fingers are holding me so tightly I'm certain they will leave quarter-sized bruises. I make a little noise to hint that he's gripping me too hard. We break apart briefly to catch our breath.

"I wasn't expecting you-" he doesn't let me finish as our mouths crash together again, his lips warm and hurried.

He slides his hands into my hair and tugs my head back painfully by the roots to work on my throat, covering it with hard kisses. The happy butterflies in my stomach have morphed into nervous moths. He's devouring me, and while it's not unpleasant, he is hurting me.

"Cato-" I murmur, and he freezes. Like the spell broke. He lets me go, and he's gone. I'm left in the dark basement with a rapid pulse and a lonely heart.

I'd expect nothing less of a ghost.

Mr. George is snoozing away when I check in on him, so I make his bed with fresh, blue sheets, organize his pill box, and venture out into the chilly night. I try to block out thoughts of my encounter in the basement, but it's like trying to block out noise at a rock concert. My thoughts are so loud. *Why did you kiss him? Why did he kiss you back? And so aggressively? What was that about? And he ran...after I said his name.*

When Cato's dark sedan pulls up behind my car, I glare at it. What kind of stupid game is he playing?

"What are you doing here?" I bark at him as soon as he gets out of his car.

"It's half past eight on a Wednesday night. We always meet here." He looks at me like I'm an idiot.

"Why did you leave and come back? We could have stayed in the basement." I scratch my head and look away.

"What?" A look of confusion creases his brow. Is he playing dumb?

"What do you mean *what*?" I snap. My voice cracks as my breathing increases.

"I got here two minutes ago," he says.

A lump forms in my throat and threatens to choke my voice.

"You're going to pretend like nothing happened?"

"Like *what* happened?" he asks impatiently. Cold realization washes over me like a heavy wet blanket on my shoulders.

When Mr. George said his grandson was in the cellar, he was talking about his *other* grandson. Not Cato. That means... I kissed...

"I thought–I thought–" I try to choke the words out, but I can't speak. He looks at me like I'm about to burst into flames, and at this point, I might. I turn and walk a few paces into the woods and proceed to puke behind a bush.

I inhale a shaky, gasping breath of fresh air to calm my stomach. The roadside smell of greasy food and car exhaust is sucked into my nose, inspiring my stomach to give up the last of its contents. I wipe my mouth with the back of my hand and stabilize myself against a tree, grimacing at the vile taste left behind on my tongue.

To my surprise, Cato stands behind me, his arm extended out with a bottle of water in his hand. I silently take it from him and march back to the woods to rinse my mouth. Once I'm confident I'm done, I walk over to him and take a deep breath.

He raises his brows in question, but thankfully he doesn't ask out loud. We continue our routine. Kazak is long gone, but I can't help feeling nauseous again as we descend the cellar steps. I pass Cato an applesauce pouch and a water bottle. He thanks me.

After weeks of work, our piles have finally merged. I sit beside him as I flip through a lab report.

I catch him staring at me as I suck on the applesauce pouch, and I flip him off as he snickers. He's slipped on a pair of glasses to read, and my face heats. My thumb knuckle pops from squeezing my fists so tight. He's so good-looking. He sweeps his dark hair back with one tan hand. My mind wanders with reckless abandon. Would we have dated if circumstances were different? I think back to the night we met.

The Incident with Howard had occurred the week prior, and I had good reason to drink my worries away. And it was my birthday. Tee's mother promised to be our sober driver, and after dropping us off at my favorite bar, she firmly pressed her shiny blue credit card in Trish's hand.

"Whatever she wants, spare no expense on our Ruby, darling. See you girls at two." She kissed us on our heads and drove off in her black Rolls Royce, lovingly named Danny Zuko.

Trish dolled me up in a sexy little cocktail dress. For herself, she had chosen a low-cut jumpsuit that drew every male gaze in the room. She's been a show-stopper since the day she was born. After dancing and indulging in a few libations, I caught a man watching me. When I saw him staring, he didn't look away. Handsome, tall, dark hair cut in an Ivy League style. Maybe a bit longer. Roman nose. Chiseled jaw. Big shoulders. All black business clothes, down to his polished black shoes. He looked like he had stepped out of an office romance. Or a funeral.

He was a light, and I was a moth. I had no conscious control of my feet as I walked over to him. I stumbled on my heels and caught myself on his hard shoulder. I looked up, horrified. A rakish smile greeted me.

"I am so sorry, I didn't mean to –" I rushed out and dared to meet his chocolate eyes.

"Watch your step, birthday girl." The smile on his face was gone, replaced with an annoyed look. My face heats as I remember the obnoxious tiara on my head and the pink banner across my chest. I gulped and threw on a cheeky smile. I'm not flirty and beautiful like Trish, but I can be fun.

"I'm Ruby. Dance with me." I offered him my hand. A strange look flickered across his face. I barely caught it. Recognition. This is a small town, maybe we had a class together. He ignored my hand, reached for my waist, and stopped an inch before touching me, looking down at me for permission. I nodded, blushing with sudden shyness.

When his large hands touched the curve of my hip, a spark in my chest popped. I sucked in a calming breath and tried to ignore it. My hands felt warm, but not too warm. If anything changed, I could always slip into the bathroom and cool my hands off under the tap. He was unsurprisingly a bit stiff, but otherwise not a terrible partner.

When the euphoria of three drinks overwhelms my brain, I become blunt. What can I say? I'm a Sagittarius.

His eyes softened, and we danced for hours. We didn't speak much, but it wasn't necessary. His cold exterior thawed quickly as we danced and laughed. His large hands never left my waist. I welcomed the intimate touch and savored the feeling of desire bubbling in my chest and humming in my core. The previous weeks had been tough. It was magical to let go and be a bit naughty and selfish for a few hours.

When he dipped his head to kiss me, butterflies with sparklers for wings erupted in my chest. It had been a long time since I felt that alive. Free.

I pulled him into a corner so we could kiss more privately. His hands climbed high on my waist, and I pressed my body into him as he cupped the back of my neck with a large hand. Warm fingers sent delightful sensations to my neurons.

He broke our kiss and stalked away without looking back. I stood there, stunned, hands floating frozen in the air where they were just pressed into his chest.

The burn of rejection rolled through my chest as I watched his dark silhouette weave through the crowded bar and exit into the rainy night.

13

He removes his glasses and rubs his eyes.

"I need to pay a visit to Hadrian Pharma. Tonight."

"Cool, let me just check on Mr. George first. I'm coming with you, right?"

"Not this time." His sigh that follows is short and annoyed.

"What?" I put my hands on my hips.

"I changed my mind."

"You're being an asshole," I proclaim to the basement.

I don't miss the ghost of a smirk on his mouth. Of course, he's going to ask for something in return.

"I'll let you come if you enlighten me. Share a secret." His dark eyes pin me to the spot, greedy for vulnerable information.

"*Enlighten you?*" I mock him and nervously laugh. I have a bad feeling about what he wants to know.

"What happened earlier? When you hacked in the bushes?"

My mouth twists as I try and think of a lie, but I'm so tired of it. Tired of lying. I'm so close to clocking out of that horrible hobby I might as well give it up now. I want to go on this mission. I want to prove to him I'm a capable woman. But...

"I can't–" I choke on the air.

"You can't come with me. Sorry," he cooly replies, a scheming twinkle in his eye. I scrub my cheeks with warm hands.

"Fine."

He reclines back in the pile of papers, balancing the tumbler of water on his thigh.

"Go on. I'm listening."

Word vomit pours from my mouth as I confess:

"I made out with your brother in the cellar because the stupid fucking bulb from 1927 burned out and it was dark and I thought it was you because Mr.George said his grandson was here and I *thought* he meant *you* and not *him* but you were so rough and hurting me so I said your name and you left but it wasn't you, it was your psychotic brother!"

His mouth opens slightly, and his gaze drops to my mouth. His chest contracts with a sharp inhale.

"Tell me you're lying," he rasps out. I stare at him in confusion. I thought he'd laugh. I'd been sure he'd throw his head back and chuckle at my fatal mistake.

"I wish I was," I whisper back. He swallows hard, and suddenly, he can't seem to look at me anymore.

"You can come."

We don't speak in the car. We don't converse when he sneaks us into the building through an elevator shaft under repair. I glare at his back as we walk the long, dark halls. I'm an expert at it. I don't know why he's so mad at me. He wanted to know even though I warned him.

"Wow," I breathe as we enter a large room of cubicles. This is the nicest office I've ever seen. Every workspace has this year's model of luxury brand computers, plush leather chairs, and built-in mug warmers at each desk.

"Oops." My mini flashlight falls out of my jacket and rolls across the smooth floor. I stomp on it with my shoe to stop it and bend over to pick it up. Before I stand, I notice the reflection of Cato behind me in the triangular blue glass of an award on a desk. A pained look crosses his face, eyebrows sewn together. He closes his eyes and runs a hand over his face.

"What?" I snap, stand up quickly, and discreetly brush a hand over my ass. Did I sit in something? Why did he look like his fingernails were being plucked out?

"Nothing. Don't touch anything. Follow me," he growls impatiently and pushes past me. I roll my eyes. He needs to sort out his daddy issues with a professional. I can't keep up with his mood swings. One moment he dotes on me, and the next, I'm an annoying little bug on his windshield.

"This is where staff with the highest security clearance operate. Destroy the computers, and I'll grab the paper files. Hurry. Go," he orders. I run over to a computer and pop it open by knocking it off the desk with a swat of my hand. This knocks over the desk owner's "Cat of The Day" calendar and a framed picture of a preschooler in graduation regalia. I look at the wires and colored pieces on the open electronic box and decide it all needs to go.

After a moment of hesitation, a wave of my hand turns the internal hardware into a bubbling, gooey mess of molten plastic and metal. I jump to the next desk and do the same.

Swat. Pop the cover. Melt it all. Swat. Pop the cover. Melt it all.

Cato shoves tan folders and paperclipped stacks of files into a trash bag with an attitude. I pause my task of melting internal hardware into bubbling globs. My pink nails hover over an uncompromised motherboard.

"How much time do we have left before the security cameras come back?"

"Twenty-seven minutes. Why?"

"Can we log into one? I need to know what Howard told your brother. He must have had an interview or something. Can we check?"

"What? Why?"

"It might be nothing, but I need to know."

He glances at his watch and concedes, to my surprise. He never does what I ask on the first try. After tapping away at one of the undestroyed computers, he pulls up a video.

"This is his interview with Kazak." He presses the spacebar, and Howard reclines in an oversized chair, hands behind his head, facing us.

"Tell us about Ruby Auclair," Kazak says from behind the camera. A nasty grin spreads across Howard's face.

"What do you want to know? I know lots about her." He runs his tongue over his canine teeth like a frat boy teasing his brothers with the details of his latest carnal conquest. My heartbeat stutters. *Don't back out. I need to know what he said. I need to know.*

"Start from the beginning. How did you meet?" Kazak's voice has the same impatient edge as Cato has when I push his buttons. I zone out while he talks about how I'm a perfect employee with perfect ratings from clients and their families and how I usually do whatever he asks without pushback.

"She's a good little dog, but she sure knows how to bite." He raises his hand and shows Kazak and the camera his scar. "That little bitch gave me this."

I slam the spacebar. That's enough.

"I've heard enough," I say. Cato shrugs.

"That guy hates you." He turns to me, an almost playful light in his eyes. Unfortunately for him, I'm not in the mood for teasing anymore. Or talking about Howard.

"Noted," I say.

"While your Strawberry Shortcake personality and loud mouth are annoying, I can't imagine anyone hating you so much that they essentially sign your death warrant."

"Hmm…" I say as nonchalantly as I can. *Drop it, drop it, drop it, please.*

"What happened? How did you manage to piss off Half-moon?"

My stomach drops, and I finally turn toward him.

"Who?"

"Half-moon," he raises a curious brow at me, "Bones said all the guys at the agency call Howard that because of how proud he is of that big semi-circle scar on his hand. He told the whole squad it was from rough sex. I didn't believe it, but–"

"I think I'm gonna be sick," I croak and grip the sides of the desk with trembling fingers. The color drains from my face. Half-moon. Howard is proud of it. He wears it like a badge. What a sick fuck.

"Auclair–"

"He snuck up behind me in the office locker room and shoved his fingers inside me so hard I bled for two days. I gave him that scar when he put his hand over my mouth."

The silence of the room is so loud my eardrums could burst. The light hum of the air conditioning is drowned out by this consuming silence between us.

Cato's dark eyes lock on me, and his body is as stiff as a board. I shove my trembling fingers under my thighs and continue.

"I had my earbuds in like a careless idiot, and before I could pull on my scrub pants, he assaulted me. He covered my mouth with his hand. The scar is an imprint of my teeth."

"Why isn't he in jail right now?" he asks calmly. Too calmly.

"A client suffering from dementia fell on my watch the week before. I-I turned my back to unfold her walker, and she fell. Broke her arm through the skin. It was horrific. I beat myself up about it–"

My voice breaks, and I take a moment to collect myself before continuing. I can't look at him, but I know he's looking at me. His incendiary stare burns the side of my face.

"He said if I told anyone, he'd make it look like I assaulted her. He told me her family owed him an old debt, and they would file an assault charge against me with a snap of his fingers...Cato, I love my job. I'm good at it too. It's healing me–"

I dare to glance up at him. He hasn't moved since I opened my mouth. I'm not even sure he's taken a breath. A dark piece of hair has fallen between his eyes, and he remains as still as the Athena statue in his grandfather's greenhouse.

"I rinsed his blood out from my mouth and kept my head down."

When my brother gets mad, he stomps his feet and raises his voice. Seth used to run his fingers through his hair and pull at the roots. Trish shouts her head off. Cato, however, is in a category of his own.

The rage radiates off of his form. His eyes are black. He twists his head and pops his jaw. My heartbeat races as if I'm the one in trouble.

"They'll never find his body. No need to worry about that." He offers me a sharp smirk of dark reassurance, and I can't help but feel turned on and terrified. My thighs shift uncomfortably as the heat between them intensifies. He stands quickly as if he means to go take care of Howard himself right now. I grab his arm.

"No. It's not worth it. He's not worth it."

"How can you say that?" he snaps at me.

"I've made peace with it; it's not your responsibility to avenge me."

"You're lying. You haven't made peace with it. Look at you. You can't stop shaking."

He's right. I let go of his arm and take his hand, intertwining our fingers.

"I-I appreciate you listening to me. I'll let you know if I need help with the situation."

We destroy the rest of the computers and take the documents we need. Before we sneak out, we pass a staff restroom.

"I have to pee."

He looks at me like I've told him Santa Clause is my ex-boyfriend.

"What?"

"I've been holding it all night. Just give me a minute. I'll meet you outside."

"Fine," he grumbles and goes on ahead. I slip into the bathroom and lock the door behind me. I let out the loudest scream I possibly can. I scream out all the pain, the fear, and the shame. It pops my own ears. I scream until my breath is spent. I inhale deeply and scream again. I grab a vase from the vanity and throw it into the wall. It shatters on impact.

When the pieces hit the ground, a sensation of peace washes over me like a wave. My next swallow burns my throat, but it felt so good to let it all out.

I step out of the building into a torrential downpour. Cato drives us to my townhouse, and we sneak in through my bedroom window to avoid my sister. His fingers slip under my shirt as he lifts me by the waist, warm hands against my icy skin. His wet shirt clings to his thick arms and chest. A shiver runs through me, but it's not from my wet clothes, heavy with rainwater.

"Towels?" he asks.

"In the-that closet, t-top shelf," I stutter, unable to stop my teeth from clicking together. He picks out my two fluffiest ones and passes them both to me. He chooses an older, worn-down towel for himself.

I thank him and bury my freezing face in the warmth of the towel. I inhale the sweetness of the fabric softener and rub the towel over my soaked locks. I peer at him from under the towel and catch him staring at me. I give him a small smile. He doesn't return it. Instead, he brings a knuckle under my chin and tilts my head up. His thumb traces my numb lower lip.

"What?"

"Your lips are purple, Ruby," he says. His frown deepens. "I'll start the shower."

I stutter out a thank you, and he exits to the bathroom to turn on the shower.

As he fumbles around in the bathroom, I challenge myself to peel off my icy clothes and cover myself with a towel before he returns. My unique and highly complicated shower knobs should keep him occupied for at least three minutes. When my sister and I moved in, we had to google how to turn on our showers.

A risky gamble, but if I sit in these icy clothes for another second, my skin will turn blue. My skin is so cold that it hurts. Cato catches me as I slink out of my top.

"The water is warm–oh fuck, I didn't–"

"It's fine, whatever." If I pretend it isn't a big deal, maybe it won't be. He draws my window shut and turns to face the wall. I avoid his eyes and pull the other towel around me quickly.

I close the bathroom door behind me but don't lock it. I don't know why. Okay, fine, I know why but I'm not going to admit it out loud.

I jump in the shower with my bra and panties still on, desperate for heat. I let out a soft moan as the hot water flows over my icy skin and hair. After I savor the warmth for a moment, I pull off the rest of my garments and throw them out of the shower.

In my enthusiasm, I accidentally knock the tissue box off the top of my toilet tank, which quickly knocks the bottles of shampoos and lotions off the rim of my tub with a loud crash. Cato bursts into the bathroom and rips back the shower curtain. I stare at him in all my naked glory, frozen under the steamy cascade of water, and he stares back, open-mouthed like a fish out of water.

"I-I thought you fell-"

"No, I'm fine. The bottles fell...." I pause and force myself to look right at him. His eyes drop down my body and make their way up. Undeniable desire crosses his perfect features. He exits the bathroom as fast as a lightning bolt. I scrub myself with my pink loofah and smile as I think of how flustered he was.

Clean, dry, and fully dressed, I open the door to find him staring out my window.

"We should stay at my place tonight for safety. I have a guest room you can occupy. Will your sister be okay?"

I blush at his concern for my younger sister. His understanding that I want to protect her is sweet.

"She stays at her girlfriend's place on Tuesday nights, so I'm not worried. Let's go."

He doesn't look at me on the drive to his house and ignores me when I gawk at it. It's hard not to. It gives Trish's house a run for her money. He leads me up the stone-carved steps and into his spotless foyer. Tasteful artwork draws my eyes first, followed by a beautiful spiral staircase.

A black blur whizzes into the foyer and launches itself at me. Cato catches the tiny black kitten mid-flight with one hand.

"This is Bouguereau, Bou for short." He passes me the fat kitten, and I feel like I may die from delight. The raven-colored baby chews on my thumb. My heart thumps as I reflect on her name. My favorite painter is William Adolph Bouguereau. Cato and I have more in common than I thought. I tell him this, and he swallows and awkwardly nods, scratching the back of his head.

"Go on up. The first room on the left is yours." With that, he stalks away into the dark of his house.

After kissing her tiny head, I place the chunker of a kitten on the dark wood floor and carry my bag to the large guest bedroom. I can't help myself and snoop in the bathroom down the hall. It's spotless. Maybe he has a maid.

I wander back downstairs and deeper into his home. He's in his spacious kitchen, pouring himself a glass of amber liquid. I could use a healthy gulp of that after the night we've had.

I look back, and the charcoal puffball is fast asleep in a basket of blankets by the door, no doubt exhausted from a long day of being precious.

"Can I make you a drink?" He still doesn't look at me, but his tone is polite as he opens his refrigerator.

"Yes, please."

"You're old enough to drink, right?" He twists open a bottle of ginger beer. I roll my eyes and wander over to his bookshelf to browse.

His shelves remind me of my own. He has Emerson, Frost, Austen, Dickens, Hemingway, Twain, Woolf, and Vonnegut. Color me impressed. I knew he was smart, but I had no idea we had such similar book collections.

A gentle touch on my back alerts me that my drink is ready. Cato doesn't look at me as he passes it to me.

"Thank you." I wrap my hands around the icy beverage and bring it to my lips. It's delightful. Spicy and cold, with a touch of cinnamon sugar sweetness.

We drink by his stone fireplace like lovers spending a quiet autumn evening together. We stay like that for a few quiet moments and listen to the fire crackle. I feel his eyes finally turn to me, burning a hole in my face. I dare to return his stare, unsure of what emotion I might find in his gaze. The light from the fireplace plays cruel tricks on me as shadows dance across his face. He's looking at me like I'm edible.

"Touch yourself for me," he blurts.

I nearly spit out my drink.

"What?!" I'm overwhelmed by the desire to honor his request, yet I'm frozen where I stand. This can't be happening. He still hates me. He can barely look me in the eyes at the best of times. My touch burns him even when my flames are fast asleep under my skin.

But the proof is right there. His molten gaze is unmistakable. He's dead serious.

"Come on, Auclair, I know you aren't a shy woman." He steps closer.

"You broke my nose." Another step.

"Stabbed a man without regret." Another.

Now he's right in front of me, and all I can focus on is the heat in his eyes and the delicious curve of his cupid's bow.

"Show me how so that, once this fucking mess is all over, I can do it myself." The desire in his expression compels me to slowly lower myself onto his loveseat.

He sets his drink on the coffee table, grabs a kitchen bar stool, and pulls it up in front of me. Front row seat to a show by firelight. I swallow hard, nerves overcoming the desire in my gut.

"I've never done anything like this before. For an …audience." My voice is barely a whisper as I fight the nerves begging me to give up and go home and use a vibrator while I think about his hand around my throat. He nods, encouraging me.

"I'll help. You're so good at following my instructions. Get more comfortable for me."

A dark little part of me rears her horned head. The same part of me stares at his butt when we take water breaks on training days, leers at his broad shoulders during cellar searches, and obsesses about how he called me a good girl when I helped bandage his busted nose.

He wants a show, Ruby. So let's give him a show.

Slowly, I slip off my pajama shorts and kick them to the floor. No turning back now.

His eyes grow impossibly wider as he realizes this is happening. Next, I roll off my Halloween 1978 tee up and over my chest, revealing my bare breasts and torso. I look up at him to check if he likes what he sees.

"Holy fuck," he moans low and bites his fist. I sweep my hair up and out of the way, feeling more confident from his almost-compliment.

He strokes himself through his lecherous gray sweatpants. The ones that hug his butt in all the right places.

"Make yourself feel good, baby. Show me how." Hearing him call me a name besides my surname or a mean nickname tightens the excited little knot under my belly button. He called me baby.

"You liked that, didn't you, baby? You like when I call you sweet names?" He smiles salaciously at me as he strokes himself up and down.

I nod, slip my hand into my panties, and draw a slow, wide circle around my clit, teasing myself. Cato's eyes are blown wide, and it's truly a treat to watch him grow more and more undone by the second.

His chest muscles expand and contract quickly with his rapid breaths, and the hand not stroking himself up and down is fisted in his pants.

"Do you…" he has to pause for breath, "…do you like to touch your breasts?" I nod coyly and bite my lip to keep from smiling.

"For the love of…please show me. Don't make me beg," he huffs. He's impatient and entranced, and I love it. I massage my breasts with the other free hand, occasionally tugging on a sensitive peaked nipple.

"Gorgeous girl…" he groans. He once told me he couldn't stand me, and now he's panting at the sight of my tits. This is the naughtiest, filthiest, most depraved activity I've ever done in my entire life. And I've never felt more alive and powerful than I do now. Getting myself off while Cato watches like a man bewitched.

He's fully pulled himself out of his pants, and it takes everything in me to not reach out and mount him. He's huge. Like, "uh oh, that might be too much" huge. I'm dying to find out. I want him to fill me up and spank me and pull my hair and throw me around his stupidly large bed and tell me what a good girl I am.

I want him to kiss my most sensitive places and crave their taste. I can't believe this beautiful, dark-eyed jerk is coming undone right in front of me. The revenge he's handed me is sweeter than honey. He used to look down his nose at me in disgust, and now he's stroking himself while I climb to new heights, nearly naked on his couch.

"Do you want to know a secret, Miss Auclair?" he breathes. He's back to using my surname, and I'm not mad about it. As I lean back on his expensive couch, I continue to circle myself lazily.

"Tell me," I whisper back. I want to know all of his secrets, each scar, every shadow.

"I've wanted you since the night we met…wanted to watch those pretty eyes struggle to look at me as you come undone beneath me. But, God, when you outsmart me… fight me…I want to grab you by your hair and make you scream. You consume my thoughts, little fire witch." His voice is deep and thick with desire, breath coming shallow and fast.

My pace speeds up at his revelation, and a little moan escapes the back of my throat. He winces like it caused him pain.

"Faster, please, baby…I'm getting close. You're doing so good… so fucking hot…perfect, just like that…don't you dare fucking stop…" he pants as he watches me slip a couple of fingers into myself, my pace now frantic. He's breathless and disheveled because of me. He's about to come all over his hand because of me. The most embarrassing noises escape from my throat as I fall apart right before him.

"Cato, I'm—"

I finish, writhing on his couch as stars burst on the edge of my vision. He gasps and moans as he follows me right over the cliff of pleasure we built together. In the midst of recovery, our eyes meet again. His cheeks are flushed from his orgasm.

"You sure know how to put on a show, Auclair." A smile tips up his mouth. I match it and pull my tee back on.

"Not so bad yourself, Hadrian."

"Can't the girls stay out a little longer? We've only just met." His devilish grin in the firelight makes me want to indulge in another round. I want to sit in his lap and let them become fully acquainted, but I want to savor it another time. I need to recover from this dramatic shift in our relationship first.

"Next time. I'm cold." I yawn and move to stand by the still blazing fire. He cleans himself off and passes me a baby wipe and tissue paper.

My eyes water as the brilliance of the morning sun attacks my face from the open window. White satin curtains move in the unusually warm fall breeze. I blink at them sleepily and lick my dry lips.

I gasp and jump up.

He's fully clothed beside me, arm slung over his eyes in sleep. Soft snores come from under his arm. I've never seen him with his guard down like this.

He's shockingly attractive when he's not bitching at me. Perfect skin, soft lips, wide shoulders. His shirt is unbuttoned slightly to reveal the muscles underneath. I swallow and tear my lecherous eyes away to study our surroundings.

This room bleeds casual wealth. A high ceiling bordered by crown molding. Freshly shined, unscratched, dark hardwood floors. They match the enormous four-poster bed. The sheets are so soft and white, angels might have manufactured them. My pink toes look tacky on the beautiful floor.

I'm embarrassed that he's seen, poked, and prodded around my tiny, messy bedroom when his own looks like it belongs on the cover of a lavish home design magazine.

"Called out sick for you," he grumbles from under his arm, "you've come down with a terrible sore throat, and I've done the kindness of calling in for you. Violet is a peach, by the way."

"I–"

I'm caught between saying "Thank you" and "Fuck you," so instead, I stomp over to the bathroom and slam the door.

14

"What do you want for breakfast?" he asks, voice slow and husky from sleep. My whole face heats up to the tips of my ears. He's maintained such a mean streak that an ounce of kindness from him towards me flusters me speechless.

"Whatever is easiest for you is fine."

A slow, wicked smile spreads across his face when he notices my blush.

"Why are you blushing?"

"I'm not." Then, with my nose in the air and my jaw set, I twist my unruly locks into a top knot and move toward the bathroom.

Suddenly he's right beside me, blocking my path with an arm. He tips my chin up with a knuckle, so I have to meet his eyes.

"You are."

I shove his hand off and push past him to the bathroom. I don't have time for this. The luxury of flirty playtime can't be afforded to me. I have a curse to break. My heartbeat still hammers against my ribs, and the insatiable burning desire to pounce on him heats my thighs.

My phone buzzes with a text from Rain.

Rain: We need to talk.

I run out of the bathroom and grab my bag. He watches me silently.

"Something is going on with my little sister. I have to go. Now."

"Can I do anything?"

"No, no. Thanks, I'll see you tonight." I step out of his bedroom before whirling around. He's sitting up in his grand bed with messy hair and a quizzical brow. I want to devour him.

"Thank you. For...last night."

"I didn't do anything." His dark eyes glint at me.

"Uh, yeah, well…see ya." I dash away, face on fire and a storm of butterflies in my stomach.

"Thanks so much." I smile apologetically at the stressed barista and try to balance our drinks and croissants as I weave through the busy cafe. I rip the fluffy confection in two and pass a warm half to Rain.

"What would you say to bugs once science figures out the secret to human-bug communication?" I muse and take a generous bite. She snorts. I love this. A moment to relax and talk about meaningless topics with my sister. I haven't even looked over my shoulder since we got here, clenched my jaw, or even checked Cato's location. For only a moment, I can pretend to be a normal girl with menial worries and an ordinary life.

"You're a weirdo. You don't even care about my answer."

"Well, first of all, let them know I want to move them to a safe place outside, biting is not polite, and finally, I'd offer crumbs that I'm willing to share as a peace offering. Your turn."

"You're giving me a headache." She rolls her eyes. "But I'd tell them to stay out of our house."

"What did you want to tell me?"

"I proposed to Syd. We're going to get married in March." She beams with pride.

"Oh, my God!" I drop my food and reach across the table to pull her into my arms. My baby sister deserves all the happiness in the world. I was skeptical and protective when she told me she met a fantastic woman at her internship last year. Sydney is kind, patient, and fun. She's the perfect partner for my sister.

"I'm so happy for you both. But, God, I was worried something was wrong."

She tells me about the surprise proposal she planned and the wedding venues under consideration. It's nice to talk about good news for a change. My life feels like lately it's been nothing but bad news and bad guys for too long.

"Anyways, um…" she pauses, raises a brow, and lowers her voice to a whisper, "do you know that guy?" She nods subtly to the space behind my right shoulder.

I already know who it is, but I turn and pretend to pluck chapstick from my purse and glance up. I lock eyes with Cato. Instead of instinctively giving him the finger, I smile and give him a polite little wave demurely.

He looks off-put like he expects me to throw my drink or a vulgar hand signal. Instead, I turn back to my sister. "Former classmate. We usually sat in the same row in physics. Nice guy."

"Hm. What's his name?"

Bitch. Drop it. "Andrew." I sip my steamy hot mocha casually and stare at the wall art. The picture depicts a watercolor black cat on a flower-filled windowsill. I suck at lying to her.

"You suck at lying," she scoffs, "that was the fakest smile I've ever seen. You love everyone you've ever met, so what did that guy do?"

She looks concerned, and I immediately wish we had gone to a different cafe. I try to dodge and deflect, but she's always been good at drilling into me and carving out the truth. All my years of practice and little to show for it.

"What? No, I'm stressed about work. I didn't mean to give him a fake smile. I barely know him, honestly. And I do not love everyone I've ever met! There was one guy on our trip to Orlando last summer...."

Rain narrows her blue eyes into slits at me and leans forward.

"You suck at lying," she mouths at me.

"You're a nosy bitch," I mouth back and steal the rest of her buttery pastry half.

I'll lecture the hunky dumbass later on how to be more subtle with his ogling. Isn't he supposed to be invisible? I poke my molars with my tongue. I challenge my brain to quickly come up with another dumb lie.

"Save it," she sighs, "I get it if you don't want to share. He's a hookup you want to forget about, right? So I'll drop it."

"Something like that," I mumble. I turn to glance at him again, but he's gone. My phone buzzes.

Cato: Bathroom. Now.

Me: Ok. You don't need my permission to go to the bathroom??

Cato: Meet me in the bathroom. Now.

Oh.

"Be right back. Bathroom," I tell my sister and quickly leave before she offers to come with me. I'm relieved to find it's a single, family-sized bathroom.

As soon as I double lock the door, Cato pops back into existence, his long frame leaning on the sink. His eyes are rimmed with dark circles.

"You summoned?" I nervously fuss with a stray thread on my skirt.

"We have a problem. With a search area." He straightens his tall form, scrubs his eyelids, and runs his hand through his dark hair. He's much more stressed than the lazy and flirty man I woke up next to. Something terrible must have happened. I bite my lip, and his eyes drop to my mouth.

"I'm kind of in the middle of a good day. Can this wait?" I cautiously question him.

"We need to meet my father's priest. He has a clue."

"What? Are you sure?" I search his face for a sign that he's joking, but I find nothing but perfect skin and plump lips fixed into his signature bored frown. I'm surprised his father was a religious man based on my limited knowledge of him.

"Yes, I'm sure." His tone is clipped. My lips press together firmly as I try and think of a way to get out of this.

"Alright. Why can't you go by yourself?"

"We're a team. You shook my hand. We do this together. You said whatever it takes." His dark eyes hold mine in a tense stare-off.

I did say that, and I meant it. I grind the toe of my shoe into the bathroom tile to stop myself from stomping it. Cato's eyes follow the twist of my foot, and I wonder if he can tell.

"Fine. Tell me more about it tonight. I'm going to finish brunch with my sister."

I bring baby carrots and dip for us to share while we comb the cellar.

"Mass is at nine tomorrow morning. Don't be late."

"Mmhmm. You've told me twice already." I lick dip off my thumb and turn a page on the lab report in my lap.

"You're going to have to fight him if he finds out who you are," he pops a baby carrot into his mouth.

"Uh, yeah, no. I don't do that."

"You do if you want to be normal again," he says, cracking another carrot in half with his perfect set of teeth. I press my lips together and don't engage. I'm not fighting anyone. I'm not a weapon. I'm a healer. I'll come up with an alternative. I'm smart enough to have made it this far. Howard was an exception.

The minute after I wake up and scrub the crusties out of my sleepy eyes, my panic wakes up too.

My heart pounds harder and harder as I race through my morning routine. When I brush my teeth, when I twist my hair into a French braid. I force slow, calming breaths through my nose while I dab foundation on my cheeks, sweep creamy, black mascara under my lashes, and carefully fill my brows. I can't slip under my lake. Time isn't on my side. My hands tremble as I clutch my keys. My pounding heart crescendos as I park in front of the church.

Get through this. Be brave. I've come so far in the past month. Can't quit now.

"Who roughed ya up, kid?" Bones barks at me from a black luxury sedan, concern tainting his features. I barely managed to cover up the large mark under my eye. I must have smeared my makeup off when I was driving. I have a habit of touching my face when I'm nervous.

"You should see the other guy," I smirk up at him as he approaches me. A proud smile spreads across his face.

"Aw yeah, heard you kicked the porcupine guy's ass. Nice." He gives me thumbs up, his thick thumb to the cloudy sky with pride.

"Not exactly, Bones." My mouth twists as I think about my empty threats. *What if he had attacked me first? My ass would be full of needles right now.*

"Hate that guy." He cracks a knuckle loudly against his chin, and my brows raise as I wonder what that strange, simpering man did to Bones.

"Me too. He's kinda freaky," I snort but immediately feel bad. It's not his fault he looks like that.

"There might be a time when you gotta fight, Ruby. For real. You won't be able to run or hide or outsmart these dumbfucks chasing you around." He gives me a meaningful look. I nervously rub my sweaty palms on my skirt. Talk about foreshadowing.

"I know." I solemnly nod.

"Do you?" His scarred brow raises.

"I'll cross that bridge when I come to it, Bones. But thanks."

"Knock 'em dead, kid. That's a sick-ass trick you got." Bones claps me on the back in a way that reminds me of my dad. A reassuring but firm smack on my shoulder blade meant to inspire courage. A surprised snort escapes me. I've never thought of my curse as *sick ass*.

"I'm trying to get rid of it."

"You shittin' me?" His eyebrows nearly jump off of his shaved head.

"I'd never shit you, Bones. I'm going to great lengths to make it stop."

"Well, for what it's worth, if anybody can handle a power like that, it's you."

"Thanks, Bones. That means a lot," I say.

The FUCK tattoo under his eye warps as he gives me a big grin.

"Big Guy's around here somewhere. Told him I'd wait until you showed up safe. Catch ya later!" He walks off towards the church parking lot, leaving me alone.

"Catch ya later, Bones," I say quietly as I size up the church. The black steeple pierces the enormous gray sky. A crow cries mournfully from the nearby woods.

Dead leaves tumble across the adjacent graveyard, scattering in the October breeze.

Cato's wrong. Bones is wrong, too.

Nothing is going to happen. I won't unleash my power. Everything will be fine. I shiver, but it's not from the cold.

Gentle hands touch my hair. I reach back before he can pull away. His hands are ice cold. Mine are forever warm. An electric surge passes between our skin before something small and crispy tickles my fingertips.

"Leaf." His gaze jumps away as he plucks it out.

"Oh, thanks." My eyes scan over him. We're matching in black. He's entirely in black down to his shiny licorice-colored shoes. He looks like he's stepped off a runway, and me...I wear a black blouse and skirt with Barbie pink kitten heels. I unapologetically love them. They were a gift from Trish when I graduated college and are the only designer shoes I own. There is magic in them. A spark of confidence always follows me when I slip them on.

Much needed for this ominous morning.

He raises one callous brow at them before looking back up at me. My nostrils flare. He doesn't need to say it out loud because his message is clear. *You're ridiculous.*

"Are you sure he won't recognize you? The priest?" I ask.

"The last time he saw me was at my baptism. I'll sit in the back of the church, closer to the choir loft. You find a spot near the front. Get as close as you can to the priests without being suspicious. Look out for a locket. A gold one. Watch your back and keep your arm bruises covered at all times."

"I've been covering them for years. I'm not stupid." Nonetheless, I instinctually pull my sleeves lower over my wrists.

"Sure..." is all he says before walking off, but not before I catch the upturn of his mouth as he walks away. Jerk. He's a confusing, gentle,

149

brilliant jerk. I can't stand him.

Since I acquired my power, I've felt uncomfortable in churches.

First of all, I'm surrounded by wood. Wooden crosses, wooden pews, big wooden rafters above my head. Not ideal for a lady who makes sparks shoot out of her fingertips.

Second, if church authorities knew my secret, I can only imagine how quickly the torches would be lit, and pitchforks sharpened. I use the choir's sudden swelling chorus as an excuse to look over my shoulder for him. He stands out among the crowd, all broad shoulders and dressed like he's ready for a diplomatic funeral. The corners of his mouth are turned downwards into a concentrated frown.

He's handsome.

He looks like the portrait of his young father in Mr. George's hallway. It's as if he has come to life and stepped out of the painting to scowl in the back of a church.

He notices my stare and his eyes shift so subtly I might be imagining it, but a wild feeling inside flutters to life.

This untamed spark of feeling inspires me to wink at him. The stern frown softens so quickly it's almost a smile, but he looks away. I turn back to listen to the priest's sermon. The eyelashes of the little boy next to me flutter as he dozes off to the low drone of the holy man speaking upfront. The priest has only looked up at his audience once, strictly reading from a notebook. The tone of his deep voice hasn't changed at all throughout.

The hump of his back is so prominent that you can see it when he's standing front facing.

He has to be in constant pain. He finishes his speech and steps down. I press my lips together in worry as he tries to shuffle heavy feet across the carpet to his chair. The younger priest steps forward and gently guides the Paleolithic man to his chair as the choir bursts into a transitional hymn. A nice gesture. Gentlemanly and kind. Our eyes meet after he turns back to his own chair. I hold my stare with him and smile politely. He smiles back and looks away.

He's a strange man, but I can't put my finger on why. He looks like an average, middle-aged white man in black religious robes. A gold chain around his neck disappears under the neck of his robes. After the service finishes, I meet Cato in the large rectory hall adjacent to the church. It's *Breakfast and Fellowship Hour 10-12*, according to the sign on the door.

His hands are in the pockets of his wool jacket, and he studies a stained glass window with a thoughtful look on his face. It's a station of the cross. The one where Jesus falls for the second time. I stare at the anguished Jesus on his knees for a moment before turning to Cato.

"Did anything stand out to you during the service?"

"Go get yourself coffee and a donut," he says without looking at me.

Every time he does this, it makes me want to punch him. Like if he looks at me when I speak, my eyes will burn him. He had no problem looking at me the other night on his couch.

"Not hungry. Did you notice anything?" I bounce on my heels.

"Auclair," he now turns to me and looks me in the face, a muscle in his temple jumps- "please go help yourself to a coffee and a donut. *Now.*"

The authority in his voice raises the hair on the back of my neck.

"Thank you, I will." I nod and slowly back away.

A pink sprinkled donut tempts me, and I oblige, plucking it off the tray with a napkin. The younger priest stands nearby, chatting with a large family. He notices me and stops his conversation with them, suddenly walking over to me. *Uh oh.* I look back at Cato inconspicuously watching us while pretending to talk on his phone.

"Excuse me, ma'am. I don't believe we've met before. Are you new to our congregation?"

My soul almost jumps out of my body when he gently taps my arm. I swallow my fear and decide to stick to what I do best. Lie to save my ass.

"Good morning, Father. I'm Ruby." I shake his hand. As soon as he touched me, my gut lurched. I force a friendly smile on my face, although my intuition tells me to drop the donut, punch him in his gut, and run screaming.

"I'm new to the area." I bite into the soft donut, seeking sugary comfort. He watches my mouth too closely as my teeth sink into the confection.

"Well, I must give you a proper welcome. I'm Father Kilpatrick. If you step into the rectory, we could have a more private chat about your relationship with our Lord." He gestures for me to follow him down a dark set of stairs. I would rather throw back a shot glass of thumb tacks. I'm going to kill Cato. I look back to glare at him, but he's already vanished.

We descend deeper into the heart of the church until we reach the basement. All of the warning bells in my head are sounding at full volume.

I flex my fists to try and shake off the fearful tremble that has overcome them. *I'm not afraid. I'm not. I'm a powerful fire wielder, and he's a weird holy man. I am not scared. Lake with still waters. Trees line the shore. Cold and deep.*

I follow him to the end of a hall. He unlocks a door and steps aside to reveal a modest office.

"After you," he says, eyes twinkling.

I hesitate for a moment before stepping in and sitting in the most uncomfortable chair I've ever had the displeasure of resting on. A carpentry staple painfully digs into my ass as I fight to maintain a confident and unconcerned air. He rounds the desk and sits in his ancient chair to face me.

A gentle tap on my right shoulder tells me Cato is near.

He snuck in behind me. He is the most annoying man I've ever met, but he's highly perceptive. But, of course, I'd never admit it to him.

"How did you come upon our humble congregation?" He clicks a pen and flips a notebook to a blank page.

"A distant cousin of mine was fond of this church," I lie smoothly. The easiest lies have morsels of truth. "Perseus Hadrian?" I sip my drink slowly, keeping my eyes on the round man. Although his body doesn't move, his eyes come to life when I finish speaking that last name.

"Oh, yes! I knew Perseus Hadrian well. We grew up together. You're related?" He folds his hands across his stomach and settles deeper into the chair. I remain on the edge of mine, fighting my instincts to try and appear at ease.

Without taking his eyes off me, he reaches a thick hand up to his throat and pulls the long gold chain out from under his shirt. On the end of the chain is a round locket. Cato's invisible hand clamps down on my shoulder.

Father Kilpatrick dangles it in front of me. "Gave me this before he passed on to the arms of our Most High. I'll hazard a guess that you are aware of the nature of his work." His brows raise, and he gives me a look, checking to make sure I'm in on the secret.

"I'm aware," I nod and give him a sly smile, "I work in the field myself."

"I gave him the majority of his experimental subjects!" he eagerly exclaims.

"Really? How?" I gush with false enthusiasm. He laughs low and strokes the chain of the locket, pinky aloft.

"A poor soul comes to their priest to confess their loneliness. Their family has abandoned them. They have no friends, no companions. I hear it all. Then I'd strike." He twists the locket in between his fingers thoughtfully.

"Paid handsomely too, as you can imagine. Maybe I could assist you in procuring your own studies–"

I lunge and pinch the chain with two white hot fingers. It melts away, and the heavy locket falls into my palm. I tap his notebook, and it bursts into flames.

The holy man blinks at me in disbelief. I kick open the office door, slam it shut, and melt the lock for good measure to buy myself time. I can only pray Cato got out before I locked it. As I run through the hall, my little kitten heels loudly click the tile. I throw open an unlocked door and run inside.

It's a dusty indoor basketball court, forgotten for decades. Aging, moth-bitten banners hang in tatters from the high ceiling. Broken bleachers line the walls.

There has to be an exit. I'll find one. I'll make one. I shove the locket deep into the safety of my bra cup.

A short, high cackle erupts behind me. I whip around. The priest is panting in manically heaved breaths, similar to the pig lady before she attacked. I throw my hands out to my sides and engulf them in flames. *Come and get me, you fucking insect.*

The priest's head twists and his huge black eyes focus on me. The light of my hands reflects in the tar-like orbs.

"Give it back, you filthy little bitch!" he roars. His brow creases, and his eyes screw shut. Someone behind him moves. No, *something* under his robes moves. Fabric rips as a thin black arm bursts from his back. Two more burst out. Five more. New eyeballs sprout along his jawline like shiny red pimples. He looks like a giant spider in priests' vestments.

Two fangs as long as my forearm sprout from his maxilla and dive down to his neck. Their tips drip with yellow venom.

"Give me back that locket, girl." His voice has changed to an inhuman and screechy tremor. The spider priest throws his head back, cackling. He rushes forward on the black legs at remarkable speed. It's a scene from a nightmare.

"Do it, Ruby," Cato's voice commands in my ear. He's finally by my side, but I'm more afraid now than ever. He's telling me to do something *I can't do*. I stand there. Frozen. My mind is blank. My muscles are paralyzed.

I'm under the cold water of my lake, water so cold it burns, chained to the dark mud at the bottom. Cato grabs my wrist and forces it up, aiming my hand at the giant arachnid running towards us.

I think he yells my name in my ear again, begging me to release it. The fangs are what snaps me out of it. An inferno explodes out of my hand like a firehose, engulfing the creature from hell.

Cato calls my name for a fifth time before I answer.

"Ruby!"

"I had a near-death experience, you asswipe. Give me five minutes, please." I place my head between my knees to fight back the bile threatening to come up. I try to picture my lake again, but I can't focus. Cato is tapping his foot impatiently and huffing.

"If you don't stop that, Cato, I swear on Mother Theresa I will turn you into beef jerky," I growl from my spot on the floor, sucking calming breaths through my nose.

"If you could hurry up the meditation session, please. Reinforcements will be here any minute."

My knees squeeze my temple. *Fuck. Gotta stay calm. I am calm. Calm is me.*

"Did I burn you?" I shakily ask Cato.

"No."

He stoically turns away from me and steps over the ashes of the disintegrated priest.

The shock of what happened finally shrivels away to a new feeling. Fury.

I stomp through the black ashes covering the shiny tile floor and grab Cato's jacket, he turns, and I grab his collar. Pull him to my face.

"I am NOT a weapon you can grab and aim like an object. I'm not a gun or a flamethrower. How dare you?"

"If it weren't for me, we'd both be fucking dead. Liquified spider food."

"I told you! I don't want to use it! Especially on people!"

"Why?"

"It's way too dangerous."

"Human spiders are also dangerous. You're a coward."

"I am NOT a coward! We could have come up with a plan, we could have-"

"You are," he spits this truth right in my face.

"A scared little girl. Like my father said. We better find the Dotion instructions fast. You're going to get us killed."

"I'm not," I weakly argue.

Fury colors his angular cheeks and jaw a splotchy red, and he lets loose on me.

"You're an optimistic little ditz who has no idea what she's doing! Wake up! Trying to get to know me isn't going to make me like you! Skipping around thinking you can outsmart monsters without violence is idiotic! You're annoying, impulsive, and worst of all, you're too scared to even utilize the *only* beneficial skill you have!" he shouts, the harsh words echoing around the court's high rafters. The words are poison, hitting me directly where it hurts most.

The arrows of truth deeply pierce my cheap armor.

We part from the church in silence. I sit in my car, turning the locket in my hands. It's locked, only to be opened by a minuscule key. I suppose I could melt it open, but that could destroy the contents inside. This little morsel of hope cost me a scrap of my humanity. I can't help but pray that it will be worth it in the end.

15

Tee's baby shower is magical. Her mother holds the party at her current boyfriend's swanky apartment downtown. Diana embraces me and slips a flute of champagne more expensive than my whole outfit into my hand. Trish is stunning in a shimmering gold gown. I tell her she looks like a goddess, and she playfully swats my arm.

I help pass Tee big wrapped boxes of cashmere onesies and corduroy teddy bears. Soft blankets from Peru and a fairytale scene on the most elaborate tapestry I've ever seen.

She can tell something is wrong, but she says nothing.

Today is her special day. Even after laughing over old baby pictures of Tee and overeating blue cake, I still can't get a pair of dark eyes out of my mind. I wonder if Trish would still love me as much if she knew I'm a killer. I wonder if that's why Cato always looks away or lashes out. Never stand too close. I'm a killer who will never be able to drop her weapon. We haven't spoken in days.

I sip blue cider and nibble on a blue cookie as I watch Trish chat with her guests. She glows with excitement.

Tee is going to be such a wonderful mother. She's wanted children forever. But, boy or girl, she hasn't cared as long as the sweet angel is delivered safely.

I kiss her cheek and hug Diana before taking my leave. My heels click as I walk to the parking garage.

"Mind if I walk with you, miss? Cold night to be alone, huh?" A stranger offers a wide smile. Despite his sleazy mannerisms, he reveals a set of perfect teeth. It reminds me of Cato's rare smile, a gift I've only earned on a few rare occasions. My politeness tends to get me into trouble nowadays, so I adopt Cato's "fuck off" attitude. We've spent so much time together; it's easy to imitate.

"Do whatever you want." I have to force myself not to smile politely at the man consciously. It's a reflex. My thoughts jump to Cato again. He'd be proud of the coldness I managed to conjure in my voice. Although he scowled at my coffee and cookie the other night, he did finish it. And he even thanked me. My tummy does a flip.

Oh, God.

I halt my steps as the realization hits me. A terrible burn deep in my chest. Oh, no. Please, no. I've fallen in love with an asshole.

All the signs are here, like a big neon light blinking in my face. The blushes. The urge to do small favors. Small touches. Thoughts about him all the time. The giddy leap in my tummy when I see him waiting for me before our long nights on the hunt. The vapid man is still attempting to talk to me, but I can't hear a single word he says. I'm too busy internally kicking myself. I've caught feelings for a moody bastard with a superiority complex, not to mention a brother from hell —a brother from hell that *I kissed.*

"This guy givin' you trouble, little bird?" a deep voice behind us asks. We both whirl around. Bones gives the man at my side a scary look. The poor guy nearly falls on his ass as he speed walks and trips to get as far away from us as possible.

"Not anymore, thank you," I smirk, and he smiles back at me with the cigarette between his lips.

"Smoking is bad for you, Bones." I scrunch my nose, teasing him lightly.

"So are lone walks at night, little bird."

"We both have bad habits we need to work on."

He nods and snuffs out the cancer stick. His big chest sinks inward as he exhales the last puff through flared nostrils. He takes off his big leather coat and tries to hand it to me.

"Oh, no, I'm fine, Bones, really-" I protest, but he won't hear it. The waist of the giant jacket hits the back of my knees. It smells of laundry detergent and tobacco.

He is a bull of a man with a soft spot for women. His mother must have been an incredible woman. The thought makes me smile. "Did Cato send you to fetch me?"

"Sure did."

"Lead the way." Bones drives me to a fancy restaurant. I thank him and return his jacket. He holds the door for me and wishes me goodnight. A fat stone cherub pours a pitcher of water into an elaborate fountain at the front door. Lush indoor greenery and gold details on the chairs and tables make me feel underdressed.

When Cato sees me, he immediately stops his meal and stands. He pulls out my chair for me, and I quietly thank him. I haven't felt this shy in years. If someone had told me what a gentleman he was a few weeks ago, I would have laughed in their face.

"Order anything you'd like. My treat. You've earned it."

"Oh. Thank you."

I didn't eat much at the baby shower. I can't stop thinking about burned priests and hard choices. I ask the young waiter for a flourless chocolate cake slice with raspberry mousse and a glass of champagne. It's been a rough month.

"Just dessert, Auclair?"

"I figured I should have dessert and go from there in case we're interrupted by another spider demon priest or your brother invites himself to join."

The ghost of a smile crosses his face before he hides it by sipping his drink. His eyes flick to my wrist. The spider priest incident left a significant mark. I move my hand to cover the bruises.

"Don't want anyone to get the wrong idea," I whisper.

"How bad is it?" His eyes are still on my wrist as if trying to see through my sleeve. I tilt my head at him. For someone who explicitly told me several times he does not want to be my friend and cannot stand me, he's atypically concerned.

"Don't worry about it. I'm tough." I sip my freshly arrived champagne.

"I know." He nods.

"So, what brings us here tonight?" I'm always impatient for answers.

"Can't a man enjoy a meal with a beautiful woman?" My cheeks heat as I watch him press a cherry tomato to his lips.

He called me beautiful. Not a princess. Not a brat. I swallow another gulp of champagne and shake my head at him.

"Not you, Cato. Let's get to business." I shift in my seat, still trying to calm my thrumming pulse from his compliment.

He sighs but nods.

"I'm sorry," he says. He sounds genuine.

"For which part?" I ask.

"All of it. Most especially, I'm sorry my father caused you so much harm. You aren't a coward. That wasn't fair of me to say. I apologize. You've been so brave through all of this."

"Liar." I laugh.

"I'm not lying. I have to confess something else, too. Come on." He stands and guides me to the back of the building. The restaurant has a beautiful garden and water features, illuminated by thousands of fairy lights. Fat cherubs spit streams of water into a blue pool, and stone Grecian women pour vases over their heads down a small waterfall. We walk over to an area without any patrons nearby.

"It took my brother over a year to discover your identity because of me. I kept you safe. I sabotaged documents, destroyed surveillance, and paid off informants to keep their mouths shut or give him false information."

"Why?"

"I was in the bar the night we met to kill you. I planned to lure you out back and snuff you out. The girl who ruined my family. The whole night I had a syringe in my pocket of potassium chloride to stop your heart."

The question burns through my lips before I can stop it.

"Why didn't you kill me?"

"You were kind and radiant," his voice breaks and trails off.

He was going to kill me. I made out with my would-be killer and changed his mind. He also (very recently) saw me naked. I pulled him onto the dance floor and made him dance with me to a goofy country song while he fought an internal battle with himself about whether or not to take my life.

"I thought killing you would end my father's legacy and ruin my brother's lust for your power. But I was wrong. And I'm so sorry I even thought about ever hurting you."

I should feel terrified. I should punch him in the face. He was going to slam a needle in my ass, stop my heart, and leave me cold and dead in the alleyway between a bar and a pizza shop. I should want to punch him in the face. But I don't. I cautiously reach over and take his hand.

"Thank you. For giving me a second chance."

He laughs without humor and pulls his hand away. A bitter laugh escapes him again, and he shakes his head. He puts an arm on the back of the bench.

"You're thanking me for not killing you? That's it? I swear, Ruby, I think you might be more screwed up than I am."

"Maybe. Do you blame me?"

"No," he answers softly, "you were a child that walked into the plot of a monster."

"I know," I nod, "I forgive you. But I've also been wanting to tell you that I..."

I close my eyes and force the confession out.

"Despite your shitty attitude and ruthless mouth, I've somehow fallen in love with you."

The fountain bubbles behind us. People talk inside the building, enjoying pasta primavera and eggplant casserole with red wine. Dead leaves scrape the tile path under our feet as the October breeze pushes them along. Cato stares at me blankly.

"And-and it's okay if you don't feel the same, but I need you to know how I feel with Halloween only a few days away. Because even though you can be the *worst*, you're also kind and funny and–"

He captures my mouth, and I wonder how I ever mistook his brother's kiss for his own. I push that disgusting thought to the back of my mind and savor the treat of his kiss.

This kiss is soft and hard and aggressive and gentle all at the same time. My head is spinning. When I was a teenager, I wanted to kiss boys for hours. I thought I grew out of it in my twenties. The truth is that I just hadn't met the man I wanted to kiss for hours yet. He holds the back of my neck with one hand to expertly deepen our kiss, and his other hand fists the stretchy fabric of my dress and pulls me closer to his body with a roughness that quickens my pulse. Finally, we break apart, gasping.

"Can we finish our meal first?" I giggle.

"Oh, I intend on finishing my meal," he says before pulling me into another kiss.

I spend the night with him and leave for an assignment in the morning, leaving a messy-haired man still fast asleep in my bed.

A dark cloud of panic builds over my head as the water for Mrs. Pepper Vogel's tea boils. I fold and press her sheets, gently comb her hair, and sort her vitamins. As I drive to Trish's place to help paint the baby's room, my ears ring so loud I can't hear my car stereo. It's a goddamn blaze under my skin, boiling in my blood. Cinders glow in the marrow of my bones. Tomorrow is Halloween.

I think about my younger self when I open my trunk and take the green paint can in my hands. I want to grab her face, look deep into her hazel eyes, and tell her never to eat anything in the woods. Never.

The harsh sting of a slap on my ass stops my panic attack in its tracks. The small size of the hand and the aggressiveness in the swing clue me into the attacker.

"Trish Bartlow! That one was too hard." I rub the spot she hit. Her swollen belly pokes out from her blue wool coat. She grins wickedly at me.

"Not hard enough, if you ask me," she says to her belly.

"Your mommy is so mean to me. Can't wait until you get here and set her straight," I tell her tummy.

"Come on inside, hot stuff." She plops down in a fancy modern version of a rocking chair.

"Don't forget to grab my dress for tomorrow night before you leave."

I stare at her blankly. She's going to kill me. The stress of my recent misadventures has pushed all other life events out of my mind.

"Tomorrow...night?" I ask.

"Holy shit, you idiot. You forgot, didn't you? My mother's bar? The party?"

"I didn't forget. I have a date," I say.

"What?!"

My mouth forms an evil little grin. "My boyfriend."

"Congrats on a great quarter, team. I'm so grateful for everyone and your dedication to safety." Meredith beams at the room as we all applaud. Our incident rates are minimal, and our reviews are outstanding.

The staff is seated in a large circle of plastic chairs. Violet claps softly on one side of me, and Howard aggressively applauds on my other.

His thigh keeps brushing mine, and I keep moving away. He beelined to the empty chair beside me at the start of the meeting. I play with my necklace and staunchly ignore him.

"Thank you all for your hard work and dedication–" Meredith starts, but another voice cuts her off.

"I'd like to say a few words," Howard says, standing up.

A flare of anger heats my cheeks. I recognize a flash of annoyance in Meredith's bright eyes, but she artistically hides it with a prim smile and steps aside for Howard to take her spot at the front of the room.

"As this quarter comes to a close, we've overcome many trials and tribulations, both personal and work-related. I, myself, have been through a lot recently."

He squeezes his eyes shut like he's blinking back tears, and I fight back a gag. His fan club nods with sympathy before he clears his throat to continue.

"After I was mugged last month, my perspective on life has changed. I want to live for each moment. Seize each opportunity. And love more freely. To do my very best every day."

Meredith and I make eye contact, and I have to look away quickly to stop myself from laughing. She looks like she's going to be sick. His gaze falls on me; thin lips upturned into a sleazy grin.

"So I would like to propose a new staff policy. Each caregiver will submit to a private weekly meeting with me in my office to discuss individual improvement, fellowship, and personal growth." His fan club claps with excitement as my mouth falls open. *Private meetings? With Howard? Weekly? His breath on my collarbone, fingers tearing my soul apart.*

I would rather pull out my fingernails.

"That's inappropriate and unnecessary." I barely recognize the sound of my brazen voice as it cuts through the dying applause.

"You–" Howard starts to sneer, but it's Meredith's turn to cut him off.

"Please let Ruby speak. This meeting is an open discussion."

He presses his lips together, eye twitching. Meredith smiles and nods for me to continue. I stand to address the room properly.

"First of all," I fight to keep a sassy tone out of my voice, "'individual improvement' and 'personal growth' are the same tasks. Second, you are accounts receivable. Required private meetings with you are not only irrelevant due to your position, but inappropriate and wasteful of caregiver time." Nods from my audience guide me to go on.

"You are not a therapist nor a human resource officer. Therefore, staff should not have private meetings with you unless it is regarding accounts receivable tasks, which does not intersect with caregiver roles in any circumstance at this company."

My hands aren't shaking. My breath is even. My cheeks are cool. My fingers aren't in flames.

I'm not under my lake. I am the lake.

"Thank you for speaking up, Ruby. I think you said what many staff members were thinking. There will be no policy change."

I can't help myself.

"Thank you, Meredith. It wasn't easy to stick my neck out like that." I finish with purposeful words and a slight smirk, eyes on my enemy. The room is silent. I've never spoken up to him before.

His eyes blaze with rage I haven't seen in a man since I told Cato what Howard did to me. I might have cowered a few weeks ago, but now a euphoric sense of pride swells in my chest. My newly earned bravery pushes him over the edge. Howard leans in so close I can smell the iodine on his neck wound.

He sneers down at me like I'm nothing.

"Just give up already, you little slut. I hope Kazak rips open your–"

A crisp slap across the face cuts him off. It happens so fast that for a moment, I think I may have struck him until I turn my head and see a purple-faced Violet step up and shove a shaking finger in his face.

"Speak to her like that again. I dare you."

Howard and I stare at her, as stunned as if she had slapped both of us. Pride and appreciation swell in my chest. She turns to the room and announces her retirement before storming out.

After Meredith dismisses the group, she asks Howard to meet her in her office. Cato pops back into vision as soon as I leave the office. He hooks a finger in my scrub pocket to pull me into his chest.

"I'm glad she hit him because your office was about to experience paranormal activity." He rests his chin on my head.

"I just hope he doesn't press charges." I scrape my lower lip with my teeth.

"He won't, babe. I'll make sure of that." He places a firm kiss on my hairline.

"You're the best." I kiss his cheek on my tiptoes.

"How would you like to spend our afternoon?" He wiggles his brows, and I smack his arm.

"I've been thinking we need to take another trip to Randy's Rooms."

No one greets us when we enter. A pancake of nerves in my stomach flips. On the drive, I explained to Cato that the riddle from Prickle may not have been a red herring. We got in a fight and didn't check the dresser thoroughly enough.

He agrees that we might as well check again. We navigate the rows of junk and treasures until I see the dresser. It's moved since the last time we visited. I analyze it like my life depends on it because it does. The grain and striations of the wood. The drawers. The size. The three bronze knobs. They each have tiny initials.

"KH. CH. AM. Kazak. Cato. And..."

"Annette Monroe. That was her maiden name."

Cato has turned ghostly pale.

163

"Your mother's greatest treasure shall reveal the secret to you. So this old dresser was her greatest treasure?" I tilt my head at it. It's a lovely piece but no treasure.

"This was intended for my older brother to find," he says.

"What makes you say that?" I ask.

"My brother was five, and I was a newborn when my father burnt our first house down. It probably survived the fire, went to storage, and was sold after her death. I was too young to remember it."

My fingers graze over the knob with Cato's initials and notice the drawers are much smaller than typical dresser drawers. It's not meant for normal clothes. I bite my lip as I realize Annette Monroe's greatest treasure was the dresser that held her sons' baby clothes.

I kneel and slip my hand underneath the bottom drawer. There's something there. I tug, and a tiny key falls into my palm.

I pass it to Cato, who has already pulled out the locket. He drops the petite key.

"My hands are shaking too fucking hard. I need you to open it for me."

I steel my nerves and shove the little key into the dainty, round locket. It pops open with help from the edge of my nail. A tiny, folded-up piece of paper falls into my palm. I unfold it and position the note so we can read it together.

Neat script fills the paper.

Cut out her heart and swallow the left chamber

Claim her power and burn the remainder

"So...I have to *die*? Is that what I'm reading?" I ask. With wide eyes, I stare at the note, the death warrant of my hope. The locket falls out of my trembling hands. I press my icy hand to my chest to try and focus on my breathing. *Calm down. Stay calm. You knew this was a possibility.* I laugh. I throw my head back and laugh hysterically.

"Auclair?"

The electric noose of a panic attack tightens my airway. My fingertips lose feeling. A shrill bell that only my ears can hear pierces the silence. I think Cato says my name. My first name. But he sounds so far away. I'm at the bottom of my lake, and he's standing on the shoreline, calling to me. Why is he far away? I need him here.

My blurry vision is no help at all. Why is everything fuzzy? It's strange to hear Cato say my first name. It's always Auclair this and Auclair that. I like the rumble of his masculine voice when he says my name.

The contact of his hand on my cheek is like a gallon of ice water over my head. I snap out of it. All this running, all of our hard work, all of it was for nothing. Perseus Hadrian is a cruel motherfucker. Cato is silent, staring at the paper with a hand on my shoulder.

"This doesn't make sense," I say.

"It doesn't make sense to you because you're a good person. You didn't know my father, but I know you're smart enough to guess what type of person he was based on his creations."

Annabelle, Prickle, the spider priest. Cato's power. My power.

"When father gave me my power, I thought Kazak's jealousy would be enough to break him. He was livid. He broke three of my ribs and smashed his bedroom door in half. I think he was hoping our father would finally give him power. But mom found out what our father was doing. She walked in on him in the middle of dissecting a child, a live boy, and she jumped off the top of the Hadrian Pharmaceuticals roof. Then I killed him, destroying any chance of power for my brother. Kazak got the letter revealing your existence, and he finally snapped. Our dad gave you his most powerful and final creation, something he had promised Kazak. It was his final revenge. To create a villain so full of hatred and anger that the earth would shake when he finally got his claws on the Morningstar Dotion. He'd usurp governments and wash opponents in waves of flames. He can never, never know what's in this locket. Never."

I hold the horrible little locket in my palm. I set it on fire with an exhale and watch it shrink and burn in my hand. Cato and I watch it until it's an indiscernible smear of ashes.

"What now?" I whisper.

"As long as my brother never finds this out, you can stay. Screw the deadline," his thumb brushes my cheek, "I won't make you leave the country. I trust in your grasp of your powers now. It's best in the hands of a healer."

"This power is mine. Forever."

He stares. I swallow heavily.

"It's mine, but my heart is yours," I confess.

He surges forward and captures my mouth with his own. He pulls me into his lap as I reach for his hair. He kisses along my neck and jaw, and I squirm as he attacks the sensitive area, breathless like I've sprinted a mile.

"Been wanting to kiss you here forever…cruel little Ruby…torturing me for weeks…months."

"Poor little rich boy had to wait for his treat...." I gasp when he punishes me with a bite to my neck. Desire rushes between my thighs at the attack, and naughty thoughts speed up my heavy breathing into a pant. He kisses my mouth again and again until I'm dizzy from it, and I put my hand on his chest and gently push. He immediately pulls back.

"As much as I would like to continue, we need to get out of here," I smirk up at him. He blinks and realizes that we're still in a furniture store. We're making out on the floor of Randy's Rooms.

16

"You look amazing," he says, grinning down at me. It's a shame I couldn't seduce him into wearing a whole Peter Pan costume, but he does look handsome in his emerald green sweater. He said the public isn't ready to see him in green tights.

Diana's bar is bursting with people when we enter the noisy scene. Trish greets me with a kiss on the cheek and a hug for Cato. "It's about damn time. Nice to meet you. Have a drink. I'll catch up in a bit." Then, she wanders away, greeting her next guest.

Tee's mom mouths, "He's hot!" at me and gives me a thumbs up with a wink from across the room. I look up at Cato, and he's staring at a person across the room with a cocky grin.

"What?" I whisper. He leans down, lips a breath away from the shell of my ear, nuzzling my hair with his scarred nose.

"Your old friend." He points.

Now I see him. Seth shifts to grab hold of his beer on the counter and reveals a small man beside him. Prickle. He pulls on an earlobe and bites his lip, eyes glued to the floor. He might be hyperventilating. He's stressed out tonight.

"Ay! Ruby! What's up?!" Seth waves me over. I pull Cato along, and he dutifully follows. We make pleasantries, and I introduce Cato as my boyfriend. Prickle stares openly at me. I shake my head slightly at him in a subtle warning. *I'll throttle you if you speak to me.*

"Be right back." Cato frowns as he steps away, and my heartbeat stutters. Something is wrong. Something must be drastically wrong for him to leave me alone with Prickle and my ex.

Seth grins widely at me. He's high as a kite and looking at me the way Cato did the other night. I can't believe I once wanted him to be my boyfriend. My fingers nervously pull the frilly edge of my tiny dress down to hide my legs from his leering, bloodshot eyes. It's useless.

"Miss Ruby with the booty, you look like a whole snack tonight." He slurs too loudly and throws an arm around me. The side-hug painfully tugs on my earring. I push him off gently and force a smile.

"What are you supposed to be, Seth?" I'm at a loss for what literary classic he's supposed to represent. He's wearing overalls and nothing else. Even his feet are bare.

"Of Mice and Men." He pokes himself in the chest. I smile and nod, folding my hands together to hide potential sparks. I hate that horrible book.

"I'm Wendy."

He blinks.

"From Peter Pan?"

"Oh! I didn't think that counted as a classic." He shrugs and takes a swig of his dark drink. Instead of yelling at him about how *Peter fucking Pan is a fucking classic*, I take a deep breath and ask him for a drink recommendation. He excitedly tells me about a stout that I know tastes like skunky bathwater. I turn around to order at the bar, and a dark figure in the corner catches my eye. I've become far too familiar with dark figures in the past two months. Finally, a person in the crowd shifts, and I get a better view.

Kazak.

Panic jolts my veins like electricity, and my heartbeat jumps in my throat. I turn back to Seth to tell him I'm going to find Cato. Suddenly, a wooden stool leg nails him in the forehead, and he hits the floor like a sandbag.

The room erupts into a massive brawl. Tables flip, glasses break, men yell, and women scream. I fight back panicked tears. I need to find Trish. I need to protect her and the baby. Where the hell is Cato? We need to get out of here immediately.

Prickle stumbles into me amongst the chaos. Huge tears slip down his face.

"Prickle overheard! Followed to the furniture store to help. Prickle is sorry! So sorry!"

"What did you overhear, Prickle?" I shout over the violence around us. Now he's crying so hard he can't respond, and I have to clench my fist to keep from slapping him. He overheard how to remove my

Dotion. And he told his master.

Kazak couldn't look more at home in the battle.

He leans against the stage with a big smile, like he's about to share a secret. My old friend, Annabelle, smashes a man's face into the table beside him, and he doesn't even flinch. I dodge and duck the chaos roiling around me. I look back over to the stage. He's still there.

Eyes locked on me. This fight is his doing, no doubt. Chaos, blood, fists, chairs, and tables fly all around us, but there he stands. Cool as a cucumber. Smiling. Watching. It's terrifying.

Hands grab the back of my dress and yank me backward. I hit the filthy floor. I scramble to stand, but a foot kicks my shoulder and knocks me back down. Kazak stands over me, smirking like a devil. I can't help but wonder how much it would hurt to have my heart cut out and have a chunk bitten out in front of me.

"Come on, Ruby. After our delightful kiss, I thought you might want another round." He teases and calmly pins my arms above my head and painfully presses on my thighs with his knees. I can't think. I can't move.

"I should have fucking killed you when I had the chance. You've wasted so much time and resources; you have no idea. Thank God you found the removal instructions. I was starting to worry that my dear old dad just made that shit up." He leans closer to my face as I try to scream for Cato. Then, with a fluid motion, Kazak moves both of his hands from my wrists to my throat.

"I'm going to choke the life out of you and cut out your heart." He tuts. No one's going to save me. No one. Cato is dead or worse. Prickle is useless. Seth is unconscious. *What do I do, what do I do, what do I do?*

"After I kill you, I'm going to exterminate your filthy little friend and her fetus. I'll enjoy that. Then I'm going to let your lesbo sister find your head in her toilet bowl. It'll be the last face she sees before I blow out the back of her head with a fireball."

He tells me this like he's telling me a bedtime story. Trish. Where is she? If his hands weren't pinning my throat to the floor, I could turn my head to look for her.

We were supposed to give her son his first bath together. We were supposed to laugh and squeal at his first diaper blow-out. His first steps were supposed to be recorded on my phone. His first Christmas ornament is in my sock drawer.

He'll never know how much I love him if I submit to this fate. And my sister. If I get out of this, I'll explain everything. I'll never lie to her ever again if I make it out of this... I'll never lie to anyone again... I'll hold Howard accountable for my assault... I'll be a better sister...a better friend.

"And Cato, poor, poor Cato. My stupid little brother fell hard for your whorish charms. But don't worry. You'll be together soon." His smile widens. I twist and struggle weakly beneath him. My vision fades. My lungs seize. I'm going to die, and it's all my fault. I should have run when I had the chance. So no one would get hurt or be in danger.

White noise eats away at any logical thought as panic grips me as tightly as his hands on my crushed windpipe. But then a roar rises above havoc around me, slicing through the fray.

"Ruby!" Cato bellows from across the room. He's alive. He's alive, and he's here, and he's calling my name, and we're going to be okay.

Sun rays burst from my heart with joy and relief. I finally met someone who saw all of me. Every secret. Each scar. And he kissed each one.

As I lie dying, I realize it wasn't my power that ate away at my life and ruined everything. It was me. I promised myself I would never harm another person with my curse, no matter the circumstance.

My rules have changed.

I roll my eyes back and close them to lure him in. I have to do this right the first time. One shot. My final lie. I have only seconds before I black out forever.

Kazak reaches out and disturbingly strokes my hair. He takes a deep breath from his nose as if inhaling my life as it escapes me. His eyes must be closed because he doesn't notice my right palm glow white-hot.

I clamp my hand onto the psycho's forearm and transform it into a horrible, steaming pile of goopy flesh, looking him directly in his wide eyes. His smoking radius and ulna splinter easily in my hand, the black soot smudging my pink manicure.

The bones of his wrist litter the floor around us like burnt popcorn pieces. His mouth opens in a silent scream as he rears back and falls. I take a huge breath, greedily gulping sweet air. Rolling onto my side, I keep my eyes on my enemy as I recover my oxygen. His scream is no longer silent as he clutches his gooey stump of an arm. His agonized sounds fill the already boisterous room. Cato grabs me from behind and drags me away from his howling sibling.

"We need to get out of here!" he shouts.

"Where's Trish? I need to find her!"

"Bones took her outside. She's fine."

I'm so relieved I could cry. I twist around and kiss Cato hard. He receives it with skill and tangles his fingers in my hair. I kiss both of his cheeks before pulling away.

"I love you." I kiss his mouth again as he blocks a glass from hitting my head.

"I love you, too. I've loved you for a while now." He kisses my knuckles. "You've branded my heart." He kisses me, and I bite his lip.

"I need to talk to your brother." I take his hand and weave through the crowd until I find Kazak again, still on the floor, calm and collected, clutching his missing limb. He's calmed down.

"Holy shit," Cato says. I kneel beside his brother.

"Kazak," I say.

"Ruby," He says.

"How is your arm?" I ask. He sighs and smiles at me.

"Missing thanks to a little bitch, but I can't feel any pain."

"Good. You're going to go to the emergency room now. Tell the doctor you fell into a campfire. Call your office and fire all of your employees. Tell them to free all animals and terminate all experiments effective immediately. You'll catch the next flight to Canada tomorrow morning and never return. If we ever meet again, Kazak, I will burn off your other arm and shove it down your throat."

17

Two Weeks Later

I take a deep breath and gently rap my knuckles on her door.

"Ruby! Hey girl, come on in." Meredith's white teeth appear as she greets me with a kind smile. I return it with a reserved grin. She picks up on it immediately.

"What's wrong?"

I close the door behind me and clasp my hands together behind my back. I take a breath before I unsheathe my sword of truth and plunge it into my chest.

"I need to talk to you about Howard."

Cato leans against my little blue car, hands in his jean pockets, looking so worried that when he sees me, he runs to me and crushes me in his big arms. I inhale his minty scent, and I melt into his chest.

"How was it?"

"I'm not sure, but I think they'll terminate his position and ban him from the property," I say this into his chest, voice slightly muffled in the flannel.

"Oh, baby, I'm so proud." He rubs my back.

"Thanks. I don't think Howard will press charges against Violet. It's been two weeks, and no criminal complaint has been filed yet, so we should be in the clear."

"I may have had something to do with that." His grin is devious and wide.

"Remind me to thank you for that later." I grin back, and his pupils blow wide. "Anyways, I've been dying to see Tee and Benny. Let's head over after I call Rain to tell her the good news."

"Bones is already there," he smirks, and I pinch his side, "he's obsessed with that baby."

"How could he not be?"

Bennett Bartlow has the biggest eyes and sweetest little toes I've ever seen in my life. He smells like heaven, and his pink cheeks feel like velvet on my nose when I cover them in kisses. Today he wears a onesie covered in blue ducks.

Tee hugs and kisses me and asks about my meeting while Cato cracks a beer with Bones. I rock the cooing baby in my arms as we talk.

I told Tee and my sister about my power the night after the bar brawl, and they were so excited that we giggled and made popcorn and baked potatoes over my fiery hands almost immediately. Baby Benny arrived the next day. When Tee handed him to me, I cried like a baby.

I should never have doubted her unconditional love. I pass the baby off to Cato so I can start the grill for dinner. Bones' son, David, joins me, excitedly telling me about Florida's most recent space launch. I nod and listen as I gently place thick steaks and colorful peppers on the sizzling grill.

Bones looks at Tee like she hung the moon. I only introduced them last week. Watching him twirl her black licorice hair in his massive fingers is such a lovely sight. But my favorite sight in the world is the image of Cato holding a chunky Bennett in his arms. Penetrating dark eyes catch my stare. My breath catches as he kisses the infant on his fluffy head.

We enter his house, and I hold onto his thick shoulder as I step out of my heels. I kiss our snoozing black fur ball on the head before I shimmy out of my jacket. I turn to catch him staring at me.

"Can I help you?"

He steps closer. "Your top is indecent."

I glance down at my modest sweater as he closes in, hands at my waist.

"Oh really?"

"...not to mention those distracting little pink heels. God." His eyes flutter closed, and he kisses my forehead with force.

"I thought you hated my pink heels. If I remember correctly, you *sneered* at them–"

"Love them. You should wear them every single day. I'll buy you a hundred fucking pairs." His knuckles brush just under my ribs. I roll my eyes.

"You should have told me that instead of acting like an asshole—"

Suddenly, he falls back onto our couch and yanks me down with him, so I'm straddling his thighs. The undeniable proof of his arousal is right there, yet I still can't believe it. He groans as I lower my weight there.

"Don't. Tease. Me," he growls as I shift my weight to my knees on either side of his hips.

"You. Deserve. It."

I roll my hips with each word, and his pupils are blown wide. Electrifying satisfaction heats my core. Sweet torture has become our favorite kind of foreplay. Last week he played with my hands under a dinner table and lightly stroked my thighs until I pleaded for him to take me. We enjoyed a long interlude in my shower. The night I banished Kazak, I wore nothing but a smile to bed, and ignored him until he was on his knees begging.

"Brat," he chokes out and flips us over, pressing his knee between my legs. I try to wiggle out from under him just to frustrate him more but he grabs my face and pulls me into a rough kiss.

Our clothing quickly disappears. Warm lips reverently explore my exposed throat and chest, patiently worshiping my body.

As if I'm precious and lovely, not dangerous.

My eyes flutter closed, and I greedily savor the lovely tingle shooting up my spine. I'm a glutton for his attention. Drunk on carnal desires and physical attention.

His mouth vanishes, and my eyes shoot open with the loss.

He's admiring my body, studying the details with those dark eyes. Instinctually, I move my arms to hide, but he quickly and firmly pins my wrists and silently shapes his head. He kisses my mouth, then my breasts, my navel....

My eyes widen as I realize the trail he's confidently marching down leads to one activity. My crappy ex-boyfriends never introduced me to the female-receiving end of third base, and I'm woefully unprepared for the activity.

"Oh- I um-" I try to squirm away, but he's in total control and squeezes my thigh with the hand not currently holding my wrists. He releases them after telling me not to move. Then, he bites my hip bone, and I squeak.

"Can I please—"

I'm interrupted by his mouth planting a full kiss on the most sensitive part of my body. My back arches, and I gasp embarrassingly loudly. I slap a hand over my mouth.

"Hand down. I want to hear everything." He pauses in between his words to lick me thoroughly. He swirls his tongue around my clit, and I immediately slap my hand over my mouth again to stifle an embarrassing whimper from escaping.

He cruelly pulls away, leaving me cold and exposed. He looks up at me in the low light, eyes ablaze with lust.

"Auclair?"

"Y-yes?"

"Do you know what's been on my mind for the past four hours?" he grumbles into the skin of my thigh. His forefinger stimulates my clit delicately as he stares up, waiting for my guess. It's terribly distracting.

"Uh, maybe beer and burgers-ouch!"

He sunk his teeth into the soft spot of my inner knee. Rude.

"Try. Again."

"Why don't you act like a big boy and tell me, jerk?"

"This. Only this. I want to devour you like a dessert. Has anyone ever done this to you?" He kisses my inner thigh and blinks up at me through thick lashes.

"No...." I gasp as he circles my clit faster, his hungry eyes flashing at my reactions.

"Let me hear you. Let me give this to you. Please?"

How could I say no to that?

I dig my fingers into the fabric of the couch to keep my promise as he dives back into his previous conquest. It's not my fault if I burn his stupidly fancy couch. He quite literally asked for it.

I stop worrying if he's enjoying it himself because the pace and passion of his mouth is making my eyes cross. My panting breaths and moans heighten in pitch and become more and more explicit with each movement of his mouth. It's embarrassing and liberating and erotic. His fingers release my hips and reach up to hold mine. Our fingers weave together, and his eyes flutter shut. He tastes every part of me. Before I burn the couch with my fingers, I push him up, climb into his lap, and look him in the eye as I lower myself onto him, pink-lipped and gasping with pleasure. He kisses the back of my hand as I ride him. The angle is heavenly. The pressure building in my center is too much.

"You're so fucking beautiful," he moans and before I know it, my orgasm hits so hard that I may have ascended to another plane of existence. Head thrown back, I grip his bare shoulders like a lifeline. Sparks explode in the corners of my vision. My skin is on fire and ice cold at the same time.

He follows me over the edge shortly after, calling my name as he finishes. His chocolate eyes hold mine with such tenderness my chest aches. No one has ever made me feel like this. He lazily kisses my face and chest as I come down from the high and whispers in my ear how much he loves me.

Now I light candles with my pinky finger for the fun of it. In the fall, my home is lit by candlelight by sunset. The anxiety behind a sudden sneeze or forgetful hand movement has melted away. I'll let Cato try and start the bonfire on camping trips by himself, subtly flicking a finger to help him get some sparks going. If he catches on to my unsolicited help, I'm assaulted with a healthy smack on the ass. My torturous fear has dissolved into laughable strife from my past, and I can't wait to face the future with a new spark in my heart. Trish's bouncing baby boy is the love of my life, right after Cato.